# SHERLOCK HOLMES

## The Monster of the Mere

## ALSO AVAILABLE FROM TITAN BOOKS

*Sherlock Holmes:*
*Cry of the Innocents*
Cavan Scott

*Sherlock Holmes:*
*The Patchwork Devil*
Cavan Scott

*Sherlock Holmes:*
*The Labyrinth of Death*
James Lovegrove

*Sherlock Holmes:*
*The Thinking Engine*
James Lovegrove

*Sherlock Holmes:*
*Gods of War*
James Lovegrove

*Sherlock Holmes:*
*The Stuff of Nightmares*
James Lovegrove

*Sherlock Holmes:*
*The Spirit Box*
George Mann

*Sherlock Holmes:*
*The Will of the Dead*
George Mann

*Sherlock Holmes:*
*The Breath of God*
Guy Adams

*Sherlock Holmes:*
*The Army of Doctor Moreau*
Guy Adams

*Sherlock Holmes:*
*A Betrayal in Blood*
Mark A. Latham

*Sherlock Holmes:*
*The Legacy of Deeds*
Nick Kyme

*Sherlock Holmes:*
*The Red Tower*
Mark A. Latham

*Sherlock Holmes:*
*The Vanishing Man*
Philip Purser-Hallard

*Sherlock Holmes:*
*The Spider's Web*
Philip Purser-Hallard

*Sherlock Holmes:*
*Masters of Lies*
Philip Purser-Hallard

*Sherlock Holmes:*
*The Back-to-Front Murder*
Tim Major

# SHERLOCK HOLMES

The Monster of the Mere

## PHILIP PURSER-HALLARD

**TITAN** BOOKS

Sherlock Holmes: The Monster of the Mere
Print edition ISBN: 9781789099263
E-book edition ISBN: 9781789099270

Published by Titan Books
A division of Titan Publishing Group Ltd
144 Southwark Street, London SE1 0UP
www.titanbooks.com

First edition: May 2023
1 3 5 7 9 10 8 6 4 2

A CIP catalogue record for this title is available from the British Library.

Printed and bound in the United Kingdom by
CPI Group (UK) Ltd, Croydon, CR0 4YY.

# SHERLOCK HOLMES

## The Monster of the Mere

# CHAPTER ONE

In June of 1899 I was engaged in a walking tour of the Lake District, that unlikely pocket of alpine territory hidden away in the far north-western corner of our English countryside. As I wandered the landscape walked before me by shepherds and poets, the serenity and grandeur of its vistas reminded me of my visit some years previously to Switzerland. That earlier journey had brought with it considerable trials, culminating in what I had believed at the time – erroneously, thank Heavens – to be the tragic death of my friend, Sherlock Holmes, at the hands of Professor Moriarty. On this occasion, I had more restful company in the person of my schoolfriend Percy Phelps, with whom I spent a pleasant time interspersing energetic walks with convivial interludes in inns and hostelries.

As we reached the town of Ravensfoot on the northern shores of Lake Wermewater, Phelps received word of a minor family emergency and was forced to cut short our sojourn. Resolving to persevere alone, I bade him farewell at Ravensfoot railway station, and continued in solitary progress around the lake's shore until I neared Wermeholt, the smaller town facing Ravensfoot across the waters from the south.

Murray's *Westmorland, Cumberland, and the Lakes* had
promised me a fine walk from there up to the summit of Netherfell,
from which a panorama of Wermewater and the neighbouring
peaks would be visible. I was to spend the afternoon of Thursday
the fifteenth exploring Wermeholt, and intended to stay there
for the night before walking the recommended path on the
morrow. From Netherfell's heights I should make my way down
to Hartsmere, reaching the town of Hartsdale by Friday evening.

The locals in Ravensfoot had warned me to make my way
westward around the lake, as much of the eastern shore belonged
to the Wermeston family and was closed to the public, and so I
approached Wermeholt with the fell to my right, and the morning
sun glinting from the lake before me. A large wooded islet,
Glissenholm according to my map, interrupted its waters like the
pupil of an eye, and I reflected on that peculiarity of local dialect,
inherited from our Celtic forebears, that transforms the lakes in
this part of England into *meres*, its mountains into *fells*, its streams
into *becks* and its islands, amusingly to me, into *holms*.

From Ravensfoot, Wermeholt had seemed a pretty enough
place, nestled beneath the slopes of the fell, but as I commenced
the downward approach towards the town, it came to seem less
picturesque. I had not appreciated quite how overshadowed
it would be by Netherfell; only now, at mid-morning, was the
town beginning to welcome the sun's illumination. Like many
settlements in the area, Wermeholt was built mainly from the
local black slate, but few of its buildings boasted the cheerful
white limewash that brightens many of those in the more
popular wayside stops. Some way beyond the town, a tall spur of
rock stretched out from the fell almost to the side of the lake, its
nearer slope scarred and grey.

I paused at a fork in the path, one track leading up towards
Netherfell's summit, the other the route that would take me

down past the lakeside to Wermeholt. An ornate way-marker stood at the divide, carved from some dark stone.

I peered north across the lake towards the friendlier waterfront of Ravensfoot. A train, the first since Phelps' departure, was approaching the town around the base of Ravensfell, and I heard the distant note of its whistle, as puffs of steam sketched a line across the side of that further slope. To the south, Wermeholt glowered at me like the town's dark reflection, an impression amplified by the shadowed peak above.

I considered simply continuing up the fell and so on to Hartsmere, arriving at my next destination a day early. It would make for a long day's walk, though, with no opportunity for luncheon or other refreshment, and so I resolved to adhere to my original itinerary.

I strode on into the gloom, through meadows cropped and fouled by sheep and demarcated with drystone walls, and shortly found myself in a grey, unlovely high street. A churchyard with a stone church tower lay close by the shore, and along the street a dilapidated pub sign proclaimed a dilapidated pub. A grey dog of indeterminate breed was tethered outside the latter, and it stirred fretfully and whined at me as I approached. I patted and complimented it before moving on. Between an ironmongery and a butcher's shop bearing the name F.H. BATTERBY stood a grocery-cum-post-office, and I considered whether, in Phelps' absence, I should write to Holmes suggesting he come up and join me in my meanderings.

I feared, though, that without the mental stimulation of the criminal cases that normally brought us to such far-flung regions, he would simply find them dull. When I had first proposed such a tour he demurred, pleading an inseparable attachment to the pavements and byways of London that had for so long constituted his native domain.

"Come now, Holmes," I had cajoled him. "You have not had a holiday for ages. It will do you good to get out of the city. A change is as good as a rest, you know."

He smiled. "Ah, but I prefer to take my rest in familiar territory. The atrocities of the countryside have their charms, to be sure," he conceded jovially, "and I have no doubt that I shall sample them again. But, for the present, I prefer the more comfortable crimes of our fair metropolis."

And so I had instead spent a week in restful companionship with Phelps, a more peaceable traveller, and if I had found his talk of his young family and modestly distinguished career at the Foreign Office somewhat lacking in excitement, he compensated for it with a tolerance for late mornings and idle lunches that I have yet to discover among Holmes's admirable qualities. When Phelps had been summoned home to Woking, I too had considered hastening back to the old shared rooms in Baker Street, but I found myself too enchanted by the majesty of my surroundings to give up on my planned peregrinations.

Wermeholt did not, on its showing so far, live up to the promise of its surroundings. Still, while not perhaps the most idyllic haven the Lake District had to offer, it was to be my resting-place for but a night, and I resolved that I should make the best of it. Having ascertained the location of the Mereside Hotel, where I purposed to stay, I turned back along the high street and returned to the church of St Michael the Archangel to pursue my plan for exploration. Returning the rather indifferent nod of a woman walking home carrying her groceries, I entered the churchyard and strolled around it, inspecting its slate roof and battlemented bell-tower.

Like many of the older churches in the area, St Michael's was sturdy and squat, as if constructed for defence rather than worship. The graveyard, crowded with centuries of the dead, stretched all the way to the lakeside, where a crumbling stone wall shored it up, for now at least, against a collapse into the mere. A gate there gave onto some steps, which led down to a wooden jetty.

The church door stood open to visitors, so I doffed my hat and stepped inside.

The inner walls were as rough as the exterior, and windows of plain glass failed to make much of the pitiful sunlight. Though inevitably lacking the grandeur of our city churches, the edifice nonetheless conveyed a simple honesty of faith that would, or so I endeavoured to convince myself, impress the folk of so humble a town.

The church's only notable decoration stood in the vestibule: a statue, perhaps three feet tall, of its patron saint engaged in energetic combat with Satan in the form of a dragon. It was executed in the same dark volcanic stone as the way-marker I had seen earlier, and perhaps by the same sculptor, as that had been in the shape of a globe held in a dragon's foot. St George's Church in Ravensfoot had, I recalled, made similar use of a scene from the legends of its own patron, but that building was a relatively modern one, and its statue had been tame in comparison. This sculptor had made his sainted angel stern and warriorlike in his armour, but his devil was truly terrifying – its snout abrim with teeth, its wings leathery and clawed, its coils constricting the saint as if they would snap him in two.

"A vivid vision of evil, is it not?" a man's voice observed, close behind me, and I started. Turning quickly, I found a man in clerical garb, his face becoming apologetic as he beheld my surprise.

"It is," I said, recovering myself. "Is it very old?"

"I believe it dates back to the sixteen-hundreds. But I apologise, sir," the priest added nervously. "I had no intention of startling you. You were quite absorbed in your contemplation, and did not hear me approach. I share your fascination with this piece. You will find that it continues to haunt the imagination long after it is first seen. My name is Felspar, sir, the Reverend Gervaise Felspar, and I am the vicar here."

"I am Dr John Watson," I told him. "I am pleased to meet you, sir. My walking companion left me this morning, and I am now roving alone wherever my Murray's chooses to take me."

"You have chosen your destination well, Doctor," Mr Felspar replied. "This is a most lovely part of the country. I am no native, and to the good-humoured scorn of my parishioners I cannot abide boats, but nevertheless I have come to consider it my home."

While he was correct about the loveliness of the Lakes as a whole, I found it difficult to concur regarding Wermeholt, at least on the basis of what I had seen so far. I made some noncommittal response.

After his initial forwardness, Felspar seemed rather a timid soul, and was clearly pleased that I had not taken offence at his intrusion. He told me that he had been the incumbent at Wermeholt for some six years, having moved from a parish somewhere in the Midlands. "An honest people," was how he described his current parishioners, "though superstitious at times, and set in their rustic ways. My parish houses perhaps a hundred souls, and I serve them as best I may."

He told me that the churchyard was unusual in having two lych-gates, or corpse-gates as they are called in those parts – one approached in the normal way by a lych-path from the road, and the other giving on to the jetty, where the inhabitants of Ravensfoot had once been wont to deliver their dead by barge for burial in St Michael's churchyard. "There was a time," Felspar said, "when Ravensfoot was a mere hamlet, and Wermeholt the largest settlement for many miles. The Ravensfoot slate mine changed that. We have no comparable industry on this side of the mere. That is why the railway passes instead along the northern shore."

He confirmed that the inn I had seen earlier would provide me with lunch, and as the church clock struck twelve I pleaded the demands of my stomach and left him to his devotions. In truth I was looking forward to some hearty refreshment after my morning's exertion.

As I stepped outside the church, I saw that the woman I had seen earlier was still positioned across the road, groceries now at her feet. She was speaking animatedly in the local dialect to a younger woman, who was stoically ignoring the complaints of a small child tugging at her hand. As I emerged from the churchyard, the older woman turned to glance at me before returning her attention to her friend. Her face was grey and craggy, and she wore widow's black.

Outside the hostelry I found the grey dog I had met earlier untied, and lying at the feet of a muscular man who sat on a bench, smoking a pipe and seemingly guarding the entrance. The sign above him was a dilapidated representation of a coat of arms, presumably that of the local landowner. The seated man nodded curtly, as if granting me permission to enter. The wag of the dog's tail was friendlier.

Inside, I found the building in poor repair, with peeling paint and a pervading smell of damp. However, the barmaid was pretty enough, and willing to sell me a pint of adequate porter, which will endear me more closely to anyone. With a promised mutton pie to follow, I soon cheered up, and settled myself at a rickety table with my mug of beer. I leaned my walking-stick against the wall, took my writing materials from my haversack, and began a letter to Holmes while I awaited my food. I had used the last of my stamps in Ravensfoot, but doubtless the Wermeholt post office would oblige.

"Is thou – are you up from London, sir?" said the girl when she brought me my pie with peas and potatoes. "I thinks thou – you must be, from your accent. I hope you don't mind me asking,"

she went on. Her own accent was strong, but after a week spent
in the region I found it easier to follow. "I like to know where
our visitors come from. My da and me don't get away from
Wermeholt over often, with t'pub to run. Over til Ravensfoot
for market days is all, and once two year ago til Keswick, for my
cousin's wedding there. But we get a lot of folk from other places
coming through, and I like to meet them. I's – I'm Effie, sir, Effie
Scorpe. My da Ben's t'publican here. My auntie does t'cooking
for t'pub, but it's just him and me lives here since my ma died."

"Well, I am pleased to meet you, Effie," I told her, though a little
warily. She was pretty, as I have said, and young, with a freckled
face and hair all curls, and while there was no sign of any other
presence behind the bar, I did not wish her father to overhear us
and conclude that I was being overfamiliar. "I am Dr Watson, I am
indeed from London, and I'm on a walking tour of the Lakes."

"Lots of gentlemen comes here for t'walking," she agreed with
me eagerly. "They say travel broadens t'mind, sir, and perhaps
talking to travellers does t'same, for those of us stays in one place.
London's a fearful long way, I ken, and so big – a town bigger than
any of our lakes, they say, though I can scarce believe that."

"Effie," I said, "Regent's Park, close by where I live in London,
is perhaps half the size of Wermewater by itself. It's the tiniest
scrap of green in the smoggy grey sprawl of the capital."

"Now I ken thou's joking wi' me, sir," said Effie Scorpe,
forgetting her careful grammar. She affected a scornful expression,
but I could see the excitement in her eyes.

"It's absolutely true," I told her. "Perhaps one day you'll see
it for yourself."

"Stop pestering t'gentleman, Effie, and gan thou back til t'bar.
Let him eat his dinner in quiet." The rough voice belonged to the
surly, burly man from outside, who had returned. Though his face
was certainly not one that I would have described as pretty, now

that I saw them together I could detect a certain resemblance.

"Mr Scorpe, I presume," I said apologetically. "It's my fault, I'm afraid. I've been keeping your daughter from her duties. I've been walking alone all morning, and welcomed the conversation."

"That's as maybe," Ben Scorpe grunted, ushering Effie back to the bar nevertheless. "She has her work."

I finished my lunch in a less convivial mood, reluctant even to ask for my mug to be refilled lest I get my young friend into further trouble with her father. However, as I left with my completed missive, I asked her whether I would find the post office open, and she confirmed that I should. "Don't get talking to Mrs Trice, though," she warned me with a smile. "She'll have your business all over town afore sundown."

Thanking her for her help, and nodding a cordial farewell to her father, which he acknowledged reluctantly, I left the inn and walked up the street to the premises I had observed earlier. Rather than anything the average Londoner would recognise as a post office, this turned out to be a village shop with shelves displaying everything from carbolic soap to mustard powder, a row of bottles containing tinctures of variously dubious medical efficacy, and a counter for taking parcels and telegrams. It was adequate to my purposes, nevertheless.

The lady in charge proved as loquacious as Effie had promised me on the subject of visitors to the town, and just as fascinated by my own affairs. She even opened our conversation with the same question. "Are you up from London, then, sir?" she asked me with keen interest. She was in late middle age, with a peevish look behind her half-moon spectacles and an ingratiating manner. When I told her my name, she added, "Are you with those scientists at t'Mereside?"

"Scientists?" I asked. It seemed an unlikely spot for a scientific project, but perhaps there were some experiments that might best be conducted in such an isolated area as this. "How many are they?" I had merely checked the position of the Mereside Hotel earlier, not considering that it might already be full. Again I wondered whether I could manage the walk to Hartsdale that afternoon, should it prove necessary.

"Four of them," said Mrs Trice promptly, "and a lady. Two older gentlemen and two younger. Friends of Sir Howard Woodwose, they are."

"I see." From what I had observed, the hotel was surely more than large enough to accommodate such a group and myself. "No, I'm not of their party. I'm a medical man, here on holiday. Isn't Sir Howard Woodwose a student of folklore, though, not a scientist?" I had seen the name in newspapers, mentioned in connection with the study of such things as medieval ballads, fairy tales and the legends of Robin Hood. While I knew little of such matters, I understood that his books were well thought of by those better versed than I.

"Oh, he knows about all kinds of things, Sir Howard does," said Mrs Trice. "A fearfully learned man, they say. Oh!" she remarked, for at this point she glanced down at the envelope that I had carelessly placed on the counter. "I see you're writing to Mr Sherlock Holmes, in London. Would he be a friend of yours, then, sir?"

I realised that I should have anticipated her interest, and cursed myself. Since most of those who write to Holmes are seeking his assistance with some mystery, criminal or otherwise, I was a little surprised that she had jumped to the conclusion that we were acquainted, but perhaps she simply assumed that everyone in London knew everyone else.

"As it happens, he is," I replied. As Effie had warned me, this busybody would doubtless broadcast my affairs to all and sundry before the day was out. Still, I did not suppose I could prevent that by dissembling now.

"Then you must be the Dr Watson that writes t'stories!" she declared, her eyes alight with gossip's glee. "I dare say you'll have a great many tales to tell us, then."

"I have told most of them," I assured her, allowing myself considerable latitude from the truth, "in my stories for the magazines. If you have read them, then you know already virtually all that is of interest."

"Read them?" She frowned, as if the suggestion were indelicate. "No, I can't say I've read them. But I'm sure we're pleased to have you here, Dr Watson. Tell me" – and I was able to predict with absolute accuracy what her next words would be – "will Mr Holmes be joining you? It'd be an honour for us in Wermeholt to welcome a man of such distinction. Perhaps there's some matter he sent you ahead to investigate?" she added insinuatingly.

I sighed. "No, Mrs Trice, I'm afraid I really am here on holiday, and Mr Holmes has no plans to join me. He is very busy with affairs in London at present." I tried to change the subject. "I'm more interested in these scientists you mentioned, Sir Howard's friends. Do you know what their purpose is in coming here?"

But my reticence had perhaps offended the postmistress. "I wouldn't know anything about that, sir. You'd have to speak to them."

I bade her a hasty good day and left the shop, pausing only to place my stamped letter into the box outside. Though I had little confidence in its privacy, given the hungry way Mrs Trice had been eyeing it, its contents were innocuous, and I did not care to carry it all the way to the post office in Hartsdale.

As I left the post office, I was surprised to see the craggy-faced widow for the third time, this time without her groceries, but once again glancing at me, with a curt nod of acknowledgement, from across the road. I was sure that, when I had first seen her outside the church, she had been heading in the opposite direction.

# CHAPTER TWO

Although it was but early afternoon, the sun was vanishing already behind the western slopes of the fell. In view of the information I had just received, I felt that I had better proceed to the Mereside Hotel and secure a room for the night. There had been no other walkers on the trail from Ravensfoot that morning, but others could have set out later, or have approached the town the other way, from Hartsdale.

Accordingly I presented myself at the Mereside, and was rewarded with a serviceable enough room. "It's all we have," the proprietor told me. A melancholy man named Mr Dormer, he spoke with a mild local accent, lacking the telltale signs of dialect that Effie Scorpe had been struggling to shake. "We've a party taking up the rest. No view of the water, I'm afraid. You're welcome to it if it serves."

I agreed that it would, and took up residence therein. As my host had warned me, the window looked back along the length of the high street towards the church, with little visible of the promised lakeshore. The prospect was entirely overshadowed by the fell. I washed and unpacked my haversack, then took my guidebook downstairs to a gloomy sitting-room, intending to make notes on prospective sights in Hartsdale and points beyond. My aim was to finish my tour at Ullswater, and to return home to Baker Street before the month was out.

The lounge was somewhat threadbare, with a fireplace that might have been cosy in winter but on a summer's afternoon seemed dismally superfluous. Shabby tapestry sofas and armchairs promised a little comfort, and a picture window gave a view across the garden to the lakeshore, with Glissenholm and Ravensfell beyond. Beneath the far hill's slopes, Ravensfoot gleamed in sunshine above serene waters, a glimpse of a better world.

As I was taking all this in, to my surprise a tall, gaunt figure sprang up from one of the armchairs, took the briar pipe from his mouth and calmly stated my name. "Dr Watson."

For a moment my heart leapt, thinking that Holmes had changed his mind about a holiday together and had thought to surprise me here, but this man was not he. It took me a moment to place him.

"Dr Summerlee?" I said. "Summerlee, the anatomist?" He had been a junior lecturer at my medical school, and had instructed me sternly on the inferences to be drawn by comparisons between human and animal skeletons and organs. Though I admired his fierce intellect, I had never found him congenial company.

"I am Professor Summerlee now," he told me, shaking my hand. "I hold the Chair of Comparative Anatomy at University College."

It had easily been twenty years since I had last seen Summerlee, whose austere and precise manner had, despite his absolute adherence to scientific rationalism, earned him the nickname "the Jesuit" among his students. Though he was but a few years older than myself, his familiar goatee and moustache had gone quite grey. As ever, he carried about him a mingled smell of stale tobacco-smoke and other odours that suggested he had not washed for several days.

"I have been following your own work with interest," he told me. "I do not mean your medical career, which I understand is undistinguished, but your popular publications. Your accounts of Mr Holmes's exploits are sensationalised, inevitably, but I find the records of his deductive technique and accomplishments to be inspiring."

"He would be gratified to hear it," I told him. It was in keeping with Summerlee's personality that what he most appreciated about my writing was the abstract intellectual theory Holmes himself was always encouraging me to emphasise, to my publishers' despair. "Personally I enjoy the sensational events and details. They're indispensable when selling the stories to publishers and readers."

Summerlee nodded. "As I said, such trivialities are inevitable. For my part I am not averse to adventure, but it is a means to scientific enquiry, not an end in itself." I recalled being told that as a younger man he had joined a number of expeditions, both zoological and anthropological, to various uncivilised climes, and had returned professing a thorough indifference to his experiences, though never to the knowledge he had acquired by them.

"I say, Professor," I said, "I suppose you must be a friend of Sir Howard Woodwose. I heard there was a scientific party staying here."

Summerlee frowned. "To be frank, I am not very well acquainted with Woodwose. He is a friend of my colleague Professor Creavesey, the palaeontologist. But yes, it is at his invitation that I am here, along with Creavesey, his students Gramascene and Topkins, and Mrs Creavesey." He stared at me, a little warily. "You have heard tell, then, of our investigative enterprise?"

I shook my head. "Only that you are here. I must say, I found it difficult to imagine what you might find to investigate in such an out-of-the-way place. But if Professor Creavesey's field is palaeontology, I suppose there must be fossils here." I remembered passing a museum of such things in Ravensfoot, though I had not been tempted to visit.

Summerlee snorted. "A fossil would be more concrete evidence than Creavesey has managed to amass so far. No, our errand is an absolute wild-goose chase, but a scientist must be as committed to falsifying theories as to proving them. Even so, it was frivolous of me to come during term time; that, I fear, has been a disservice to my students." His beard bobbed self-censoriously as he spoke.

"How intriguing." I was conscious that I was echoing the prurient interest of Mrs Trice, but was unable to restrain my curiosity. "Can you tell me no more?"

He sighed. "The secret of our purpose here is not mine to divulge. Perhaps Creavesey or Woodwose will take you into their confidence, although I doubt it. There will be an opportunity at dinner tonight, I believe."

There being some time still until then, I elected to walk a little way beyond the Mereside Hotel to the east. The professor declined to join me, pleading a paper he was to review, and I set off alone.

There was little enough left of the town in this direction. Beyond it, a rough track led across more meadows towards the spur of hill that reached down almost to the stagnant water. Though I knew that the recommended route up the fell, which I should take on the morrow, lay to the west, I was curious to see whether or not there might be another approach to the summit from this direction.

The fell's shadow lay across all the land here, and the grass was sparser than it had been even on the other side of the town. As I approached, I saw that there was certainly no route up Netherfell this way. Along the ridge of the spur ran a drystone wall, constructed from large rocks settling together under their own weight without mortar, but that would be an easy enough barrier to pass. The problem would lie in reaching it, since the slope ahead was scree, a mass of dust and rubble that covered bare rock, and would make ascent all but impossible for any but the most experienced mountaineer.

At the end of the ridge, where it sloped sharply down to meet the lake, the drystone wall met a more formal construction, and the track ahead was bisected by a high wall of cemented limestone that extended some distance beyond the shore into the lake itself. This wall was broken by a large gate, which from my vantage looked large enough for a cart or carriage.

This, then, must be the way to Wermeston Hall, which I had been told barred the walker's route on the eastern side of the lake. As I had been warned, it held no welcome for visitors, and I was not surprised that the locals saw fit to avoid it. I, too, turned back without going any closer, seeing no good reason to probe the shadows under the fell, and returned to the Mereside Hotel to dress for dinner.

At dinner, Professor Summerlee introduced me to his colleagues, and also to Sir Howard Woodwose, who came from his cottage on the other side of the town to dine with us. I was the hotel's only guest not of their party, and they seemed disinclined to be forthcoming on the nature of their undertakings. I did, however, gather that they intended an expedition onto Wermewater the next day, where they intended to circumnavigate Glissenholm, the wooded island out in the mere.

To me this sounded more like a pleasure jaunt than a scientific endeavour, but I supposed that Creavesey and the rest must have their reasons, however frivolous Summerlee considered them. I had seen on my arrival that the hotel had its own mooring and a rowing-boat for the use of guests, but for my own part I had no intention of making use of the facility. In my mind boats have always been a necessary form of transport rather than a leisure pursuit. I was finding the dank shadows of Wermeholt oppressive, and frankly I was looking forward to quitting it for what I hoped would be the superior comforts of Hartsdale. Besides, I gathered that my dining companions intended to rise at six, and that in my view is no way to conduct oneself on holiday.

"I say, though," Henry Gramascene suggested, "if you'd waited a bit until old lady Wermeston pops off, whoever inherits the estate might have given us permission to land on Glissenholm, rather than just rowing around it. I must say I'm curious about what's there." The student was loud and hearty, and seemed tolerantly amused by both his elders and his friend, the quieter Topkins. Despite his irreverence, I liked him instinctively.

"That is hardly respectful to Lady Ophelia, Henry," suggested Edith Creavesey. "Her manservant explained to Sir Howard that her family burial plot is on the island. I can quite see why she would not want outsiders treating it as a curiosity." Mrs Creavesey was a handsome woman, less than half the age of her balding, gnomelike husband. I gathered that she, too, had been a student of his before their marriage, and she had clearly profited intellectually from the experience. She was articulate and curious, asking intelligent questions that drew out fascinating strands of knowledge from her companions.

"Besides, her ladyship, though advanced in years, is hale and spry. Who can say how long she has left – or any of us for that matter?" Sir Howard Woodwose said. "Such things are not given to us to know."

His voice was mournful, but his eye held an amused gleam. Though of advanced years, the great man had a relentless energy that I could tell after our few minutes' acquaintance would make him the largest presence in any room. He was a huge man physically too, not overly broad nor muscular but quite six and a half feet in height, with a spade-like beard, and no sign of the self-effacing stoop that sometimes afflicts tall men.

"Well, she isn't immortal," Gramascene pointed out reasonably. "Or, if she is, that really is a scientific curiosity worth investigating. Have you known the family long, Sir Howard?" he asked, with an interest that sounded more than perfunctory.

"Only since my arrival in Wermeholt," said the knight, "some ten years ago. At that time Lady Ophelia was not quite the recluse she has since become. She still walked the hills beyond her estate, and we encountered one another on the far side of Netherfell. I was able to tell her more than she had known of some of her family's legends, and it seems she found the conversation sufficiently stimulating to seek out more of it. Sadly, her ladyship is unmarried with no living relatives, and it is a moot point to whom Wermeston Hall and its lands shall pass."

"Why did she never marry?" I wondered.

"Really, Watson, do you imagine that the human animal can find fulfilment only with a mate?" snapped Summerlee, whom I knew to be a lifelong bachelor.

"On the contrary," I said, "I have known several women who have been quite as devoid of interest in our own sex as some men are in theirs." I was thinking of Holmes, of course, among others. "But I suppose that whatever her own feelings on the matter, the pressure on an heiress to continue the line must be very great." Summerlee merely grunted in reply.

In some ways the Professor reminded me of Sherlock Holmes. His commitment to the facts, and his merciless application of logic, certainly explained his interest in my published reminiscences of my friend's activities. But he shared none of Holmes's passion nor his zest for adventure, and certainly none of his considerable personal charm. While Holmes could be sardonic and impatient, Summerlee responded to lesser intellects – which in his view included almost everyone – with the disdain that Holmes reserved for criminals alone.

I had heard both men characterised as thinking machines merely, lacking in emotion and empathy, as indifferent to others' suffering as to their own, but nobody who read my stories closely, let alone met Holmes himself in all his glorious humanity, could sustain such a view of him. And in fairness, though many among my fellow medical students had described Summerlee as such, I could not believe that it was wholly true in his case either.

As I was the only one at dinner not privy to their secret purpose, the conversation of necessity turned to more general matters, and I asked Woodwose what had led him into such an unusual career as the study of myth and folklore.

"In my youth," he confided in his deep, compelling voice, "I aspired to the priesthood, if you can believe such a thing. I was a pious young man, or so I imagined, and I talked my way into a theological college with a view to ordination." His beard bristled white and his eyes shone with humour, though I could well imagine them burning instead with religious zeal.

I sensed as well that expounding upon his personal history was something of a habit with Woodwose, as he continued with practised ease: "Alas, as I read more widely in the religions of the world and their attendant mythologies, I came to realise that what excited me was not faith itself, but the legends and stories that surround it. I came to many of the same conclusions that Mr Frazer has popularised recently in his *Golden Bough*, though I did not, alas, think to publish them for myself."

I searched my memory for what I might have read about this Frazer, but unearthed nothing beyond a vague sense that he sought to relegate Christianity to the moribund status of the pagan religions. The folklorist continued, "I left the college under something of a cloud, after questioning the morality of the ancient Christian evangelists who turned our ancestors away from the worship of their national gods, Woden and Thor and their peers. Who were those missionary saints, I asked, to decide that the destiny of our people lay with a deity from the Middle East, so foreign to these shores? Needless to say, this was not the kind of question that my prospective superiors appreciated from a priest-in-training.

"And so I parted company with both the seminary and the church, and turned my attention to the work that has consumed me since."

"And the world of scholarship has been the beneficiary, Sir Howard," Professor Creavesey assured him. "As have I, through the intersection of our fields of study." The palaeontologist displayed a childlike enthusiasm for almost any subject of conversation, but the awe with which he deferred to Woodwose seemed excessive to me.

"I'm surprised that they intersect at all," I said, prompting a look of concern as Creavesey realised that he might have said more than he intended.

"Oh, but they do, Doctor," Woodwose assured me at once. "Fossils may inspire folklore, and folklore may influence our interpretation of fossils. You are familiar, perhaps, with the legend of St Hilda?" I admitted that I was not. "The story tells us that when the area around Whitby suffered a plague of snakes, the abbess prayed for a miracle, whereupon the reptiles all curled up and turned to stone, becoming the fossils known as ammonites. The coiled snake has become an essential part of her iconography, and appears on the town's coat of arms. I understand a species has also been named after her, Professor?"

"Oh yes, I believe so," Creavesey agreed, blinking.

"*Hildoceras bifrons*," said James Topkins, the quieter student, eager enough now to share his knowledge of their shared subject. "The creature was never a snake, of course. It's a mollusc with a coiled shell, similar to the nautilus. They're one of the commoner types of fossil, and I believe especially prevalent around the Yorkshire coast. I suppose that's why the locals felt the need to explain them."

"Hilda of Whitby was a real historical figure, though," Edith Creavesey observed. "The new women's college at Oxford is named after her."

"Of course, my dear," the professor agreed at once. "A most intelligent and able woman, like yourself," he added, with a fond smile.

"She played no small part in the Christianisation of these isles," said Woodwose, a little censoriously, "but as with many so-called saints, some fascinating tales have accreted around her."

"Isn't there a similar legend of St Patrick?" I asked. "Didn't he drive the snakes out of Ireland?"

"Ah yes," beamed Woodwose, "but that story exists to explain an absence, not a prevalence, since the curious fact is that Ireland has no native snakes."

"Shrewd of old Patrick to take the credit for that," Gramascene observed. "I blush to mention it, but I myself banished all the tigers from Shropshire some years ago." While it was clear that Topkins would one day follow in the footsteps of the older men, it seemed to me that Gramascene was concealing a certain impatience with their whole purpose, whatever it might be. I wondered whether he had come along solely to keep his friend company.

"Must you, Henry?" Topkins complained affectionately.

Woodwose gave a good-humoured laugh. "No, Topkins, Gramascene is quite right to prick my pomposity. I am afraid you have hit upon a subject upon which I threaten to become a bore, Dr Watson. The lore of serpents and their relatives is a particular area of interest of mine."

I am afraid that at that point I rather closed my ears to his conversation, but it was in any case not long before we finished dinner. Shortly afterwards Woodwose bade us all farewell and left for the short walk back to his cottage, while Summerlee and the Creaveseys announced their intention to retire. Topkins and Gramascene were all set to stay up with brandy and cigars, and invited me to join them, but by now I, too, had had enough of company. I made my excuses and retired to my room, where I read for a while then tried to sleep.

Despite my weary limbs, I was unable to. Against my habit, I had taken a small cup of coffee after dinner, and I should have remembered how this always affects me. Sufficient time with the brandy decanter might have remedied the problem, but I was certainly too tired now to get dressed again and join the conversation between Gramascene and Topkins downstairs.

I lay awake for some time, then finally I got up, opened the window of my bedroom to the damp night air, and sat there smoking for a while. Having no need to see clearly, I did not light a lamp. The sky above was cloudless, though much occluded by the ominous bulk of Netherfell, and such stars as I could see were bright and clear. Although I could discern even less of the lake, it too was calm, and reflected the celestial lights perfectly. There was an otherworldly beauty to be found even in Wermeholt, it seemed, even if it was a paradoxical beauty bestowed by lights astronomical distances away.

Thinking of beauty reminded me of Mrs Creavesey, a striking woman with a penetrating mind. Her grace and intelligence seemed wasted on the elderly, weak-willed Professor Creavesey, and I felt it a shame that her husband seemed more under Sir Howard Woodwose's influence than her own.

Why was she here, I wondered, or for that matter Summerlee or the students? I could imagine that Creavesey was sufficiently in thrall to Woodwose to welcome some eccentric collaboration that impinged upon both their disciplines, and perhaps it did make sense for him to bring his wife with him on such a visit, but his undergraduate students, not to mention an eminent anatomist, surely had more important calls upon their time.

It was a mystery, and for a moment I indulged myself by wondering whether it was one that would interest Holmes. My friend was wont to occasional protestations that it was the grotesque and surprising that interested him in the mysteries we investigated together, not the criminal element in itself, and there was perhaps some of that here. Yet I could hardly suppose that he would find this academic secret sufficiently alluring to draw him away from the bloodstains and fingerprints of the capital.

My musings were interrupted by the sound of a door being quietly opened, and then just as carefully closed. Had my window been shut I might never have heard it at all, but in my position by the casement I recognised the sound of the hotel's front door. A moment later, I watched a dark figure appear in the street outside, stepping away in the direction of the church. From his broad back and youthful stride, I saw at once that it was Henry Gramascene.

I recalled being told that Sir Howard Woodwose's cottage was beyond the church. Indeed, I must have passed it on my way into the town that morning, though I had of course been unaware of it at the time. Perhaps, I thought, Woodwose had left something behind here when he departed, though it would have to be some item of great importance to need to be returned to him that night. I could think of no other reason why Professor Creavesey's student would be abroad at such an hour.

I was startled, then, when a moment later I heard the sound of the front door again, even more quietly this time, and a second figure appeared, silently following the first. This one was slender, and crept nervously, keeping to the shadows, but I thought that it could only be that of Topkins.

This was still more curious, but nevertheless hardly my business. If Gramascene had some nocturnal errand in Wermeholt, and Topkins some interest in following him, that was no concern of mine. I was on holiday, after all, and both men had seemed quite harmless at dinner. I had no reason to imagine any ill intent on the part of either, and there was no Holmes here to persuade me that their choice of tobacco or the state of their shirt-cuffs was proof of some nefarious intent.

In any case, it was long past time for me to be asleep, and I felt that my fatigue might now be great enough to overcome the stimulant in the coffee. As the second figure rounded a crook in the road ahead, vanishing from my sight after the first, I made to close the window.

As I did so, however, I was baffled to discern a third figure in the high street, following Topkins every bit as surreptitiously as he was pursuing Gramascene. I was quite certain that I had not heard the hotel door close for a third time.

I saw this person only for a moment before they, too, disappeared beyond my view, but it was clear enough that the silhouette was that of a woman. More perplexing still, I was more than half convinced that it had been Wermeholt's inquisitive postmistress, Mrs Trice.

# CHAPTER THREE

In the end I slept, though fitfully and with ominous dreams. At one point in the night I was convinced that I heard phantom music from the mere, a mournful piping. I had resolved, during a second spell of wakefulness at around four o'clock, to lie in and beg Mr Dormer to indulge me with a late breakfast, but instead I awoke with a sense of dread at around half past six, to loud voices ringing through the hotel.

Reluctantly, I concluded that I could expect no more sleep tonight. In annoyance I washed, dressed and presented myself for breakfast in the hotel's dining room, where the research party was gathered in some agitation. Outside, despite the time of year, the streets were dark, and a sticky mist could be seen clinging to the mere. A scent of damp, with a hint even of rot, pervaded the morning air.

"I tell you, I don't know where he is!" James Topkins was insisting plaintively. "If he's not interested in coming, we must simply leave without him."

"There's no need to be so upset, James," Mrs Creavesey advised him, with sympathy but some impatience. "He has probably only gone for an early morning walk and lost track of the time."

"I think not, my dear," her husband said distractedly. "I have looked just now, and his bed has not been slept in. I know that he has expressed interest in some books Woodwose has at his cottage. Perhaps he returned with Woodwose, and stayed overnight?" He looked a little lost without Woodwose to appeal to on the matter.

"No. No, we stayed up long after Sir Howard left, until – that is, until about two," said Topkins, quieter suddenly.

"If the young man has any sense at all," Professor Summerlee observed, "he will have packed up and gone home." He, at least, was perfectly composed, sitting and smoking his pipe in the corner of the room. "He could have caught the early train from Ravensfoot. If you ask my opinion, we should all follow his example."

"Observations of that kind are not helpful, Summerlee," snapped Professor Creavesey with surprising force. More mildly, he added, "Besides, all his things are still in his room."

I wanted nothing more than for them all to leave so that I could have my breakfast in peace. Still rather befuddled in the head, I asked, "Did Mr Gramascene not return last night, then?"

From the corner of my eye I saw Topkins frown slightly, but nobody else appeared to have noticed my inadvertent implication.

"Henry has vanished, as far as we can see," Mrs Creavesey replied. "We were to set out on our excursion half an hour ago, and he's our strongest oarsman."

"He strokes for the college First Eight," Topkins acknowledged, rather distantly. "If the boat were not still at the mooring, I might have thought he'd gone out for an early morning row."

"Ah," I said sagely, wondering in my exhausted state why Topkins was not telling the whole truth, but still reluctant to put any malign interpretation on the matter. "Perhaps he borrowed a different boat?"

"Why on earth would he do that?" Topkins asked, a little shortly. "No, Henry has let us down. Perhaps Professor Summerlee's right and he's gone home. We'll need to proceed to Glissenholm without him. I'm no college blade, but I can stroke in a crisis."

"I, too, am perfectly capable of paddling a canoe if called upon to do so," said Summerlee placidly.

"Is Sir Howard not joining you?" I asked. Though elderly, the folklorist's frame was a powerful one, and I thought he must be nothing like as frail as Creavesey.

"He says he has seen Glissenholm quite enough times for his own satisfaction," said Creavesey. "This trip is one for scientific eyes, and instruments too of course. We carry cameras and a phonograph, and we intend also to take depth soundings." He paused, as if remembering suddenly that I was not privy to the purpose of their excursion.

"Well, I still say we should proceed," insisted Topkins, and the company reluctantly acceded.

Mrs Creavesey said, "Of course, if you would care to join us, Dr Watson, then the gentlemen could share the work more evenly and we might make better time." Her husband glanced at her in mild alarm, but he need not have worried. Intrigued though I might be by the enigma the scientists presented, I had no wish to prolong my presence in Wermeholt.

I said, "Thank you for the offer, but I must set out for Hartsmere today if I am to keep to my itinerary."

"Well, that is a shame, but understandable," said Creavesey.

"Yes, I don't blame you in the slightest," Summerlee muttered.

I promised that I would convey their displeasure to Gramascene, if I should happen to see him before I left, and I saw them off from the mooring. Despite Topkins' offer, it was the stoical Summerlee who rowed them away.

Returning indoors, I was finally allowed to address myself to a leisurely breakfast. I read the previous day's newspapers again, Mr Dormer having informed me that those for the new day would arrive around noon. They were brought up by the early train from London and then by boat from Ravensfoot, but I had no intention of staying in Wermeholt long enough to see them. No doubt there would be papers in Hartsdale.

I packed away my belongings into my haversack, settled my bill, took up once more the ashplant I had borrowed from Holmes, and took my leave of Wermeholt with a morning stroll.

The air was chilly, and the lakewater plashed sluggishly against the hotel's mooring-post. The townsfolk were already about, and the post office was open. I did not call in, having no particular need to renew my acquaintance with Mrs Trice.

I purposed to take a final walk along the high street, past the Scorpes' inn and St Michael's church, before ascending to the dragon's-foot way-marker where the paths had divided, and continuing my interrupted journey to Netherfell's summit and points beyond. I would, I supposed, pass Sir Howard Woodwose's cottage as well, and knowing that he was not out on the mere with the rest of the previous night's party I considered calling upon him to say goodbye. I concluded, however, that our acquaintance of the previous night had been insufficient to require or justify that I disturb him at home. I should indeed be happy to press on and to leave Wermeholt, with its gloom and damp, behind me.

As I approached the church, however, I began to hear a hubbub ahead. The voices had the hushed, excited quality one hears from idlers in London at the scene of some tragedy like a suicide or a coach crash, but I thought there was another note as well. It was the distinctive tone of fear. I hastened forward, heading for the churchyard whence I thought the noise was coming.

To my alarm, however, Mrs Trice suddenly stood before me in the street, having interspersed herself from Heaven only knew where. She looked concerned, but none the worse for her late night. I was surprised when she said, "Dr Watson! Thank all t'stars thou's here. There's no doctor here in town, thou sees, none but Dr Kebbelwhite over in Ravensfoot, and thou – you are needed straight away, if you please." Her manner was markedly changed since her prurient friendliness the previous day. Though forthright, she seemed conciliatory, and even a little subdued.

She hustled me quickly away to, as I had expected, the churchyard, where a small knot of locals stood in what would have been the shadow of the church tower, had the whole graveyard not lain in the shadow of the fell. Among the bystanders I recognised the Reverend Felspar, and Ben Scorpe the publican, along with a few others whom I had seen about the streets the previous day. The grey-faced widow was there too, and this time as she glanced at me she made some reflexive gesture with her hand that I did not catch.

All of them seemed sombre. As Mrs Trice led me up, they parted guiltily, as if ashamed of their fascination with the inert body that lay sprawled on the ground among the gravestones, several yards from the path. I could see at a glance that it was grievously damaged.

I thought at first that the young man must have jumped or fallen from the bell-tower, but then I saw the bloody trail behind him. It seemed he had been making a beeline for the vestry door at the base of the tower, directly from where the churchyard met the lakeside at the corpse-gate.

It was an apt entrance for his arrival, since he was evidently lifeless. There was no possibility that Henry Gramascene could have survived such injuries for long.

"Stand aside," I instructed them all sharply. "I'm a doctor. I need to examine this man. Are you in charge here, Constable?" I asked a scrawny young man with deep-set eyes and an unfortunate nose, who wore a police constable's uniform and ill-fitting helmet.

"Aye, that I is," he said defiantly, as if he expected me to insist otherwise. He could scarcely be more than twenty years old. "I's Batterby, t'police constable here. Who'd thou be?"

"My name is Watson," I told him, realising in dismay that Mrs Trice had probably told everyone present that she was going to fetch the associate of the famous Sherlock Holmes. "As I said, I am a medical man, and there will need to be a medical report. Someone must confirm how this man died."

"I's in charge here," he reiterated, but he stood back and let me kneel beside the body.

Gramascene wore the remains of an overcoat over the clothes he had dined in the night before. He had been badly mauled. The flesh had been ripped from his left side along with his coat and shirt, and his head bore a deep and jagged gash across the scalp. The rest of his body was covered with cuts and bruises. He was soaking wet and a pool of bloody mud surrounded him. He lay on his intact side, his arm splayed out towards the gravestone of one Reverend Laertes Wilfredson, 1754–1799. For all his bulk and muscle, he looked like nothing more than the sad and soggy remains of a rat that had been mauled by a housecat. I was amazed that he had been able to crawl so far.

"Good God," I whispered into the sudden hush. "What happened to you, man?"

A superstitious murmur followed my words, and even Constable Batterby shook his head fearfully, rubbing his misshapen nose. "Nowt that's good," said a voice finally, and I looked across to see an older man in a butcher's apron, hurriedly avoiding my gaze. I remembered that the local butcher shared the constable's name, and there was indeed a family resemblance between the men, but that was hardly to the point at present.

"Have any of you seen injuries like this before?" I asked.

There was a lengthy silence, then at last a man I did not

recognise replied, "Aye, as it might be." He went on, "One on my
ewes down by t'mere's shore, two month gone."

"Aye, and I, maybe," another admitted reluctantly. "Another
ewe too. Back last summer, but. And Josh Thoroughby said his
old dog Shem was just t'same."

I turned my attention back to the body. Gramascene's wounds
were torn and ragged, and I returned to my instinctive comparison
with a cat's prey. Had he been mauled by some animal? But surely
no rogue dog, such as might have worried a sheep, could have
done such damage to a healthy specimen like Gramascene. As I
inspected the horrible marks, I heard the Reverend Felspar burst
out, "Oh, but I can't bear it! That poor young man!"

"There, vicar," said a female voice soothingly, and I recognised
it as that of Effie Scorpe, the publican's daughter. "He can't suffer
no more. He's wi't'Lord now, wouldn't thou say?" Though she
clearly intended to comfort the priest, I noted that she professed
no such belief herself.

"Of course, my child, of course. But still – it must have been
such a ghastly death. To drag himself all that way, so awfully
injured…" Felspar's voice quavered, and I thought he was about
to burst into tears.

"Aye. It'd be a shock for anyone, t'way thou found him like
that," Effie commiserated.

"You found the body, Mr Felspar?" I asked, hoping to persuade
the priest to focus his thoughts on a practical point. He had struck
me on our earlier meeting as a man with no great resources of
resilience, and it would do little for his authority among his flock
if he were to break down crying over a stranger like Gramascene.

"I – I did," the vicar admitted. "I was coming to prepare for
matins. I say the liturgy every morning at nine o'clock, even if it
is… sparsely attended. The routine is a comfort to the parishioners
nevertheless," he mumbled, though I suspected that the only

person his regular morning prayers comforted was himself. "I was looking up at the bell-tower, and I almost stumbled over him. The poor wretched fellow..."

"There, vicar," Effie said again, patting his shoulder.

A few minutes later, I had finished my investigation. I closed Henry Gramascene's staring eyes, reflecting as I did so that he was the kind of man many would mourn. I had learned nothing of his private life, but even if he had no parents or sweetheart to weep for him, his wit and charm must have won him many friends. He had not been, I supposed, such a promising student as Topkins, and probably had had no great scientific career awaiting him after university, but with his physique and intellect he could have been an athlete, a military man, or something in the colonial service, had he been so inclined. His loss was a tragic waste, whether or not it was the result of any human agency.

Affecting a businesslike manner, I stood up. "This young man died of loss of blood, following severe trauma to the head and torso."

"Aye," said Constable Batterby truculently. "Doesn't take a doctor to see that."

I went on, "It's most unlikely that he would have survived this, even had there been a well-equipped surgeon on hand. I've seen a few men live after being wounded this badly on the battlefield, but they were very lucky."

At the mention of my war service, the constable bit back another rude retort. Instead he said gruffly, "Nearest doctor's Ravensfoot, and there's no hospital closer than Keswick. There's none here could've helped him, saving thou."

"Well, in my opinion he's been dead for several hours." He had probably been expiring, in fact, at the very moment that his friends had been bemoaning his absence from the hotel. "I imagine many of you recognise him," I went on to the crowd at large, remembering what I, and I realised Mrs Trice too, knew of his movements last night. "This is Henry Gramascene, a palaeontological student of Professor Creavesey's party, staying at the Mereside Hotel. He was missed early this morning. Have you got anything to cover him up with, Mr Felspar?" I asked.

The priest turned helplessly to another man, who wore the black vestments of the church verger. In a local accent this man said, "There's t'old altar cloth," and hurried away.

As I stretched my back and looked around me, I noticed for the first time, with an unaccountable unease, that a few of the nearby gravestones were carved with a serpent motif of a kind I had never seen in a graveyard before. It reminded me of the dragon sculpture in the church, and I supposed must be connected with it in some way.

"Did he arrive here in a boat?" I asked the constable, though the question clearly lay beyond my medical purview. Gramascene was wet through, but it was impossible to imagine him capable of swimming in his condition. After a moment's thought I rejected the idea that he might have sculled here, either. If he had been in a boat, he must have been attacked while disembarking.

"Aye, down at t'jetty," Batterby said reluctantly. "Not one from Wermeholt, but."

"Don't you recognise it?" I asked. "There can't be that many boats on the lake." But it seemed from the general shrugging and mumbling that no one did.

I suggested to Batterby, as tactfully as I could, that the boat should be carried up from the jetty into the churchyard, where it could be inspected in its entirety. With poor grace he agreed, and a few of the local men obliged.

It was an ordinary rowing-boat of simple design, with no identifying marks that I could see. I did not recognise it either, but, as I have said, I am no boatman. The one remaining oar had been left lying loose in the bilge, and was brought up separately.

The vessel had been in good condition, recently varnished I supposed, but the hull was scraped near the stern and stained with blood. A narrow cable lashed to a hook in the centre of the transom had been neatly severed a foot or so below the gunwale.

"Lord preserve us," I muttered, horribly shaken by the sight. And then an even worse thought struck me.

"Great Scott!" I cried. "The Professor's party is out on the lake now, with Mrs Creavesey! Whatever happened to Mr Gramascene could happen to them too!"

"Then they gets what they came here for," Ben Scorpe said callously. "Let them see how they likes it."

"Now then, Ben," Batterby scolded him half-heartedly. "T'doctor's right, we must bring them in. I've questions to ask on them. Ned, Luke, hie out in your boat and tell them to come right back in," he told a wiry man and younger boy lurking on the fringes of the crowd. With more good sense than I had expected, he added, "Don't tell them what's happened, mind. See you leave that on me."

The older boatman gave a lazy salute then sloped off, taking the boy with him.

"It seems thou's looking to leave us, Doctor," the constable noted with a nod at my haversack, as the vicar and the verger covered up Gramascene's body, and the crowd began reluctantly to disperse. "I reckon thou'd better bide a while. There may be more we needs to ask on thou."

"I had realised as much, Constable," I told him, but that was not the only conclusion that I had come to. With this development, horrible as it was, it had become clear to me that the mystery of Summerlee's and Creavesey's purpose here was, after all, a question likely to be of interest to Sherlock Holmes.

# CHAPTER FOUR

I returned at once to the Mereside Hotel, where I extended my reservation for the next two nights and unpacked once more in my room, which Mr Dormer fortunately had not let in the meantime.

Then, hoping that Constable Batterby would have successfully dispersed the throng at the churchyard, I stepped out quickly to the post office, to send a telegram to Holmes:

```
MYSTERIOUS DEATH WERMEHOLT NR
WERMEWATER STOP MEMBER OF SECRETIVE
SCIENTIFIC EXPEDITION FATALLY WOUNDED
GUILTY PARTY UNKNOWN INTRIGUING
CIRCUMSTANCES STOP WATSON.
```

If that failed to attract my friend's attention, then I knew him less well than I thought.

I found Mrs Trice quite returned to her familiar self. "So, he'll be gracing us with his presence now, will he?" she asked pointedly when I had dictated this missive to her. "Finds Wermeholt interesting enough for him now? Well, fancy. Who'd have thought a death's what was needed to bring him here."

I made no reply, not least because her assessment was uncomfortably accurate. "But there was something else I wanted to ask you, Mrs Trice," I said instead.

"Aye?" She glared at me suspiciously. "What would that be, then?"

"You were following James Topkins and Henry Gramascene last night," I told her, and was rather gratified to see her eyes become quite wide with shock. "Pray don't trouble to deny it," I told her, feeling rather as I fancied Holmes must when confronting a wrongdoer. "I saw you from my hotel room window. Gramascene left at around two, then Topkins followed him." Two o'clock was the time when Topkins had told the party that he and Gramascene had retired, but it had also been the time, according to my repeater watch, when they had set out separately on their single errand. "And then you followed Topkins."

"And what if I did?" she demanded defiantly. "That'd be my business, wouldn't it?"

"Normally I would say yes, but since one of the men you followed was dead a few hours later, I think my interest is a legitimate one, don't you?" Again I found myself imagining the thrill Holmes would have felt. "I'm sorry to have to tell you, Mrs Trice, but the reputation you enjoy among your neighbours is not one of discretion, especially concerning others' secrets. It would be remarkable, and not a little suspicious, if you began to keep them for the first time in connection with a young man's death."

"Oh, very clever," Mrs Trice sneered. "I suppose your friend taught you that, did he?"

I deflated slightly under her withering gaze. "You will surely allow that it's a valid question," I insisted.

"Aye, well." She sniffed. "Seeing as you ask, I did follow those two lads. I saw them out of my window going down the street, first one and then t'other, and I thought they might be up to no good, so I followed them."

"You were close on their heels, and yet you were fully dressed," I objected. "At two in the morning?"

"I'm not much of a sleeper, not that it's any business of yours. I often walk abroad at night. I was about to go out when I saw them both, creeping down the high street like a pair of schoolboys up to mischief."

"Very well," I said again. I nodded, as if satisfied of her innocence, though I was no more so than I had been before our conversation. Now, though, came the more interesting question. "If you followed them, can you tell me where they went and what they did?"

"I saw them stop outside the Serpent's Arms, though they were wasting their time there." The Serpent's Arms was the somewhat paradoxical name of the town's inn. "Ben Scorpe would never have the place open at that time of night, certainly not for those two. The big gentleman stopped first, Mr Gramascene who's dead now, then t'other stopped too, but when he did, the first one saw him. 'That you, James?' he said, and t'other lad stepped out and said 'Of course it's me. What the devil do you think you're doing?'"

"And did Mr Gramascene say what he was doing?" I asked.

"No. He said, 'Come away from the street, for' – well, I won't tell you whose sake he said – 'and let's talk about this like gentlemen.' And then they went off into the alley next to the Arms and I couldn't hear them any more."

"That must have been very provoking for you," I said, though in truth I felt equally frustrated. "Did you hear nothing further?"

"Oh, they argued," she told me, with great certainty. "There were raised voices, though I couldn't tell you over what. I won't say they came to blows, but they weren't far short of it. Then I heard one of them coming out again and I went on my way."

"Rather hastily, I should imagine," I said. "Thank you, Mrs Trice, that's potentially helpful."

"I don't see why you're asking," she said truculently. "It's not like that lad killed his friend, is it?"

"We still don't know what he was doing out on the mere," I admitted, aware that any nugget of information I gave her would soon be all over the town. "It sounds as if Mr Topkins may be able to set me right on that point, though, so I'll have a word with him."

"Aye, you do that," she said sceptically. "I'm sure he'll tell you what his friend was doing that he thought he needed to follow him, and why they fought about it. It's not like he's anything to hide now, is it?" she sneered. "With his friend dead and all."

Curse the poisonous woman, I thought as I left the post office, but she was right. Whatever secret Henry Gramascene was keeping that his friend had felt important enough to follow him covertly and confront him over in the street, it hardly seemed likely that Topkins would be willing to confide the details to me.

I returned to the hotel to find the rest of Creavesey's party tying up their boat. It seemed that they had noticed the commotion on the shore, and turned back before Ned and Luke had even reached them. The other boat was floating nearby even so, the boatman and his boy watching their return with unconcealed curiosity.

Constable Batterby had been awaiting the party, and once they were all safely ashore, with an awkward mixture of embarrassment and self-importance, he informed them of Henry Gramascene's death. Mrs Creavesey cried out, and James Topkins went deathly pale. Professor Creavesey tried manfully to comfort his wife, while also protesting that Batterby must have made a mistake and that the body he found must have been some other young man, some stranger to the town who merely resembled Gramascene, a tramp perhaps.

Summerlee placed a hand on his fellow professor's shoulder and said, "No doubt the constable knows his work better than we, Creavesey. Besides, I see from Watson's face that he too knows all about this business. It is a tragic loss, of course." He nodded several times, as if satisfying himself that it might be justly described in such terms. "How did he die?" he asked the constable.

Batterby hesitated. I had been wondering whether he would be more forthcoming about his suspicions away from his compatriots in the churchyard. Instead, to my surprise, the young policeman turned to me. "Dr Watson can tell thou better than I," he informed Summerlee.

I, too, paused before replying. Picking my words carefully, I said, "He appears to have been seriously injured while tying up his boat at the corpse-gate. I can't say what hurt him, but it may have been an animal of some kind. He managed to make his way into the churchyard, where he collapsed. The vicar found his body earlier this morning."

There was a stunned pause. Then Topkins cried angrily, "Is this a joke? Is this supposed to be funny, Dr Watson? Was this Henry's idea? Did he put you up to this?"

"Topkins, you are upset," I told him sternly. "I assure you that I am not in the habit of playing practical jokes, especially about the deaths of others. Nor, I am quite certain, is Constable Batterby. Henry Gramascene is dead, I am sorry to say, and his death was as I have described. I have no theory to explain it, only the facts."

"Good God," Professor Creavesey whispered. "Good God. To have it all confirmed like this!"

"Have what confirmed?" I asked, but the question went unanswered, and for all I could tell unheard.

Summerlee's hand was still on his shoulder. His face was grim. He said, "We cannot regard anything as confirmed until we have seen the body." I could tell, as clearly as if I could hear his thoughts, that he was weighing up this new information and finding its evidentiary value dubious, whatever it was that he and his colleagues were seeking evidence for. Scant though his native reserves of tact might be, they were sufficient not to stress that argument at such a time.

"Yes," Creavesey said. "Yes, you are right. It will be terrible, of course, but our duty is clear. We must examine the body, Constable."

Batterby seemed at a loss as to whether to allow this or not. Fearing that he might forbid it out of nothing more than a desire to reassert his authority, I said mildly, "I have no objection to hearing a second or third opinion, Constable. And these people are young Gramascene's friends."

"Aye," the policeman said. "Well, thou can't hurt him now."

"I'll stay here with Mrs Creavesey," said Topkins hurriedly. "Someone should."

"There's really no need, James," Edith Creavesey replied, and for a moment I thought that she would insist on joining the viewing party. However, seeing Topkins queasily reaching the same conclusion, she added, "Though it would be a comfort, of course." The student looked relieved.

While I had been otherwise occupied, Gramascene's body had been moved to the town hall, a grand name for a building considerably smaller than the church. It lay a little way back from the high street, where the streets began to slope up towards the skirts of Netherfell, and, as well as a public hall that I supposed was used for public meetings, dances and the like, it housed the tiny office that served as Constable Batterby's police station.

Henry Gramascene was laid out on a trestle table in the hall still covered with the second-best altar cloth from St Michael's. Old newspapers had been set across it, and upon the floor beneath, to soak up the lake water from his clothing.

Poor Creavesey was deeply affected at the sight, and cried out. Summerlee, by contrast, seemed to dismiss any dismay at the young man's passing in favour of his status as evidence, and, ignoring his

colleague's distress, crossed the room to peer at the body. After
a few moments' hesitation, Creavesey joined him, and the two
men leaned in close to inspect the fearsome wounds, conferring
in murmurs between themselves. I hung back in the dubious
company of Constable Batterby, unwilling either to intrude upon
their grief or to appear to influence their conclusions.

It was clear to me that Batterby was ill-equipped to take
charge of an investigation into the violent death of a gentleman
from outside the area, but when I gently suggested calling in the
county constabulary, he adamantly refused. "Why'd I want to
call in them in Keswick?" he objected petulantly. "They thinks
they're pretty smart there, wi' their incomers and their tourists.
If I tell them I can't handle this mysel', they'll laugh in my face."

"Then let them laugh," I told him forcefully. "They'll change
their tune when they come here and see the body."

"This ain't one on thy Mr Holmes's murder cases down
in London," Batterby persisted. "It wasn't a man killed Henry
Gramascene."

"We haven't established that," I pointed out, though it
was interesting to know for sure that the constable thought
so. Despite the savagery of the wounds, there was no reason I
could see why they might not have been inflicted with a weapon,
though it would have had to be serrated and heavy; I thought
perhaps a timber-saw might fit the bill. It was a mystery why any
human assailant would also damage the boat, unless it was to
increase the impression of an animal attack. "And if you're right,
then whatever creature did it must be captured, or at least its
threat assessed. It's your duty to protect the public," I reminded
him. "And there are procedures to be followed."

Reluctantly, he conceded. "All right. I'll send word til
them at Keswick," he agreed, with very poor grace. "But I's not
answerable for what they tells me."

While we had been speaking, Gramascene's boat had arrived, carried by four ill-tempered local men, and that, too, was laid down on newspaper so that the eminent scientists could examine its abrasions.

At length they were finished. "It is the very evidence we needed," Creavesey sighed heavily. He glanced at me and Batterby. "We must go and tell the others. Sir Howard in particular will need to know."

"Wait," I said. "If you know more of this, then you must share it with the authorities. I claim no such status for myself," I added hurriedly, gesturing towards Batterby, "but the constable must know, at least."

Creavesey gazed at us for a time, then shook his head. "Perhaps, but we must speak to Sir Howard first. Besides, I think the constable already knows."

"Knows what?" I asked Batterby indignantly as the scientists left, but he just shook his head.

"Them in Keswick'll laugh in my face," he said again, bitterly.

I left the town hall and began to walk back to the Mereside Hotel, noting as I did so that the streets of Wermeholt, while busy, were largely silent, the folk grim-faced in response to this tragedy that had occurred in their midst. Few boats were out upon the lake. I thought I saw the craggy woman in black walking away from me in the distance, towards the end of town where Woodwose's cottage was located, but shortly afterwards I passed her coming out of the ironmonger's. Again she made that quick movement of her hand that eluded me, following it with a curt nod before walking away.

Confused, I returned to the hotel. The front door stood open, and in the hallway Summerlee and Creavesey were speaking in urgent whispers with Sir Howard Woodwose. Not wishing to be thought to be eavesdropping, I walked round to the garden, and the rear door overlooking the hotel's own mooring. That led into the sitting-room, and it too stood open. As I approached, I heard low voices from within.

"…and yet you will not help me to dissuade him, even now," a female speaker was saying.

Well, if both routes had become venues for furtive conversations, I could only take my choice. I stepped up to the door.

"That is not what concerns me, as you know," said a male voice. "If the professor suspects as much as we fear…"

"The consequences of that will not be so disastrous," replied the first. "Provided—"

But at that point I entered the sitting-room. I saw James Topkins and Mrs Creavesey, engaged in earnest and intense talk, before they saw me and stopped immediately.

Topkins greeted me stiffly, though Edith Creavesey managed a facsimile of her usual warmth. I made my apologies as I passed them and went up to my room. I could not help but wonder, though, what it was that Topkins feared Mrs Creavesey's husband suspected, and what its possible consequences might be.

Upstairs in my room, I wrote a full account of what had occurred since my arrival in Wermeholt, omitting nothing, for Holmes to peruse on his arrival. If I heard nothing, I could always send it to him, perhaps asking some traveller to post it in Ravensfoot so as to bypass the eagle eye of Mrs Trice. If he did not come, my friend might at least offer his views by post.

I was contemplating what I might best do next, given my enforced stay in Wermeholt, when there was a tap upon my door. "Watson," said Professor Summerlee when I opened it to him. "I have spoken to Creavesey and Woodwose, and to Topkins and Mrs Creavesey too, and we have come to a decision. You are correct that the information that we have, such as it is, should be laid before the authorities. As I have mentioned, I am not entirely of one mind with my colleagues over the import of said information, but we are at least agreed that you should be taken into our confidence regarding the purpose of our mission here, before we tell the constable."

"I see," I said. "Well, that is gratifying, Professor, and I shall endeavour to repay the compliment."

"Do not be too eager to take it as such," Summerlee said wryly. "As I say, the whole affair is, in my view, quite absurd, but it has acquired a relevance that I decidedly did not foresee. Tell me, Watson, have you heard about the legend of the Hagworm?"

"The... Hagworm?" Something of the kind had been mentioned in my guidebook. I tried to remember the details. "Some sort of creature said to live in Lake Wermewater, like the one in Loch Ness? The lake is named after it, as I recall."

"Precisely so." Professor Summerlee shook his head, his beard waggling from side to side. "Woodwose is certain that it exists, and summoned us here to discover whether there was a single atom of truth in the matter. I was invited as the party's sceptic. You will understand the critical importance of such a role when I tell you that Creavesey and Topkins are quite convinced that the beast is a surviving dinosaur."

# CHAPTER FIVE

"I have no hesitation now," Professor Creavesey pronounced, once we had joined him and the others downstairs, "in saying that a specimen of some unknown and predatory species lurks in these waters, and that poor Gramascene has fallen victim to it. There can surely be little doubt that it is the Hagworm of legend. Confirming that it is indeed a plesiosaurus or similar aquatic saurian will only be a matter of observation."

"Such a calamity." Woodwose's declaration rang with melancholy. "And yet in its way, as we must surely accept, an opportunity as well. Poor Gramascene would have found it little comfort, perhaps, to know that his sad passing would so further the cause of human knowledge, but we may take some solace in it nevertheless."

Creavesey took heart from Woodwose's presence, as he was wont to do. "We will complete the work we came here for, in Gramascene's honour," he declared. "No lesser recognition than naming the creature after him – *Plesiosaurus gramascenensis*, if plesiosaurus it be – will suffice."

"Let us find it first." Summerlee's beard wagged severely. "There is no sense in naming a creature we have not seen, and whose existence we have little more proof of than we had yesterday."

"On that point," I said, "I could not be certain that the wounds I saw were inflicted by an animal. Can you?"

Carefully, Summerlee said, "At present I can say nothing more definite than that they could have been the work of some large-jawed predator. I am not, of course, an expert in animal dentition. Since we already knew of the recent deaths of sheep and other livestock, I cannot say that Gramascene's demise has offered us evidence enough to change my view, whatever my personal feelings for the fellow."

I said, "Some of the townsfolk mentioned sheep dying. And a dog, one of them said."

Woodwose nodded gravely. "Indeed," he assented, "though the dog was an elderly one, well past its prime. I have of course long been familiar with the legend of the Hagworm, as one among many of lake monsters and their kind. The creature has been seen for centuries in these parts, and its appearances are said to foretell the deaths of members of the Wermeston family, with which it has an ancient connection.

"Since I moved to Wermeholt I have been collecting accounts of these appearances. In the past year, there have been rather more of them, and of course these attacks, the likes of which have not been known for some time. I am sure they would be of little enough interest to your Mr Holmes, Doctor, but they interest me. There have been no wolves in Cumbria, or anywhere in England, for a hundred years, and no wild bears or big cats for much longer."

"Another dog, perhaps?" I suggested, remembering my earlier speculation. "Some stray gone rogue?"

Woodwose said, "Such a thing would be unusual, but hardly unprecedented. Even if no local farmer admitted to owning such an animal, they would all recognise the signs for what they were. And the wounds in question seem to have been inflicted by a rather bigger creature. The locals are hard-headed when it comes to farming and its hazards, and yet many of them are perfectly convinced that the Hagworm is roaming abroad. Some are quite terrified, I'm afraid."

I realised that such a superstitious fear would certainly explain the atmosphere at the churchyard when Gramascene had been found, and since then in the town at large. It was, I assumed, what Creavesey had suggested that Constable Batterby already knew, although I agreed with Summerlee that "knew" was putting it unjustifiably strongly. It was surely also why Batterby feared that his report would meet with derision among his superiors in Keswick.

Despite the grave mood, James Topkins could restrain his scientific enthusiasm no longer. "A dinosaur would explain everything, you see," he told us quietly, yet forcefully. "There were many aquatic species, but they could probably move onto land like seals or walruses. Our theory is that the sightings represent a small population of surviving plesiosaurs. Their long necks would fit the bill perfectly. And some of the fossil specimens I've seen are huge."

"But dinosaurs have been extinct for millions of years," I said, as reasonably as I felt able under the circumstances. It seemed to me that James Topkins must have read Monsieur Verne's *Journey to the Centre of the Earth* at rather too impressionable a time of life.

"You may say that, Dr Watson," said Creavesey quickly, "but 'dinosaur' is simply the name we give to these large extinct reptiles. If we had been familiar all our lives with plesiosaurs, would it ever occur to us to class them with late monsters such as the diplodocus or stegosaur? And, on the contrary, had we learned of the latter's existence before the first explorer set eyes upon a crocodile, would we not dismiss his tales of huge predatory lizards as a scientifically unsound fantasy?"

This argument was so preposterous that it temporarily silenced me. I wished I had Holmes at hand to bring his razor-sharp logic to bear, along with his equally cutting wit.

Instead, I said again, "But why now? That is, why would... such a creature, whatever it is... emerge now, after so long?"

"Perhaps a juvenile specimen has only now reached maturity," Creavesey suggested, with a tentative glance at his wife.

"With respect, Professor, I have an alternative idea," Topkins said. "I think it may be our fault."

"Yours? But you've only recently arrived here," I pointed out patiently.

Hastily, Topkins corrected himself. "Mankind's, I mean. With the arrival of the railway, the population of Ravensfoot has grown, and what was formerly a modest local fishing industry has grown with it. This would reduce the food supply for the creatures in the lake, who must also live on the fish. Such a body of water could never have supported a large population of the beasts, but perhaps it can no longer sustain the few that live here. Perhaps that's why they are beginning to seek their prey on dry land."

"Might not a smaller lake also limit the size of the specimens, like fish kept in a small aquarium that never reach their full size?" Mrs Creavesey asked quietly. "Land animals isolated on an island often become smaller over many generations, after all. The same would surely happen with aquatic creatures cut off from the sea. And any plesiosaur population must have resided here for many generations indeed."

Topkins looked surprised. After a moment he said, "Well, I suppose it might. But since it is a large specimen we have to explain, it would appear not."

"Circular logic, Topkins," snapped Summerlee. "You are begging the question. If Mrs Creavesey is correct, then she has reduced the explanatory power of the plesiosaurus hypothesis.

You must prove her wrong or admit as much."

"Summerlee plays the role of official sceptic in our party," Creavesey explained to me, with a sad smile. "It is his function to point out the flaws in our thinking, so that we may strive to overcome them."

"Strive, and certainly fail. We are here on a perfect fools' errand." I wondered whether Summerlee numbered himself among the perfect fools. "As Watson's friend Mr Holmes would say, I am here to eliminate the impossible."

"So what is your explanation for the mutilated animals, Summerlee?" rumbled Woodwose in a soothing tone. "Something must have butchered them."

"Poor Henry said that we should ask the butcher where he was at the time," Topkins reflected ruefully.

"Given that the constable is Mr Batterby's son, that line of investigation is unlikely to find favour with the police," smiled Woodwose. "But you were about to enlighten us, Summerlee."

"If the creature you hypothesise did indeed attack Gramascene, then why has it come ashore at all in search of sheep and dogs? There are boatsful of nourishing human beings afloat on the lake daily," Summerlee responded acerbically. "And while the alternative hypothesis of a rogue dog may not receive much favour from the superstitious locals, dogs have the merit of existing in the present day. Indeed, I find it less unlikely that a lion or tiger might somehow make the journey unobserved from present-day Africa or India to the shores of Lake Wermewater, than that a plesiosaurus could find its way here from the Jurassic Era."

"And yet there are some creatures that survive from earlier ages," Topkins urged. "Darwin mentions several such living fossils. Both the platypus and the lungfish, for instance."

"Each of which is a perfectly mundane animal, to the natives of those regions where they are endemic," Summerlee said. "A plesiosaurus is not mundane anywhere." As if unable to restrain himself any longer, he burst out, "It beggars belief that a giant aquatic reptile, or even a dwarf form of one, should persist in an English lake with nothing more to attest to its existence than the ramblings of a handful of witnesses over the centuries. Where are the remains? If there is a population of such creatures here, any number of them must have died since this lake was cut off from the sea. How is it that none of their bones have ever found their way to the shore – especially if, as you maintain, they are capable of amphibious behaviour? Do the beasts never damage boats or piers? Has none ever become tangled in a fisherman's line?"

While this seemed to me a cogent point, the others, Woodwose and Creavesey in particular, were looking frustrated at Summerlee's obtuseness. I had the sense that it was a line of argument the professor had employed before, to equally little effect. I had been surprised at first to hear Summerlee's reasons for being in the vicinity, but it was quite in keeping with what I knew of him that he would relish his intellectual duty to be present, provided he could pour scorn on the credulousness of his colleagues.

"Well, nevertheless," said Creavesey after a little pause, "whether this new information changes everything or nothing, we must resume our expedition as soon as decency allows."

"You surely do not intend to venture out upon the lake again?" I asked. "Think of the danger if you're correct. Something certainly attacked Gramascene, human or otherwise."

"A sturdier boat would surely be a sensible precaution," Woodwose agreed. "One with a metal hull, perhaps, and stable in the water."

"Obtaining and transporting such a vessel could take weeks," Summerlee objected. "There is none already on Wermewater, and there can be few in any of the Lakes."

"I shall make enquiries among my local contacts," rumbled Woodwose. "I've no doubt something can be found, for a price."

Finding no sense among the older men, I left them to their disputation and turned to their disciple. "Shall you go along with this foolishness, Mr Topkins?"

"In the name of science? Of course." Despite the understandable qualms he had felt earlier at facing his friend's corpse, Topkins seemed willing enough to defy danger in such a cause. "The import of such a discovery remains incalculable."

"I see," I said. Though I considered all these men foolhardy, I could only respect their courage and commitment, even for so misplaced a purpose – although I suspected that, for all Woodwose's enthusiasm to continue the project, he planned to take no personal part in their excursions onto Wermewater. "And shall this venture have your blessing also, Mrs Creavesey?" I asked.

She smiled. "Since I cannot expect now that I will be permitted to participate in person, my blessing is all that I can give it. This expedition means a great deal to my husband, Dr Watson, and his happiness means a great deal to me."

"But if they go disturbing this creature…" I began, hurriedly adding, "if creature it is…" I did not wish to be thought to be tacitly accepting the Hagworm's existence.

Edith Creavesey sighed. "I cannot deny my misgivings about their safety, but Wermewater has not suddenly become a more dangerous place overnight. People row and sail on it daily, and Henry is the first we know to have perished. He could be impulsive, I am afraid, and none of us knows why he saw fit to set out on the lake alone. It's possible that he did something to provoke what happened."

On that point, I remembered anew that Topkins might know more than he had told us so far. "Yes, I wonder what Mr Gramascene *was* doing abroad so early, and in a strange boat?"

I speculated. The young man did not respond, so I asked him directly, "Did he say – or do – anything last night to suggest that he had such plans?"

"He did nothing out of the ordinary," Topkins said promptly. More thoughtfully, he added, "I'm quite as surprised as anybody else by this whole terrible business. And as devastated, to be frank with you. Henry wasn't merely my best friend; he was engaged to be married to my sister. I can't imagine how I shall tell her of this."

I remembered my conviction that Gramascene would leave broken hearts behind him, and expressed my condolences once more – but not without privately noting that Topkins had been less candid with me than he had professed.

There might of course have been some perfectly innocuous reason why the young man had followed his friend and quarrelled with him the night before, but if so, it was difficult to see why he would not have admitted it, now that the friend was dead. Nor was it merely my silence on the matter that stood between him and the suspicion that would naturally descend were his behaviour known. Mrs Trice could also tell what she had seen, and she could hardly be considered the soul of discretion. Young Topkins was playing a dangerous game, whatever it was; and that was quite apart from whatever it was that he and Mrs Creavesey feared that her husband might suspect.

Even if Gramascene's death had indeed been the work of this Hagworm, some secret errand had propelled him out onto Wermewater during the night, and so far, nobody had admitted to knowing what it was. Was it possible that that knowledge was in Topkins' possession, and that he considered it best that it should stay secret?

However, it would do no good to confront him on the matter in front of the others, and perhaps it would be better in any case to await Holmes's arrival – for I had no doubt that, when he learned what had transpired, my friend would come. It had become just the kind of grotesque mystery that always exerted a special fascination upon him.

It was soon agreed that Woodwose, as a local by adoption, would speak to Constable Batterby on behalf of the research party, and accordingly the group broke apart, each to his or her own sombre reflections on their friend's passing. Reminding myself that I had come here for a holiday, and that I was not the close friend of Henry Gramascene's that these people had been, I walked out instead for a constitutional.

With what I had learned, though, the demeanour of the townsfolk took on a new meaning. These people's faces were not sombre, but scared. They scurried from place to place, hunched as if in dread, though surely an attack by this Hagworm could not come here, upon the dry land of a populated high street. The few boats I could see out on the lake were across the water near Ravensfoot, where I doubted that the Wermeholt folk's fears of the monster in the lake were widely shared. The sun was above me by now, and that morning's dank chill had given way to an oppressive humidity.

I stepped into the pub, hoping to see the sympathetic face of Effie Scorpe, and perhaps ask the young barmaid her views on the legend, and on the fate of Henry Gramascene. I respected the good sense she had shown when comforting Felspar, and I imagined that she would be eager to impress me further, as a visitor from the far-off, fabled land of London.

Effie, however, was nowhere to be seen. Instead her father Ben stood behind the bar, scowling his usual unfriendly welcome at me as I came in. I stayed for a beer, but following the angry clatter with which he set it down, I did not venture to ask after the whereabouts of his daughter.

I drank up quickly, and as I did so it occurred to me that Effie Scorpe was just the kind of pretty young thing who might catch the eye of a young gentleman visiting the countryside, far from his fiancée and feeling the need of the companionship of the opposite sex. I did not like to think such a thing of the late Gramascene, who had seemed to me a decent young man, nor for that matter of Effie, but I reminded myself that I knew neither of them well. And after all, what else might have drawn the young man to the Serpent's Arms at such a time of night? If such an assignation had been in his mind, and his prospective brother-in-law had got wind of it, it was not difficult to see how the two might have come to harsh words.

Blows were another matter, though, let alone the violence that had been visited upon Gramascene. However, I told myself sternly, I did not know Topkins particularly well either, and my time with Holmes had taught me that the mildest of men, and of women, may sometimes be driven to murder. Being so much slighter and less fit than his companion, Topkins might the sooner have recourse to weapons if their friendship came to such a desperate pass.

I shook my head to free it of such forebodings, and moved on, first taking the opportunity to renew my friendship with the inn's dog. Outside, I looked up once more at the inn's sign. The Serpent's Arms were arms in the heraldic sense, a shield whose central device was a knotted silver snake superimposed on a green oak tree. I guessed that it would be the coat of arms of the Wermeston family, and presumably like many family arms arose from a pun on their name. They too had a connection with the Hagworm, from what Woodwose had told me, in its capacity as a portent of doom in their family history.

As though my observation of the inn sign had unlocked something in my mind, I became aware with new eyes of the town around me. I had already noticed the snakes carved on the gravestones in the churchyard, and of course I had seen the dragon's foot way-marker, and the statue of St Michael in the church itself. But now I began to realise how prevalent such references to the creatures were in Wermeholt.

I noticed a drinking fountain in the shape of a snake's head, gushing water unappealingly between its twin fangs and forked tongue, and a mosaic in the tiny, scrubby public gardens that depicted many small serpents following a large one. The Netherfell Tea Shop displayed a large painting of a Parsee snake-charmer in its bay window. Many of the street names – Werme Street, Sloughskin Street, Hag Way – followed the theme. Even some children playing hopscotch had chalked out part of the pavement, not in the conventional pattern of squares, but in a long, sinuous shape that I could not fail to recognise.

As I looked up from their childish game, its innocence peculiarly tainted by this strange imagery, I met the eyes of the widow who seemed to take such an interest in me. She made her finger gesture once again, and now I realised that this, too, was a motion as of a snake striking: her fist its head, her first and fourth fingers turned down to form its fangs. Then she turned as if dismissing me and disappeared among the houses, leaving me strangely shaken.

I considered visiting the Reverend Felspar, but felt that given his state of mind in the morning, the vicar would be of little help in making sense of the events overtaking his parish. Still, it had been a few hours since I had sent my telegram to Holmes, and it was conceivable that by now there might be a reply. Somewhat in desperation, I admit, I called in once more at the post office and spoke to Mrs Trice.

"There's nothing as yet," she told me, the instant she saw me. "Give it time."

# CHAPTER SIX

That night's dinner at the Mereside Hotel was a sombre affair. Woodwose had left us to our own devices, after inviting Summerlee and myself to dine at his cottage the following evening, and the company at the table was subdued and all but silent. Nobody felt inclined to stay up smoking and drinking.

I, too, retired, and slept no better than the previous night, though this time I had dutifully eschewed the postprandial coffee. Eventually I slumbered, though uneasily and with frequent wakings. I slept with the window ajar, and more than once I thought that I heard strange slithering noises coming from outside the hotel, but leaping up and gazing through the window revealed nothing of any greater note than a pair of cats resolving a territorial disagreement.

On the morning of the seventeenth, there was still no word from Holmes. As I was restricted to the area for the time being, I decided that I would once again try walking along the shoreline to Wermeston Hall, and find out whether this time I might not gain entry to visit Lady Ophelia Wermeston. It had occurred to me, during a sleepless hour, that she might know more about the legend of the Hagworm than even Woodwose, or that there might be books containing such knowledge in the library at the Hall. If Gramascene had died by human hands, then the creature he was chasing might well hold the key. And if, of course, he had not, then it was imperative to identify what manner of beast we faced, if possible without the risk of a direct encounter.

If nothing else, I felt that the last scion of the Wermestons deserved to be informed of the matter. After all, if the legend held true, the Hagworm might be here to portend her own death.

Conscientiously, I asked permission for my excursion from Constable Batterby, who told me rudely, and not without self-contradiction, that provided I did not leave the shore of Wermewater I could go to the Devil for all he cared. I guessed from his demeanour that his request for assistance from Keswick had met with the derision he had feared.

Thus emboldened, I struck out once again away from the town, towards the spur of fell and the narrow, gated pass where it met the water. I quickly crossed the sheep-fouled fields that I had seen before, and proceeded ever deeper into the shadow of the fell. The air was clammy, and the ground damp beneath my boots and walking-stick.

As I came closer, I was accorded a better view of the high stone wall that I had seen before only from a distance, and the stout oak gates that barred the track through it. I had observed that the limestone gateposts were ornate, but now I perceived that each was carved with a representation of the Hagworm itself, entwined around the pillar.

To the right of these carvings, as I approached, the wall met the spur of hill and joined with its drystone counterpart, which continued up the steep slope of the fell. I confess that I had wondered whether the wall might not, in fact, prove to be scalable, but I was now convinced that it would take a ladder to enter that way.

To the stone monsters' left, the wall continued out into the mere some ten yards. It was, I presumed, sufficient to prevent access by wading, though I supposed that it would still be possible to swim, or even to enter the estate by boat. I knew, from my view across the lake when I had first approached the town, that the shoreline itself was not walled or fenced.

To land a boat unannounced on Lady Ophelia's property would hardly be polite, of course. On the other hand, there could be little hope that the gate would be manned by somebody authorised to permit me entry. My impression was that her ladyship was, if not a hermit, at least somebody who expected to see guests only by prior arrangement. Nevertheless, I had to try.

In the event I was fortunate, to a point. As I neared the gates, I became aware of a cart approaching along the track behind me, drawn by two horses. I was able to reach the gates a little before it, and examined the Hagworm carvings while I awaited its arrival.

Though these depictions, unlike most of those in town, had legs, each body was tiny compared with the monstrous lengths of neck and tail that coiled up and downwards, making of each of the creatures a serpent whose four limbs were mere afterthoughts. Atop the posts the two heads, broad and arrow-shaped like those of lizards, gazed fiercely at one another, their toothed jaws wide. The oaken gate was carved with the same armorial that graced the Serpent's Arms in town.

The cart drew up and stopped beside me. It held crates and boxes whose labels suggested they held bread, meat, beer, lamp-oil and the like, such as might keep a small household for a week or a large one for a day or two, and was driven by a burly, bearded man of saturnine appearance. He ignored my greeting, climbing down from his seat and stepping forward to the oaken gate. He drew an iron key from his pocket as he did so.

"I say, fellow," I repeated. "My name is Watson. I am hoping to call upon Lady Ophelia Wermeston, if she is available."

The man glanced at me again, and grunted. He unlocked the gate and swung it open, but as I stepped towards it he raised a huge hand to bar my way. It was dirty and calloused, and looked as if it would make a fist the size of a child's head. Indeed, it looked like the kind of hand that was well used to doing so.

"She's not," he told me shortly, and spat on the ground. "Available," he clarified. There was something faintly familiar about his face, but it eluded me.

"And what might your name be, my man?" I asked. I remembered Mrs Creavesey referring to a manservant, one who had informed Woodwose that the Wermeston family burial plot was on Glissenholm. If this was he, I hoped that he had taken a more polite tone with the knight.

The insolent fellow looked me up and down. Behind him the gate stood open, but all I could see was the track continuing around the line of the spur, with the lake beyond. "Modon," he said, and since the word meant nothing else to me I assumed it was indeed his name. "Who's thou?"

"As I told you, my name is Watson, Dr John Watson. I have some business to discuss with Lady Ophelia. It concerns her family."

Modon spat again. "There's no family."

"Her family history, I should say. The history of the Wermestons. You've been in the town, I suppose, so you must have heard about the unfortunate death of that young man, Henry Gramascene." I wondered whether he was one of those I had seen the previous morning at the churchyard, but was unable to decide.

He looked me levelly in the eye. "Aye."

"And you must have heard the rumours that he was killed by... well, some kind of wild animal. Something in the lake."

The faintest ghost of a smile touched his lips, then his face was as stony as before. "Aye."

"I believe that his death may be connected with the Wermeston family," I said, a little desperate now. "I need to discuss the matter with Lady Ophelia."

Modon stared at me for a while, considering. "There's naught to discuss," he said at last. "Good riddance, that's all."

That was at least a more definitive statement than anyone in the town had been willing to provide me with. I contained my anger. "My good man, whatever your views may be upon the matter, I assure you that Lady Ophelia will wish to hear what I have to say. If you do not allow me to speak to her, I promise that it will go the worse with you."

He snorted. "Her ladyship won't talk til thou," he said derisively. He led the horses forward through the gate, his eyes on me the whole time. I could have followed, but I had little doubt that those huge hands would be capable of ejecting me from the grounds, and that they would do so with few concessions to gentleness.

"For goodness' sake, at least tell her that I called!" I begged the uncooperative oaf as he came back to lock the gate.

"Aye, when hogs fly," he responded calmly, and slammed it in my face. A moment later came the heavy clatter of the key in the lock, and I was left fuming and impotent as the trot of the horses' hooves receded into the distance.

I wondered whether there was some other way onto the estate. The further boundary must lie to the north, on the route I had been advised not to take from Ravensfoot, but there was no reason to imagine that I should find it any more accessible than this approach. Reaching it would take many hours' walk around the lake, or a boat ride; but, of course, if one were taking to the water, then one might as well land on the estate's shore and avoid the boundary altogether.

Reluctant to give up entirely in the face of the churl's rudeness, I essayed an ascent of the nearest bank of fell, which this close to the wall was surfaced with grass and mud, rather than with scree. It was, however, very steep, and I was soon clinging to it with both my hands, my feet dug into the earth around the point where the wall changed its structure. I could perhaps have clambered over at that point, but not without causing noticeable damage to the uncemented drystone construction, which would hardly endear me to my prospective hostess or her manservant.

I could, however, lean sufficiently far outward, dangling precariously from a clump of damp grass clutched in my right hand, that I could see over the wall and into the estate.

It seemed that the fell on the far side was wooded down to the waterline, with the same forest of ancient oak and ash that covered Glissenholm. The leaves gleamed green in the sun that failed to reach us on this side of the pass. I thought that the lowland area extended some way back, into a hollow created between the spurs of the fell; that must be where Wermeston Hall itself stood, since it was certainly not visible from where I perched. The cart and its unwelcoming driver had long since vanished from view.

The only sign of human habitation I could detect was a jetty down by the shoreline, next to an inlet leading into a stream, or rather a beck, that vanished into the treeline.

Out of the water of that inlet, as I watched, something rose up, dark and glistening like a beaching whale, and then subsided. It was visible for only a few seconds in the distance, but as the sun glanced across its wet surface I thought that I saw the glittering of scales.

I gasped, and gripped convulsively at my clump of grass, the roots of which gave way at once. I tumbled inelegantly down into the mud at the foot of the nearer gatepost.

I climbed to my feet, cursing. As I turned to make the journey back towards Wermeholt, I could have sworn I heard a hissing sound from the wall itself, as if the serpents on the gate were deriding my ill luck. Trudging back to the hotel, I damned the insolent Modon and his truculence, and did not allow myself to question too closely what else I might, or might not, have seen.

After luncheon I set out again. I called in first at the tavern, where neither Effie Scorpe nor the friendly dog were in evidence, and then at the post office, where I was relieved to find that Mrs Trice had left a monosyllabic girl, perhaps her daughter, attending customers in her stead. There was, however, still no reply from Holmes. This was unlike him, and I wondered whether he was perhaps no longer at Baker Street at all, having embarked on some adventure without me.

As I left, I passed the superstitious widow whom I had seen on several occasions since my arrival in the town, on her way into the post office. Face to face as we suddenly were, we both recoiled slightly, and this time her snake gesture was unmistakeable. Then she said, "How do," quite calmly and proceeded into the shop, where she was shortly greeting the shopgirl by name and asking for a stamp.

Betty, since that was apparently the shopgirl's name, had consented to become loquacious for just long enough to give me directions to the vicarage, and I proceeded thither to call upon the Reverend Gervaise Felspar. His house, of limestone rather than slate, was on Adder Lane. As befitted his station it was one of the finer in the town, but it would have been meagre by London's standards, or those of any large city.

I had avoided seeing the priest the previous day, but remembering the state he had been in at the churchyard had caused my conscience to prick me. I was not equipped for a professional consultation – my medical bag, of course, was back at Baker Street with the rest of my belongings – but I hoped a friendly visit might help him to deal with the shock of finding young Gramascene's body. If it should turn out while I was there that some informal medical advice was needed, then my visit might prove a prudent one.

His door was opened by a housekeeper – and to my shock I recognised the craggy widow herself, whom I had left but moments before in the post office. This time her gaze was level and warily professional, and there was no superstitious gesture.

"I say," I began feebly. "Is Mr Felspar at home?"

"Aye, that he is," she said, in her thick accent, "and I's pleased to see thou. Doctor Watson, isn't thou? I's Mrs Gough," she added as she invited me inside.

It seemed that I had been right to be concerned about the vicar. Mrs Gough told me that her employer had taken to his bed the previous afternoon, and had refused to emerge from his room since. She had been on the verge of sending to Ravensfoot for Dr Kebbelwhite when I arrived.

I explained that I was there merely as a friend, but that I would assess his condition as best I could, and the widow showed me into the vicar's room. He was not abed, but sat at a writing-desk, holding a pen poised over a sheet of paper, while staring vacantly out of his window.

"How are you today, Mr Felspar?" I asked him kindly.

"Oh! Dr Watson," he remarked in surprise on seeing me, and stood up sharply, causing his chair to topple. I righted it, then led him to the bed where he sat docile as I took his pulse. It was fast, but his skin was cool, and his overall demeanour suggested to me a nervous agitation rather than a fever.

"I am sorry that you see me like this, Dr Watson," he admitted meekly as I attended him. "I have not been so very well, I am afraid."

"You are having a nervous reaction to yesterday's events," I informed him. "Finding poor Mr Gramascene must have been a terrible shock."

"Oh, yes. Terrible." He shook his head vigorously. "The poor young man. To think of him like that, creeping on his belly upon the earth. Another crushed corpse through the corpse-gate."

"And yet such morbid imaginings won't do, vicar," I told him firmly. "They won't help the poor fellow now. And your parishioners need you, you know."

"Ah, yes. Their lives are so constricted," he told me sadly. "And some have become quite filled with venom, I am afraid."

"I suppose that's true," I agreed, thinking of the objectionable Modon, and of Mrs Trice. "But nevertheless, sir, they are your flock."

He gave a wry smile. "We know what happens to flocks in these parts, Dr Watson. Killed! By snakes, you know. Gramascene and the others. All the dead in the churchyard. They sought for fish, like dutiful children, but all they were given was snakes."

"Surely not," I suggested gently, but he had hold of the idea now.

"Oh yes, every last one of them. It is the fate of all in this town. Dr Harpier knew it well, so I am told, and so does Sir Howard Woodwose. Sir Howard tells me that Netherfell was once named Adder Fell, and they are everywhere here, you know, the vipers and the serpents. The adders, you see. The serpent addeth and the serpent taketh away."

"Hush, sir," I told him, alarmed by this babbling. "Don't tax your strength. You need a rest. I shall prescribe a sedative." I tried to recall whether any of the nostrums I had seen on sale at Mrs Trice's post office were likely to have the requisite effect.

"That poor young man," he said again. "Harmless as a dove. And yet we are called to be as wise as serpents? I did not know Dr Harpier personally, of course, but he had true wisdom, not that kind." He clutched my arm convulsively. "I did not ask for such wisdom, Dr Watson, I swear it!"

I did my best to soothe him while I sent his housekeeper out with a prescription for a sleeping-draught. By the time she returned, I had him settled once again in the bed.

As soon as the vicar took the medicine, he started to become drowsy. "When in the field," he told me earnestly as he slipped away into sleep, "the serpent is the subtlest of all the beasts. But in the water it becomes a very leviathan." I was unable to suppress a shudder, remembering the thing I had half-seen in the inlet, but Felspar was past being aware of my reactions now. "That old serpent… who we call the Devil, and Satan… St Michael protect us…" He fell silent, exhausted from his ravings, and began to snore.

I went to look at the writing-desk. The top sheet of paper had a drawing of a snake on it, as did a large number of crumpled pages in the waste bin. As I had rather suspected, a cursory search of the desk turned up a bottle of laudanum, a quarter full. It seemed that Mr Felspar had been trying to medicate himself, and in a most ill-advised manner.

"I think I'd better take this away," I explained, showing Mrs Gough the bottle. "I hope that Mr Felspar will be much recovered when he awakes. If he's no better, though, please let me know at once."

I made to leave, but then remembered to ask: "I say, though, Mr Felspar mentioned a Dr Harpier. Who is that, pray?" But the housekeeper either did not know or would not say.

# CHAPTER SEVEN

That evening Professor Summerlee and I dined, as arranged, with Sir Howard Woodwose at his cottage.

The professor met me in the lounge and we walked over together from the hotel. My erstwhile tutor seemed minded to distract us both from the topic of Gramascene's tragic death and its attendant circumstances, which had for the past day been casting such a pall of gloom across our fellow guests and, insofar as was possible given its permanently grim aspect, across Wermeholt itself.

Unfortunately, his idea of cheerfully diverting conversation was to discuss, with detailed examples, the post-mortems of various anatomically unusual human specimens that he had attended, on the assumption that as a medical man I would find these as fascinating as he did himself.

Summerlee meant well, I knew, but he was not a man for small talk, and the fact did not embarrass him. He regarded every conversation as an opportunity to advance the cause of human knowledge: if not his own, then that of those he was addressing. Nevertheless, I was somewhat relieved when we arrived and were greeted by Woodwose with his usual generous bonhomie.

The eminent folklorist's cottage was larger than most of the houses in the town, though Felspar's vicarage, built with the intention of accommodating a family as easily as a single man, was larger still.

While there was no escaping the serpent motif that so dominated Wermeholt, in Woodwose's domain it took a more exotic form. Snake idols from numerous nations were dotted about the shelves, some horned or maned or otherwise adorned, together with fetishes made from scaled skin that must have belonged to reptiles.

Like Gervaise Felspar, Woodwose lived alone with only a housekeeper to provide for his needs – and to my considerable confusion, it was once again the grey-faced widow who entered with the serving-dishes. Her hands were occupied when she first saw me, but I was sure that, once she had relinquished the soup-tureen, she made a furtive movement behind the cover of a chair.

Sir Howard introduced this woman as Mrs Jenkins, rather than Mrs Gough, and now that I saw her close, I realised that her face was indeed slightly different from that of Felspar's housekeeper, particularly around the chin and eyebrows. The two were uncannily alike, though, in their widows' weeds, and I was certain that they must be sisters, if not twins. I realised, not without embarrassment, that this fact might go some way towards explaining my superstitious widow's apparent ubiquity in the town.

Mrs Jenkins did not "live in", as Mrs Gough did, but kept a cottage of her own a short distance away. Our host bade us sit while she served us a lamb stew with dumplings and a decent Beaujolais. It was undistinguished but wholesome fare, and I set to with a will, my day's peregrinations having given me an appetite.

I happened to mention my visit of the morning to the gate of Wermeston Hall's grounds, and Woodwose laughed good-humouredly. "Ah yes, that sounds like Modon. An excellent fellow in his way, loyal and hard-working, but not one to offer the hand of friendship to strangers. He has been with the Wermeston family since he was a boy, like his father and grandfather before him, and during that time I don't believe he has stirred further from the estate than across the lake to Ravensfoot. His sisters married local men, but none of them moved further than here in Wermeholt. Imagine, a family spending entire lifetimes within an area no larger than Richmond Park! And yet the great majority of Englishmen lived thus, not so many generations ago.

"As you may well imagine, though, no man knows the land and its people as well as Modon does, and no man, in these parts at least, is less tolerant of those who intrude upon it from outside. It took him many years to become used to me, and I have been one of Lady Ophelia's few, if very occasional, visitors."

"You said that she was not always reclusive?" I reminded him.

"Far from it. She journeyed widely in her youth, I believe. Her father was an inveterate traveller, and he often took her with him after her mother died. But since his death she has not stirred beyond England's shores, and as she grows older she spends more and more time on her estate. Of late she leaves it even less than Modon does. These days she treats with the outside world only through him, or a few other trusted servants, except for her formal business, when her lawyers serve as more congenial proxies.

"Even to me, her invitations have become less and less frequent, and each time I see her I wonder if it will be the last. Not because her health fails her – far from it; she is hale and spry, though she must be approaching eighty years of age – but because she may simply choose to live out the remainder of her days alone."

"I am still surprised that she never married," I said, with a wary glance at Summerlee, who this time merely rolled his eyes.

"And yet," said Woodwose, "once her relatives have passed away, whence would come the pressure to do so? The late Lord

Wermeston had remarkably progressive views for his generation, and believed that a woman should be permitted her own interests, perhaps even a modest career. He saw no harm in his only issue marrying late, provided she still had some childbearing years left in her. She was but thirty when he died, and there was no male heir. Lady Ophelia has little interest in posterity, nor in her lands and title for their own sake."

"And there are no other branches of the family?" I asked.

"None that have been traced. I dare say a few relatives have been mislaid over the years – they are an old lineage, after all – but if other legitimate Wermeston descendants exist, the lawyers are ignorant of them. And they have searched." He smiled. "For all I know, the lady will leave her estate to Modon. He more or less runs it now, so it would be in capable hands."

Though Woodwose doubtless intended this as a joke, having experienced the manservant's attitude to his betters I could not laugh. It sounded as if he and his misanthropic mistress were well matched.

The knight was in expansive mood, though indeed I wondered whether he experienced any others. After the stew he plied us with cakes, cheese and port, then dismissed Mrs Jenkins as he led us through to his study for after-dinner drinks. Throughout he led us in lively and amusing conversation upon local matters, academic gossip and the doings of his London acquaintances, seasoned with an instructive discussion of the herbal knowledge to be found among traditional folkways, and its value to the modern medical practitioner.

His study was lined with books, a compendious and well-thumbed assortment bound in cloth and leather. Here too, though, snakes and other reptiles predominated, including a somewhat indecent statuette of a goddess wielding a pair of serpents, and a kite in the shape of a Chinese dragon. A large leather wall-hanging bedecked with feathers portrayed, Woodwose explained to us, an Aztec god named Quetzalcoatl, traditionally depicted as a feathered serpent. The knight selected a good Scotch whisky from a long line of decanters, and offered around a fine Persian pipe-tobacco, which Summerlee and I both availed ourselves of while he regaled us with the legend of the Hagworm.

"The records of sightings of an unknown creature in the lake date back centuries," he told us. "It has been described as a serpent, a wyrm or even a dragon, though without wings. It has, at least, a long neck that coils above the waters of the lake, and a head shaped rather like that of a horse. It may have legs like a lizard or fins like a turtle, or it may be altogether limbless. All sources are agreed, though, that it is a reptile rather than a mammal, hairless and with a scaly skin. I am no zoologist, Dr Watson, still less a palaeontologist, but I know that no known living creature could fit the bill, still less one native to the British Isles."

Sir Howard Woodwose was a persuasive speaker. His fascination with the story was quite compelling, and complemented the conviction of Summerlee's colleagues that this fabulous creature not merely existed, but was of a species unknown to science in the modern era. He made that theory seem exotic and enticing rather than merely ludicrous.

He went on, "There was a monastery at Ravensfoot in the Middle Ages, and an illuminated manuscript produced there in the 1400s depicts just such a creature, showing that the Hagworm legend was already current then. The illustration is a marginalium in a book of psalms, and such drawings often feature the fantastical imaginings of bored monks, but the depiction is nevertheless consistent with the descriptions we find centuries later.

"I have said that the beast's appearances foretell the deaths of Wermeston family members. A vicar of St Michael's with such a connection, one Thomas Wermeston, wrote of seeing the

Hagworm shortly before his death at the end of the sixteenth century, and this was taken as an omen by his parishioners.

"A more gruesome account holds that it took and consumed an infant – an ordinary local child, not a Wermeston scion – placed by the lakeside almost at this very spot, while some women washed their laundry in a nearby beck. That was in the early 1600s, though I have been unable to discover the precise year. No less an authority than the poet Coleridge claimed to have seen a *pair* of the creatures sporting in the lake while he was climbing Netherfell with Wordsworth in 1801, though it must be said that his fellow poet does not allude to the incident, and given Coleridge's enthusiasm for laudanum we might consider him a somewhat dubious witness."

I remembered the bottle of which I had relieved Gervaise Felspar, whose contents I had since tipped away. Surely, though, not everyone who saw the creature had been under the influence of opiates or other hallucinatory drugs. I was fairly certain that I was not, for instance.

Woodwose said, "More recently, however, some quite reputable observers, including a learned ornithologist not given to unscientific imaginings, have witnessed the creature's appearances. During the construction of the railway line to Ravensfoot in 1873, a group of navvies and one very level-headed engineer watched for some minutes as a lizard-like head atop a long neck broke the surface of the water and continued for some distance across the mere.

"My conversations with the local populace have turned up oral histories of other encounters, including two witnesses who state that they have seen the creature first-hand. Those who have not have often heard an unexplained slithering sound coming from the lakeshore at night, and some have found unusual tracks in their flowerbeds, though I have not had the opportunity to observe these myself.

"And then, of course, there are the ballads. Professor Child's definitive collection includes three that refer specifically to the Wermewater Hagworm. One allusion is frivolous, a man in his cups who boasts among other feats of having harnessed and ridden the beast. Another uses it as a portent, appearing to foretell the death of Lord Reynold de Wermeston in the fourteenth century.

"The third ballad, 'Lord William's Lady', is of far more interest. It purports to tell the origin of the beast, and appears to be the source of the popular name. This verse has points in common with other ballads using the Loathly Worm motif, as well as with the legend of the Lambton Worm, but it is, like its subject, a unique creature."

It was quite dark outside the house, and the gas-lamps in the study were dim. Their light flickered, and to my slightly stimulated imagination the shadows of the multiple serpent forms that haunted Woodwose's study seemed to slither across the walls, amply illustrating the story he declaimed.

"The story is dated to the time of the Crusades." His voice was sonorous, his square beard giving him the air of an Old Testament patriarch laying down the law. "It tells of how Lord William de Wermeston brings home a foreign woman whom he takes to be his bride, a graceful maiden whom he loves as life itself. In those days, of course, foreign parts might mean anywhere further than the next lake over, and the ballad refers twice to his 'finding' her, an unusual word to use. Overall, though, the impression given is that Lord William has encountered this woman during his travels in the Holy Land. She brings with her strange clothes, and manners of speech and action that baffle William's servants.

"The couple marry and are, we are told, happy, although the lady scandalises the villagers of Wermeholt, and infuriates the priest, by refusing to attend mass. Lord William, who himself is pious, tells the priest that his wife must be allowed to worship alone, as such is the way of her people. The priest will not accept this, and vows to call in the Bishop to resolve the dispute. The next day, however, the reverend gentleman is bitten by a snake while walking on Netherfell, or as the ballad calls it, Nadder Fell. *Nadder*, as you know, was the original form of the word *adder*, though this particular snake is perhaps something more dangerous.

"In any case the wound turns septic, and the priest dies. His replacement prudently decides that Lady de Wermeston's absence from the weekly services at church may thenceforth go unmentioned.

"Her next disagreement is with a doctor of physic sent to treat her handmaid, who has fallen sick, and Lady de Wermeston fiercely insists that no one but she should nurse her. The doctor takes a high-handed view of the matter, as did the priest, standing on his learning and his dignity, but her ladyship has her way in the end. The maid recovers, but the doctor dies, again from a snakebite.

"By now the villagers are whispering among themselves that Lady de Wermeston is a witch. She is with child, and some say that the infant is not Lord William's but the Devil's, while others maintain that it is indeed his lordship's, but that the mother plans to sacrifice it to Satan when it is born. For William de Wermeston's part, he is overjoyed to be expecting a child, and he loves his wife as much as ever. He punishes the villagers who speak out against her.

"However, the Bishop of Carlisle has learned of the priest's death, and arrives in person in Wermeholt, declaring that Lord William's lady is a demon and that he will exorcise her. William is unhappy with this, but cannot gainsay the authority of the church, and so reluctantly he allows the ritual to take place.

"The bishop has his servants hold the lady while he reads to her from the Bible, and sings psalms, and prays to God for her deliverance, abjuring Satan and commanding him to leave her body – but the Devil does not oblige. Instead Lady de Wermeston is transformed, there and then, into a loathsome worm, which slips away into the lake before any of those present can seize it.

"Lord William is devastated to have lost his wife, but now he cannot but acknowledge that she was a witch, and that she must have enchanted him.

"The villagers, forgetting her youth and beauty, take to calling her the Hagworm, and say they have seen her swimming in the lake, or slithering across the shores of Glyssen Holme. As the months pass, they begin to fall prey to bites that rot and fester, killing them slowly, while the serpent becomes fat on stolen animals and children.

"The people plead to Lord William to save them from the creature his wife has become. He is reluctant at first, but with the Bishop's help he learns resolution, coming to see that the woman he knew has gone for ever. Blessed by the Bishop, he puts on his armour and amasses his various weapons – that part of the ballad is long and detailed, but I will spare you the particulars – and sets out in a rowing-boat for the island.

"The beast recognises him, and bursts forth from the trees hissing and bellowing, now grown to monstrous size. They fight, and over and over again the creature bites William, but his faith keeps him safe from its venom. For his part, he lands killing blow after killing blow, but every time the serpent is seemingly mortally wounded, it retreats into the lake, emerging moments later restored to full health.

"Eventually the lord realises how he must defeat the creature. He seizes it in both hands – the size of the beast becomes somewhat ambivalent here, but that is not unusual in such tales – and ties it to the branches of an oak tree, so that it cannot slither away. There he hacks it to pieces, which he buries separately. The Hagworm is destroyed, and good has triumphed over evil.

"However, it is not forgotten that Lady de Wermeston was expecting a child at the time of her transformation. As time passes, her descendants, monstrous serpents like herself, are soon seen in the lake. And who, the balladeer asks rhetorically, will protect the Wermeston family now that Lord William is dead?"

There was silence in the study. Woodwose was an electrifying storyteller, and had held me spellbound. Though Summerlee had doubtless heard the story before, he too had listened gravely and respectfully, with a minimum of sceptical huffing noises.

In the quiet I could almost imagine that I heard, from the direction of the lake, a rustling and hissing, as of a giant serpent slithering along the shore. I remembered, too, seeing trees shaking on Glissenholm earlier that afternoon, no doubt the result of the wind, but exactly the kind of thing that might prompt tales of a monster dwelling on the island.

Then Summerlee broke the enchantment. "All this is doubtless interesting from an anthropological point of view," he observed drily. "The superstitions of the natives in these parts are not so different from some I have encountered in the furthest reaches of the Empire. But I have a question."

The knight gave him a hearty grin that nevertheless showed a lot of teeth. "My dear Professor, I would expect no less of you."

Summerlee returned him an altogether more acid smile. He said, "If Lake Wermewater is named after the creature that supposedly haunts it, and the name Wermeholt follows likewise, then how is it that Lord William de Wermeston bore that surname before the creature came to exist?"

Woodwose looked amused. "A perceptive point. Unfortunately such ballads rarely withstand the application of rigorous logic.

Perhaps the Wermeston family was not indeed so called until later, but the balladeer applied the name retrospectively for familiarity's sake. Or perhaps the family, the town and the lake are not named after the Hagworm after all, but after the adders that must have infested Netherfell when it was named."

Summerlee snorted. "A remarkable coincidence if so."

Woodwose laughed. "More likely, then, the family name attracted the legend. I said that there are variants of the story all over the north, and who is to say where they originated? It may be that you are correct, and the whole business is a series of misunderstandings and sheer fabrications. Or perhaps, after all, there is such a creature, or a small population of such creatures, and they have been here far longer than seven hundred years, giving rise to the legend, the surname and the toponymy of the area. That, after all, is what you and your colleagues have come here to discover."

I said, "And was there a real Lord William de Wermeston?"

"So the genealogies would have us believe," Woodwose replied, "though as they were compiled in later centuries they cannot be relied upon. His first wife goes unnamed even there."

I said, "He remarried, then?"

"Evidently so, as his descendants have lived here ever since. Lady Ophelia's estate includes the land where his castle stood, though it was torn down long ago and replaced with Wermeston Hall. The townsfolk retain a superstitious fear of the place, for all that some have relatives who live and work there. Barring some miracle, the family will die with her, and the ballad's ending will gain new significance."

"Was it also the Hagworm legend that brought you to Wermeholt, Sir Howard?" I asked.

"Essentially, yes. I told you that I have a special interest in legends of serpents and other reptiles. I had no connections here, but I bought this cottage when its previous owner, Dr Harpier, died." My ears pricked up at his mention of a name that I had heard for the first time only that day, but Woodwose had other matters on his mind.

He continued, "I said that the Hagworm is one of many lake monsters in legend. Dragons and their ilk are often associated with lakes and the sea, from the Lernean hydra killed by Hercules to the water dragons of Chinese myth, and such stories are found from pole to pole, from Lagarfljót in Iceland to Nahuel Huapi in Patagonia. If Creavesey and young Topkins are right about their nature, then surviving plesiosaurs may be far more prevalent than we imagine."

"Or such tales may simply appeal to human credulity," Summerlee interjected. "There might be numerous reasons for such a pattern, not involving the literal existence of such creatures."

"Indeed, Professor. I make no firm claims as to their reality. There is, for instance, a theory that memories may be inherited at an organic level, and may influence our behaviour even if we are not consciously aware of them. In that case, all human beings might retain a racial memory of the time when our distant ancestors were obliged to cower in terror from gigantic lizards."

"I am not convinced that the survival of such memories over millions of years is any more likely than that of the beasts themselves," Summerlee noted. "Nor would it account for the aquatic connection you noted, since those ancestors would surely have been likely to encounter such creatures on land."

"The theory raises questions of its own, I admit," conceded Woodwose with a smile. "There is no doubt, however, that the reptile clan holds great significance in the legends of almost all peoples, across all the continents. In the Norse myths there are dragons, of course, such as the one slain by Sigurd, but there is also Jörmungandr, the World Serpent, who circles the world beneath the oceans. By contrast, the Hindus believe that the world itself rests on the back of a different reptile, a turtle swimming in a celestial ocean.

"In the Bible, the Serpent tempts Eve with the fruit of the Tree of Knowledge of Good and Evil, and it is later identified with Satan, who in Revelation appears in the form of a dragon." (I winced a little, recalling poor Felspar's deranged babblings of the morning.) "But among the Gnostic sects, the wisdom the Serpent of Genesis brought has been seen in a more sympathetic light, like that of the snakes entwined with Apollo's caduceus or the rod of the healer god Asclepius.

"Snake gods appear in the myths of the Egyptians, the Aztecs and the Hindus, to name but three. They are found creating the world, guarding the underworld and swallowing the sun." He gestured to a statuette on his desk, this one depicting a snake rearing up from its coils, with an unlikely mane of hair and a face rather like that of a greyhound. "This serpent deity, Glycon by name, claimed thousands of worshippers during the time of the Roman Empire, including no less a figure than the Emperor Marcus Aurelius, although some of his manifestations were found to have been counterfeited by use of a glove puppet."

Summerlee snorted with mirth, but Woodwose continued serenely. "Serpents are deadly, of course, to the extent that simply to set eyes upon the mythical basilisk or snake-headed gorgon is to die. But because they shed their skins, snakes are also symbols of rebirth, and the ouroboros, the serpent forever swallowing its own tail, reminds us of the cyclical nature of life. I could continue in this vein for some time," he admitted, beaming, "and I perceive from your faces that I am in danger of doing so."

I hoped that my expression had remained one of polite interest, but Summerlee's had certainly been registering increasing impatience with Woodwose's unscientific screed.

Woodwose continued, "I will simply say, then, that the Loathly Worms of British legend are but the local representatives of a most august worldwide company, and that my interest in the folklore surrounding them had made me especially interested in the Wermewater Hagworm and its ilk. When I heard of the tragic death of Dr Harpier, whom I knew but slightly, I enquired after the disposition of the cottage that he kept here. If a bothy near Loch Ness had become available first, then I dare say I should reside there now.

"For a while I divided my time between the Lake District and London, but my research here was fruitful, and in time I found that the atmosphere here suited me, and I was able to conduct my business with publishers through correspondence, and to confine my more conventional inquiries in libraries to occasional flying visits."

"Was Dr Harpier also a folklorist?" I asked.

"No, an historian. A man of modest reputation, but highly respected, I believe, among those who study that subject on the scale of towns and shires rather than nations and empires. Like me, he was an incomer who moved here originally for his research, but who found the surroundings conducive to a partial retirement. I believe he amassed quite a quantity of notes on local matters."

"And then he died?" I prompted.

"Why, indeed." Woodwose gave a sudden hearty laugh. "As we all must, Dr Watson, in the end. He was in his seventies, I believe. But… yes, his end was sudden and rather awful, I'm afraid. He was trampled by a runaway carthorse in Wermeholt high street."

Having half expected him to say that the late doctor had been found part-eaten by the lakeshore, I felt rather let down.

A while later, Summerlee and I took our leave of the affable knight, and strolled back to the Mereside Hotel. The night was clammy and a clinging mist rolled in from the lake, bringing with it a stench of rot. I wondered how either Woodwose or his predecessor could have felt the local climate to be a congenial one, however fond they might be of the local colour.

"Woodwose is a respected academic," Summerlee observed as we walked, "but I consider him altogether too imaginative. His discipline will never be truly scientific, but even in such pursuits there are forms one must follow, not flights of fancy. His influence on Creavesey is particularly to be regretted. There is not such a profusion of adequate scientists in the world that we can afford to lose them to idle fancies," he added thoughtfully.

"Hullo," I said. "What's happening here?"

We were approaching the churchyard, the squat bulk of St Michael's a darker shadow against the grey of the fell beyond. From where we stood we could see a number of boats tied up at the corpse-gate jetty, and some indistinct figures with lanterns embarking upon them.

"What can they be doing?" I wondered. "It must be after midnight. Are they fishermen?"

Summerlee shook his head impatiently. "Wermewater is an inland lake. There is no requirement for fishing expeditions to catch a tide."

"Then whatever can be going on?" I said again. "They can hardly have been bringing a body for burial at this time of night."

Summerlee shrugged. "The ways of the local people are obscure to me," he said, "and, as Woodwose has been reminding us, are quite as superstitious as those of any Aborigine or Zulu tribesman."

I hoped to call to the boatmen and ask the purpose of their excursion, but they set out rowing quickly across the dark waters of the lake, and by the time we reached the churchyard the reflections of their lanterns were beyond hailing range. I thought perhaps that they were headed towards the wooded islet in the middle of the lake, although I had understood it to be out of bounds except with the express permission of Lady Ophelia.

We passed without further incident along the high street and back to our hotel, where I bade Summerlee good night and retreated to my room. Before retiring, I glanced out of my window to see whether I could spot the rowers.

As I have said, my window overlooked the high street down to the church. I saw no sign of the boatmen, but I did see another shadowy figure with a lantern. It stood on the church tower, gazing out across the lake, I thought towards the gloom of Glissenholm.

# CHAPTER EIGHT

Once again I slept poorly, haunted by imagined hissings and slitherings from the mere, and once again that dreadful phantom piping.

The next day was Sunday, and I was awakened by the tolling of the solitary bell at St Michael's, summoning the faithful of Wermeholt to the morning service. Nevertheless I lay in bed late, hoping thereby to avoid the press and fuss at breakfast.

I heard the two professors leave the hotel early, discussing the purchase of a boat through an agent of Woodwose. Topkins and Mrs Creavesey set out shortly afterwards, in a cart that seemed bound for Ravensfoot. I had no knowledge of their errand, but I expected the dining-room to myself when I eventually descended, yawning and craving kippers.

I was surprised then, and at first a little annoyed, to see someone already ensconced at my table and tucking into a hearty breakfast. I supposed that Gramascene's room could be considered vacant now, but Mr Dormer had given me no inkling of any other guest's arrival. My annoyance was short-lived, however, as the man stood and turned to me, and a broad smile creased his very familiar aquiline face.

"My dear Watson!" cried Sherlock Holmes, and at once I felt a surge of relief. The agency that had slaughtered Henry Gramascene might be human or prehistoric or supernatural or whatever it pleased, but there could be no monster in the world that would not seem altogether less menacing in the presence of Holmes's cool intellect, sardonic wit and steadfast bravery.

"I thought that you would slug abed all morning," my friend went on cheerfully, as I clasped his hand. "I was becoming impatient to wake you. I came up by the overnight train from St Pancras, and chartered a boat from Ravensfoot at dawn."

"A boat?" I replied, a little alarmed. "Did you see anything out of the ordinary?"

He gazed coolly at me. "Why, no. The ferryman joked that we should be wary of the lake monster, but we saw neither scale nor flipper of it. Why do you ask?"

I told him a little of what I had learned from Woodwose the previous night, and how he and the scientists thought it might pertain to the death of Gramascene.

"I see," said Holmes. "Well, for what it may be worth the view in Ravensfoot would seem to be that Wermeholt folk are a fearfully backward lot, who cry Hagworm at the smallest shadow on the water."

"I wish I could agree with them," I said, "but shadows don't tear men to pieces."

"You may be proven right. Pray tell me all," Holmes said promptly, pulling out a chair for me, "while you break your fast. I have sent word to the local constable that we expect to view the late Mr Gramascene at ten."

I conveyed to my friend everything I could remember since my arrival in Wermeholt: first having him read the account that I had written just before learning of the true purpose of the scientific party's investigation, and then repeating everything that I had heard since then. As I knew to be his preference, I endeavoured to omit no detail, no matter how insignificant or absurd.

He listened gravely, interrupting rarely with a question that was always to the point, and often thus eliciting some particular that I had not been aware of glossing over. When I reached the moment at which, looking over the wall of the Wermeston estate, I had seen what I could only believe to have been the Hagworm itself surfacing in the inlet from Wermewater, his eyebrows elevated themselves considerably, but to my relief he said nothing to call doubt upon my testimony.

At length I was finished. He set down his empty teacup and asked, "Who was it that supplied the Reverend Felspar with laudanum? Was it Mrs Trice?"

The question was not one that had occurred to me. "It's certainly not on sale in her shop," I said. "But it's not a big town, and the nearest chemist is in Ravensfoot."

"A private individual, then," said Holmes. "You said that Sir Howard Woodwose had many decanters, and that you sampled only the Scotch. Laudanum looks much like any fortified wine in dim light."

"I suppose that it does," I said. "It didn't occur to me to wonder, I'm afraid."

"You kept the flask you took from Felspar, I hope?"

"No, I poured it away," I admitted. "I didn't want the maid to find the stuff." Evidently my time away from Holmes had dulled my investigative instincts.

He clicked his tongue. "Well, it is not to be helped. I do not suppose that it was anything more than the simple tincture of opium that you assumed. That would be quite sufficient to create the effects you describe in a man of Felspar's temperament. Whose was the horse?"

"Excuse me?" As ever, my friend's processes of thought

progressed too quickly for me to follow, let alone predict them. Under ordinary circumstances I often found the habit trying, but at present I was quite prepared to bask in it.

"The carthorse that trampled the unfortunate Dr Harpier, thus freeing his cottage for Woodwose to purchase. Did Sir Howard mention the identity of its owner?"

"He did not."

"And then there is the matter of the churchyard," Holmes mused. "I must visit it quite soon."

"I'm afraid there were a lot of people around after Gramascene was found," I said. "And Constable Batterby has done nothing to prevent others from following, like those Summerlee and I observed last night. The ground will be quite churned up by now."

"No doubt it will," my friend said indifferently. "The boat, at least, was preserved?"

"Along with the body," I reminded him. "Although they will surely be wanting to bury him soon."

"Then let us commence there," Holmes proposed, it being by then nearly ten.

"Holmes…" I began.

He nodded solemnly. "I know, my friend. It is good to see you, too."

"That's not what I was going to say," I said, though I was proud to hear him say so. "I'm afraid you'll find Batterby a rather prickly young man. He is the son of the local butcher, I believe, and far from confident in his handling of such a serious case. You may need to be diplomatic with him."

"Then I shall be the very soul of tact, Watson," he promised me, with a smile to show that he knew as well as I that any such behaviour would be quite unprecedented.

As we walked the short distance to the local undertakers', Thorpe and Son, we passed Mrs Gough, unless it was Mrs Jenkins, who nodded politely at me and stared in open curiosity at Holmes. Her hand was in her coat pocket, but I saw it move even so.

In fact, in a reversal of the historical state of affairs which once had Ravensfoot send its dead to Wermeholt for burial, Thorpe and Son were based across the lake. They maintained only a small office in the town, consisting solely of an anteroom with a desk and the tiny morgue where Henry Gramascene awaited his final rest.

We found Constable Batterby waiting for us in the outer room, glowering with resentment. Before I could finish introducing Holmes, he interrupted.

"Aye, I ken who thou is, Mr Sherlock Holmes, and I'll tell thou I'm none too pleased to see thou here. I ken what my superiors are like to say, but, and for their sake I'll not get in t'way – if thou remembers that it's I in charge on t'business here, not thou. Do we understand each other, Mr Holmes?"

"Pellucidly, Constable." Holmes beamed, and strode through into the cramped back room.

Gramascene was its only occupant. He lay in a plain black coffin, its lid open to allow visitors to pay their final respects. The blood had been washed away from his face and hands, the cuts to his head cleaned, and he had been dressed in fresh, undamaged clothes. He looked peaceful, I thought, and fit to move on to the next life with dignity.

Holmes tutted. "This will not do at all. Help me to turn him on his side, Watson, and loosen his shirt. I must see the wounds you mentioned."

"Holmes!" I protested. "We cannot disturb the poor man's rest."

"I understand your misgivings, but he is quite beyond being disturbed. If I am to understand his death, and perhaps prevent others suffering the same fate, then I must examine him."

Reluctantly I complied. The cadaver's wounds had been cleaned but otherwise not interfered with, and Holmes inspected them briskly, minutely and without sentiment. I could not have maintained his calm, despite my medical training, but then I had known the poor lad, if but briefly.

After a few moments he took out his magnifying glass, and continued his perusal.

"You are slipping, Watson," he noted, finally standing. "There are distinct toothmarks here, and to the scalp also. I cannot be certain, but if this was not an animal attack, then it was staged with exceptional care to resemble one. I shall need to examine the boat. His clothes, I assume, will be with the rest of his things. You say he dragged himself some twenty yards through the churchyard before expiring? He must have enjoyed exceptional physical health."

"Aye, well, not any more," Constable Batterby noted lugubriously from the doorway.

"Indeed," said Holmes. He turned suddenly on the constable, who flinched a little. "And where are his personal effects?"

"There was little enough on him when we found him," Batterby replied. "His things is all at t'town hall wi't'boat. Clothes too. There's little enough to be gleaned there, any road," he added pessimistically.

Voices reached us from the anteroom, a man and a woman, and Batterby moved quickly to intercept them. "Finish up quick," he told us as he left. "Next of kin's here."

"I think that is Topkins' voice," I said. "It must be his sister, Gramascene's fiancée." As they were yet unmarried, the young woman was not strictly Gramascene's next of kin, but ordinary compassion would overrule any such technicality. "The constable's right, Holmes, we had better be out of their way."

"One moment, Watson," Holmes said abstractedly. He had leaned in with his glass to inspect the area around Gramascene's horrific torso wound. Staring, he fished absently in his waistcoat pocket to produce a pair of tweezers. "Kindly delay them for me."

I stepped out of the morgue at once, and found Batterby

speaking to Topkins. The student was accompanied by a pale and distressed young woman, dressed in black, whose similarity to him was clear. Edith Creavesey hovered behind them with an air of concern, in the doorway of the building.

"Dr Watson," Topkins said, immediately displeased to see me. "Whatever are you doing here?"

"Paying my respects," I prevaricated. "I assume this must be Miss Topkins?"

"Yes," the young man agreed, resentfully. "This is my sister, Mary. Mary, this is Dr Watson, the writer. I understand he's on holiday here."

"I am delighted to make your acquaintance, Miss Topkins," I told her. Her eyes were red-rimmed and her face drawn. "Did you come up on the overnight train?"

"Yes," she said hoarsely. "James and Mrs Creavesey met me at Ravensfoot."

Topkins snapped, "My sister has come to pay her last respects to her fiancé, Doctor, and isn't in any state to make small talk. Please be so good as to allow us in to see Henry." His eyes narrowed suspiciously. "Is there someone else in there with him?"

I opened my mouth to say I know not what, but Batterby forestalled me. "Aye," he said defiantly, "Dr Watson's Mr Holmes is up to see him from London, and I've asked him to help t'police out. He'll be done in a minute."

"Sherlock Holmes is here?" Topkins repeated, aghast.

I supposed that his appalled reaction could have resulted from the prospect of publicity for the family, or the horrid realisation that his friend's corpse was even now being examined for clues. Either would have been natural. However, in light of what I had learned from Mrs Trice, and overheard between him and Mrs Creavesey, I could not help but wonder whether his dismay arose instead from fear that Holmes was capable of uncovering some fact that he, Topkins, would prefer to stay hidden.

While I considered this, Topkins thrust himself between myself and Batterby, and threw open the door to the morgue. I turned to look, and saw to my relief that Gramascene was decently clothed and laid out as decorously as before. Holmes stood beside him, his head respectfully bowed, his gaunt appearance making him look himself somewhat like an undertaker in mufti.

I effected the necessary introductions, to Topkins' continuing chagrin. "I find your presence here frankly ghoulish, Mr Holmes," he informed him. "Is it not enough that my friend is dead without his needing to be pawed over by freelance sensation-seekers?"

Holmes replied, "I understand that you are a scientist, Mr Topkins. I would have thought that you would appreciate the need for dispassionate inquiry in such a case."

"And what exactly have your researches discovered?" Topkins demanded tartly.

"That will emerge in due course," Holmes said calmly, and we left the bereaved to their grieving. Topkins put his arm around his sister's shoulders, which were now silently shaking, and led her through into the morgue, from which her wails shortly thereafter emerged.

Mrs Creavesey remained in the anteroom, her face grave. She said, "You must forgive James's agitation, Mr Holmes. He and Henry were close friends, and he has been much affected by his loss, as well as being terribly concerned for his sister."

"I understand, of course," Holmes replied. Despite Topkins' pugnaciousness, he had by his own standards exercised considerable restraint. "I am sure we will meet again soon, Mrs Creavesey, under less oppressive circumstances."

"Did you find anything more?" I asked him, once we were outside in the gloomy street, but he shushed me and turned to Batterby.

"Might we now peruse Mr Gramascene's belongings, and his boat?" he asked.

"Weren't his boat," the policeman said, and then closed his mouth abruptly.

"You said you didn't recognise it," I reminded him. "Do you have any evidence it *wasn't* Mr Gramascene's?" There was little enough reason, of course, why Gramascene would own a boat in the locality, but Batterby's denial of what was a conventional turn of phrase on Holmes's part, conveyed a suspicious impression in itself. In trying to make a smart retort he had, perhaps, given away more than he intended.

"He wasn't keeping it at t'hotel," Batterby replied sullenly. "Likely he borrowed it from someone."

"Not someone you're familiar with, apparently." I received no reply.

I was sure that the constable knew more about the vessel than he was saying, but Holmes was intent on his own investigations. Accordingly, we proceeded at once to the town hall, which Batterby unlocked for us. We went first to his office, where he brought out for our inspection the belongings that had been found on Gramascene's body, and those he had left in his hotel room.

"You say that these are the clothes you saw him in the night before?" Holmes asked, turning over the ragged garments.

"I could not swear to the coat," I reminded him. "It was dark outside when I saw him leave. And of course he wore ordinary shoes at dinner, not those boots. But other than that, the items look the same."

"Hmm. Well, the boots have been washed clean, or as clean as the lake can make them, so we cannot tell where he might have been walking before his immersion. Since he was waterlogged when you found him, yet the boat was at the corpse-gate, we must assume that he was attacked while disembarking there, but was able to climb up, first into the boat and then onto the jetty, whence he made his way into the churchyard. Why there and not the hotel, I wonder?" It was not a point that had occurred to me.

He turned his attention to the young man's pocket-book, which had been on his body when found and was now a mass of flaking leather and wadded paper, in which a handful of loose change was embedded. He teased the items apart with his tweezers, but few of the papers remained legible, and they were mostly receipts and ticket-stubs and the like. A damaged but discernible photograph of Mary Topkins suggested that, whatever secrets Henry Gramascene might have been harbouring, he had at least thought of his fiancée fondly.

Holmes showed me one other paper of any interest, a stained and faded letter. The waters of the mere, and perhaps age and wear as well, had rendered it illegible, but the final signature was relatively undamaged. Unfortunately it was one of those signatures that are extremely difficult to read at the best of times. The forename was probably either *Edward* or *Edwin*, but the surname could have been almost anything. After staring at it in puzzlement for a while, I thought that either *Jasper* or *Marquis* might have been the likeliest candidates – although in truth it was such a scribble that I could scarcely have sworn it was not *Watson* or *Holmes*.

"Suggestive, is it not?" said Holmes, but it meant nothing to me, and I could see from his frown that Constable Batterby was equally at sea.

Gramascene had had nothing else on him but keys, handkerchiefs and his pipe. The baggage from his room contained no more that was remarkable, at least to my eyes – a suitcase holding a few changes of clothing, a set of pyjamas, a kit for washing and shaving, some books, his smoking materials, and another photograph of Miss Topkins, this one framed.

"No pen or inkstand, and no paper," Holmes observed. "If Mr Gramascene was making notes of any findings from the group's research, he must have relied wholly on the Mereside Hotel's facilities, and handed them to someone else for safekeeping afterwards."

"I am not sure that Gramascene had much dedication to his work," I observed. "These volumes of his are all popular novels, not scientific textbooks."

"Quite so." Holmes riffled through the pages, but nothing fell out of them except a leather bookmark.

Batterby showed us through the rear door of his modest police station into the town hall proper, where the upended rowing-boat had been laid down. As with the body, Holmes spent some time gazing through his magnifying-glass at the damage it had sustained during the attack.

"What do you make of this stain, Watson?" he asked me, indicating a reddish discolouration at the rear of the craft, where the worst scraping and splintering was visible.

"Blood, surely," I said. "Gramascene must have bled copiously." Holmes grunted.

"The marks seem consistent, at least," he noted quietly a few minutes later. The varnish was scraped and gouged, and the signs of the serrations that Holmes had suggested might be teeth were now unmistakeable. "I am no expert in reptilian dentition, but if this is an animal attack then my best guess would be an alligator or a crocodile."

"In an English lake?" I asked, incredulous.

"Well, quite," he nodded. "Still, we must eliminate the possibility before concluding that any more exotic creature was responsible. What did you say was Topkins and Creavesey's hypothesis?"

"A plesiosaurus," I told him, and recounted what little I had been able to glean about the beast from the technical discussions between the scientists. "I gather it was a dinosaur with a compact body, four flippers rather than legs, and a long neck and tail. As I understand it they believe that the neck and head, if seen alone or with the humped back, could be mistaken for a serpent."

"I see. Well, perhaps they would forgive me if I were to seek a second expert opinion."

I said, "We might ask Summerlee if he has come to any conclusions. He has been sceptical of the creature's existence, mind you."

"I had another in mind. Do you recall Dr Mossbaum, who advised us in the case of the Stepney cobra killings?"

I shuddered at being reminded of the case; but yes, I remembered Herman Mossbaum, the spry German expert on reptile behaviour who had helped us to exonerate the Indian snake-dancer Rani Ranjeet Rupresh of all blame in the matter, and establish the murderous duplicity of her employer, the music-hall impresario Jeremiah Youngblood.

Holmes said, "He is a world-renowned herpetologist. If anyone can tell us which reptile might be the owner of such teeth, it will be Mossbaum. I shall wire him to ask if he can join us here. But tell me, Watson, what do you make of this?"

He showed me that the boat was bloodstained in two places – the transom, where I had already observed this smeared patch of red just at the waterline, and here on the port side, where, as Holmes noted with some relish, "The gore is liberally slathered across the gunwale. Clearly this is where Mr Gramascene climbed back into the vessel, so whose is the blood at the stern?"

"The Hagworm's, then?" I suggested. "Perhaps Gramascene beat at it with the oar before it pulled him into the water. The other oar hasn't been recovered, you know."

"Perhaps," Holmes conceded dubiously. "Certainly it is suggestive, as are the abrasions I observed on Gramascene's skin."

"Abrasions?" I asked, wondering whether this was what Holmes had noticed at the morgue, and kept to himself in Batterby's presence. The constable had left us alone in the hall, and, while I could imagine him listening at the door of his office, he would look rather foolish doing so if one of the townsfolk arrived seeking the help of the police.

"Abrasions," Holmes elaborated, "as of vigorous contact with some very rough surface. A wrestling bout with a large and tough-hided reptile could fit the bill, but it is not the only possibility. However, I discovered this just now," he added. "It was caught in a seam of Gramascene's clothing."

He showed me a horny, almost translucent oval, the size of an eggshell, stained pinkish by its recent steeping in human blood.

"All reptiles shed their skin," he noted, "whether wholesale like an ordinary snake, or piecemeal, scale by scale. It seems that the Hagworm, if such this was, is no exception to the rule. It will be more grist to Dr Mossbaum's mill, if he is able to attend us."

# CHAPTER NINE

We proceeded, with Constable Batterby, to the churchyard. The young policeman might be keeping a close watch upon our investigation, and might, I privately suspected, have some inclination to hamper it, but having taken no steps to bar the crime scene to all comers since Gramascene's body was found, he could hardly object if we visited it ourselves.

As I had feared, we found the spot greatly disturbed by the crowds that had trodden it, both on the morning of Gramascene's death and in the days since. Indeed, as we arrived a handful of the worshippers from morning service were still hanging about the place, discussing the occasion in whispered voices. My inclination was to accuse the denizens of Wermeholt of precisely the morbid fascination that Topkins had attributed to Holmes, but I supposed that there was little enough to entertain them in such a place that they could hardly be blamed for revisiting a scene of such excitement.

Holmes paid only cursory attention to the ground where the body had lain, and less than I had expected to the grass, still stained dark in places, that the young man had flattened during his painful progress from the jetty. He did, however, look carefully at the grave of the eighteenth-century vicar Laertes Wilfredson, next to which

Gramascene had lain when he finally succumbed to his wounds. Like most of the burial plots it bore a modest headstone rather than a more elaborate memorial, though this one was ornamented slightly by a carving representing an open book.

"I did not gain the impression that Gramascene was *pointing* at the grave, Holmes," I said. I had meticulously refrained from omitting the detail when giving my account over breakfast, and I now feared that I had inadvertently placed too much emphasis upon it. "It was just where his arm happened to fall."

Holmes, closely examining the Wilfredson gravestone, did not respond. Instead he said, "There is an inscription on this carved Bible. One would expect a comforting verse about eternal rest or the like, but this, I fancy, is more unusual: 'His hand hath formed the crooked serpent,' indeed. We shall have to ask your Mr Felspar about this."

"Well, if you think it important," I agreed, though I was disagreeably reminded of the gesture that it seemed the town's housekeepers habitually made in response to my presence. That might be a crooked serpent, for all that it was formed by human rather than divine hand.

"It may prove so. Would you ask Constable Batterby where Dr Harpier's grave might be found?"

I meekly did as I was told. Batterby professed ignorance, however, and not a little disdain. Instead I was compelled to search among the graves for the historian's resting place.

As I had realised on the morning of Gramascene's death, even here among the dead the town's interest in snakes remained, with more than one gravestone wrapped around by a carven serpent. Many of the older specimens were encrusted with greenish-brown lichen, giving them the unsettling appearance of flaking scales.

Dr Harpier's headstone was recent, clean and unadorned. It gave only his name and dates, with no academic honours. It was only because those dates, 1822 to 1889, matched Woodwose's account of the historian's death that I could be certain it was the right man. I noted down the particulars, such as they were, and returned them to Holmes.

I found him in a part of the churchyard given to some of the oldest burials, scraping the lichen with a small trowel from another headstone, this one surmounted by a crude but unmistakeable representation of the Hagworm, legs and all.

"Thomas Wermeston," my friend observed, "The sixteenth-century priest, and distant relative of Lady Ophelia, whose death in 1599 the Hagworm supposedly foretold. He, at least, was not consigned to the family plot on Glissenholm. And what were Dr Harpier's first names, pray?"

"Edmund John," I told him.

"Edmund Harpier," Holmes mused. "Yes, I believe that that would fit."

I realised what he meant. "The signature on the letter in Gramascene's pocket-book?" Batterby was loitering by the town-side corpse-gate, pretending not to watch us, but he was surely out of earshot.

"I cannot say for certain, but it would be one plausible interpretation of the scrawl we saw. Ideally we should compare it with another sample of the late doctor's signature. Perhaps Woodwose has something," he mused.

"Dr Watson," a voice called timidly, and I looked across to the vestry door, from which the Reverend Gervaise Felspar had emerged.

"My word, Mr Felspar," I said, hurrying over to the vicar. "It's good to see you feeling better."

"I am indeed, I am pleased to say," he told me with a weak smile, "though most embarrassed to recall the state in which you saw me yesterday. Whatever must you think of me?"

"I'm a doctor," I reminded him. "If I judged my patients for their lapses of health, I should not find myself at all popular. This is my good friend, Mr Sherlock Holmes," I added as Holmes crossed the churchyard to join us. "He has come to look into the matter of Mr Gramascene's death."

"It is a terrible tragedy," Felspar said fervently, shaking Holmes's hand, and something returned of the haunted look that I had seen in his eyes the previous day. "I'm told that the poor man's fiancée has arrived in town." News would travel quickly, I knew, in a small community like Wermeholt, and I had no doubt that Holmes's appearance had likewise been fervently discussed among the parishioners. Certainly the vicar seemed little surprised to be introduced to him.

I glanced at Constable Batterby, who was frowning at us from the corpse-gate. "Perhaps we should talk privately," Holmes suggested, and Felspar assented with a rapidity I found surprising.

The priest led us into the vestry, a stone room lined with simple wooden cupboards holding vestments, silver plate and other ceremonial paraphernalia. A firmly shut door led, to judge by its position, to the tower above us.

The man whom I had identified as a verger was within, polishing a chalice. "Would you leave us alone for a moment, please, Peston?" the vicar asked him diffidently.

"O'course, vicar," the man said flatly. Setting down his cup and cloth, he stepped through a doorway into the church proper, pulling the thick oak door closed behind him.

The vicar fussed about getting us tea. As he did, so Holmes began the conversation, cutting through the niceties as was his wont. "We have been looking at the memorials in your fascinating churchyard, Mr Felspar. Tell me, were you acquainted with Dr Edmund Harpier?"

"Alas, no," the priest replied, rather nervously. "As I may have mentioned to Dr Watson, I arrived here several years after his death."

"Indeed. Sir Howard Woodwose you know well, however?"

Felspar swallowed. "We are acquainted, of course, but we are not often in company together. He's a prominent local citizen, but not, I am sorry to say, a churchgoer. It was not always thus. He was a promising young seminarian at one time, but he chose another path."

Holmes nodded to himself. "And did you know him better in those days?"

"A little, yes. We were contemporaries at theological college. Or near-contemporaries, I should say – I happen to be a year older, though that hardly seems significant after so many decades. He was, I believe, an exceptional scholar. It was known that our tutors harboured great hopes for him, a bishopric perhaps. However, he was seduced away by the glamour of the pagan creeds. He is not the first man to have succumbed to their allure, and I dare say he shall not be the last." Felspar shook his head sorrowfully.

"No doubt," said Holmes, a little impatiently.

Knowing what my friend hoped to ask, and that it would come more naturally from me, I asked the priest, "Was it Woodwose who gave you the laudanum that you were taking for your nerves?"

"Well, yes." Felspar blinked. He set down the tea tray on a trestle table and poured us each a cup. "I knew that he kept a supply for medicinal purposes, and I had read that it might have a calming effect on those of a nervous disposition. I should have consulted a doctor, of course, but Dr Kebbelwhite is tremendously busy and I did not like to trouble him over so trivial a matter. As it happens Woodwose's housekeeper, Mrs Jenkins, is Mrs Gough's sister, and after the shock of seeing poor Mr Gramascene—" He began to tremble at the thought, and was unable to complete the sentence.

"You asked Mrs Gough to borrow some for you?" I suggested gently.

He nodded gratefully. "It was most ill-advised of me. I shall not make the mistake again."

"Have you always suffered trouble with your nerves?" Holmes asked.

"It is a family weakness, I'm afraid." Felspar essayed a self-deprecating laugh, but it emerged at a rather higher pitch than he might have hoped. "It has troubled me more since my arrival in Wermeholt, I will admit."

"And why is that?" Holmes asked, with surprising gentleness.

"The snakes!" Felspar gave a convulsive shudder, spilling his tea. "I have a lifelong horror of the creatures, Mr Holmes, stronger even than my dislike of boats. As a boy I owned a picture-book that contained a lifelike drawing of one – a snake, that is – and if I accidentally saw it I would become literally paralysed with fear, until my nurse took the book away from me. I have the misfortune to be terrified of all reptiles, quite out of proportion to the harm they might do me."

"It isn't so very rare," I reassured him. "Some people have a similar fear of spiders, rats or even cats. It's an affliction, nothing more."

Felspar nodded quickly. "In adult life it ceased to trouble me, provided I was prudent enough to avoid zoos and their like. Here in Wermeholt, however, the creatures are everywhere. Oh, not the adders on the fell – them I have scarcely seen, although I avoid walking there if I can. No, I am referring to the art and architecture of the town, its statuary, even its toponymy. Why, even my house is on Adder Lane! The horrid beasts are inescapable. The one time I visited Woodwose at home, I am afraid that I practically fled in fear. Even in church I must constantly be passing by that statue of St Michael fighting the serpent – a fine piece of work, as I said to you, Dr Watson, but a source of inexpressible horror to me. It preys on my nerves… the serpent and all its slithering brethren…"

He was shaking hard now, having fortunately set down his tea, and I feared a relapse. "Hush, Mr Felspar," I urged him. "Please, do not tax yourself. We understand how trying life here must be for a man with your unfortunate condition. Have you not thought about seeking a new position elsewhere?"

He shook his head with an obstinate determination. "I cannot desert my flock here, Doctor. To abandon them that I might indulge my own weakness would be a failure I could not bear."

"That is most laudable," said Holmes, who had been listening with conspicuous patience throughout the foregoing. "Perhaps, however, we may move on. I am developing something of an interest in local history, Mr Felspar. Do you by any chance have a list of your predecessors as vicar here?"

Distracted from his morbid fears, Felspar cheered up at once. "Why, yes, as it happens. We are lucky enough to have a wooden plaque listing all the incumbents since the fourteenth century, so far as their identities may be determined. Dr Harpier helped my immediate precursor, Mr Hale-Grimm, to compile it." His face fell. "Unfortunately it was vandalised last year. A most regrettable incident. The culprit was never caught. We're keeping it in the bell-tower until such time as we have the wherewithal to restore it."

At Holmes's continued gentle suggestion, the vicar opened the door to the tower with an iron key. "We keep it locked," he explained, "in case of misadventure. An overly bold child could climb up to the belfry, or even the turret, and fall to their death."

The ringing-chamber was dusty, cluttered with lumber and bric-a-brac – broken pews, old hymn books, detached fragments of masonry and a pile of faded hassocks. The single bell-rope hung through a hole in the plank ceiling, and a wooden ladder led up to a hatch in a corner.

The vicar showed us where the plaque had been placed, and between us we dragged it out and set it on the trestle table in the vestry. It had been scored several times from top to bottom with some sharp implement, and was only partially legible. The incumbents' names had been laid out, with the dates of their arrivals in the parish, in two columns, with space left at the end for future arrivals to be added.

I made a careful record of the layout in my notebook, with marks for the illegible characters.

| INS_. | INCUMBEN_ |
|-------|-----------|
| c.1_20 | ANSELM |
| c.1_55 | CUTHBERT |
| c.1_70 | CRISPIN |
| c.1_80 | ROBERT W_ITE |
| c.1_00 | GEOFFREY _UNTER |
| 141_ | EDWIN FEL_ |
| 144_ | JACOB ABE_ARD |
| 147_ | JOHN HOOP |
| 149_ | HUGO BEA_D |
| 152_ | NICOLAST_ORPE |
| 153_ | CECIL ADD_SON |
| 154_ | HENRY CH_DWICK |
| 157_ | RICHARD H_WARTH |
| 158_ | THOMAS W_RMESTON |
| 159_ | STEPHEN E_DERBY |
| 160_ | BARNABAS _ECK |
| 162_ | CHARLES L_GHT |
| 166_ | EDWARD S_VAGE |
| 169_ | ANDREW T_WAITE |
| 169_ | SIMON HO_ERTON |
| 170_ | LEMUEL D_CKSON |

| INS_. | INCUMBENT |
|-------|-----------|
| 170_ | CHARLES FI_ZJAMES SPEAKE |
| 172_ | SIMEON Mc_NTIRE |
| 176_ | GEORGE CA_LE |
| 178_ | MARTIN TIM_S |
| 178_ | LAERTES W_LFREDSON |
| 179_ | ARTHUR TH_RNE |
| 182_ | WALTER CU_NINGHAM |
| 185_ | CECIL MONT_OSE |
| 187_ | JONATHAN H_LE-GRIMM |
| 189_ | GERVAISE FE_SPAR |

"Mr Hale-Grimm showed commendable optimism regarding the future of the Church," Holmes observed drily, "not to mention the longevity of his plaque. At this rate, enough room remains to accommodate your successors well into the twenty-third century. His name and yours we know in full, of course," he went on, "as well as those of Messrs Wermeston and Wilfredson. The rest are informative, if partial, additions."

For a moment the vicar seemed to be giving Holmes a pleading look, but he said nothing. Once again I wondered just how stable in his recovery the man was.

Holmes continued, "It would be useful to have the full information. The dates in particular. I assume a record was kept?"

Felspar seemed somewhat crestfallen. "Alas, no. We believe we can remember some of them, but it seems that the list was never copied down in full. And the original, together with Dr Harpier's research that produced it, went missing along with the rest of his papers."

Holmes's ears pricked up. "Really? This is the first that I have heard of such an occurrence."

The priest appeared a little surprised. "Oh, yes. There was a quiet scandal about it at the time. You see, he had bequeathed all his research materials to St Osyth's College in Camford, his alma mater, although I dare say their academic value would have been modest. From what I hear his will was most explicit, indeed emphatic, upon the point. But when his cottage was searched, not a trace of the material was found. All was lost, including his investigations into the history of Wermeholt, Ravensfoot and the Wermeston Hall estate. His executors were quite embarrassed, though I imagine St Osyth's took it philosophically enough."

Holmes asked him about the source of the biblical verse that we had found on Wilfredson's tomb.

"Ah, yes – the Book of Job, of course," Felspar informed us

readily. "'By his spirit he hath garnished the heavens; his hand hath formed the crooked serpent.' It comes as the culmination of a series of examples of God's handiwork that are singled out to illustrate his almighty power. You are right to consider it an eccentric choice for a headstone." Again, he shuddered.

After a few more careful enquiries after Mr Felspar's health, Holmes and I quitted the church, though I took a moment to show him the statue to which the priest had referred. After all I had learned of Wermeston and its traditions, I found its malevolent Satan more ominous than ever, the more so since his battle with the Archangel so clearly recapitulated that recorded in the ballad between the Hagworm and Lord William.

Outside we saw that Constable Batterby had moved from the corpse-gate to await us outside the vestry door, so we were able to evade his attentions for the moment. We proceeded to the post office, which was of course closed for the sabbath. However, Mrs Trice lived on the premises, and proved amenable to being disturbed from her Sunday rest in return for a sizeable consideration.

She was acidly delighted to meet my famous partner. "Dr Watson told us we'd no chance of meeting you, sir," she told him tartly. "Then there's a killing and you come running. Life's a funny thing."

"*Killing* is an interesting choice of word for what may have been an animal attack," Holmes observed imperturbably.

"Young Mr Gramascene was killed, wasn't he?" Mrs Trice replied promptly. "Well, then."

She took down Holmes's telegram to Dr Mossbaum, requesting his attendance on a matter that promised to be of the greatest interest to him. Her eyes gleamed with zeal as she wrote down the message, and I had no doubt that everyone in the town would know its contents long before the eminent herpetologist to whom it was addressed.

"What do you suppose Mossbaum will say about the creature?" I wondered, though I knew full well that it was never Holmes's habit to speculate in the absence of firm information.

Instead he remarked, "He should, at least, be able to tell us whether the marks were made by the jaws of a living animal."

"A living animal? Surely you don't credit the plesiosaurus hypothesis?" I asked.

"I think you know my approach in such situations, Watson. However, while it seems the killing, as Mrs Trice referred to it, was seemingly inflicted by the teeth of some large animal, it does not follow that the beast was responsible. After all, if a man is clubbed to death with the branch of an oak tree, we do not place the tree in the dock."

I tried to follow his analogy. "You believe that someone killed Gramascene using a jawbone? Like Samson and the Philistines?" Our visit to the church had evidently impressed itself upon me, as I would not normally reach for such a biblical analogy. Certainly the Hagworm was no ass.

"Scripture has never been my field, as you know," my friend replied distractedly. "But that is one possibility among several. I should like us to consider it further. When I was passing through Ravensfoot I observed a museum of fossils. We might profitably pay it a visit on the morrow."

The Serpent's Arms was just opening, and Holmes suggested that we step inside. I recalled that I had not seen Effie Scorpe since the morning of Gramascene's death, and agreed. I stopped on my way in to pay my respects to the grey dog, who once again was tied up outside.

Effie's absence continued, however, the bar being manned by her ill-tempered father. Holmes greeted him, all affability, and requested two glasses of his finest brown ale. Ben Scorpe supplied them, his glower as resentful as ever.

"Tell me, my man," said Holmes genially, "do you see many visitors here?"

Scorpe did not reciprocate his friendliness. "It's a pub," he said flatly.

"Aha, yes, of course," Holmes chuckled. "Naturally, I meant strangers to the town. I believe this is the only hostelry. Do you see much by way of out-of-town trade?"

Ben glared at him. "Don't thou try to coddle me, Sherlock Holmes. I ken who thou is and what thou wants. Thou wants to find out if I kenned that deid lad, doesn't thou?"

"Well, Ben Scorpe, perhaps I do," Holmes beamed. "Just as your work is to run a pub, mine is to solve mysteries, and the circumstances of Mr Gramascene's death certainly warrant that description."

"It's no mystery," Scorpe replied darkly. "Dare say it's a shame for them as kenned him." His voice bore little evidence of sympathy with such people.

"No doubt it is," Holmes agreed. "But you would not count yourself among their number, I gather."

"Barely met t'lad since thou asks, nobut it's any on thy business," Scorpe retorted. "I'd naught against him, if that's what thou means."

"Oh, certainly not, Mr Scorpe," Holmes smiled. "It would be most unlikely that he or his friends would be visiting these premises after hours, for instance."

Ben Scorpe's huge fist made a grab at Holmes's neck, but my friend, ever alert, had danced back from the bar just in time. "What does thou mean by that?" the publican cried. "Has thou been talking til that nosy biddy Martha Trice? I'll wring her scrawny neck for her, and thou's as well!"

I had hoped that this outburst might bring Effie running to calm her father, but we remained alone in the bar except for the inn's only other customer, an elderly man in the corner. This fellow said, "Easy now, Ben," but his tone was one of wry amusement, and he made no effort to intervene as Scorpe rounded the bar and advanced on us both.

"I assure you that Mrs Trice has said nothing whatsoever to me about you," Holmes replied evenly, with greater accuracy than honesty given that I had merely relayed her words to him. "If she had, though, Mr Scorpe, what do you suppose she would have said?"

"Naught to do good til anyone but Martha Trice, that's for sure," Scorpe replied belligerently. "She's told thou about that young goat and my Effie, then, has she?"

"Why, nothing of the kind, I promise you," Holmes repeated, more candidly this time. "Am I to take it, then, that Mr Gramascene had been paying court to your daughter?"

"Paying court?" Ben Scorpe spat on the floor. "That lad had one thing on his mind, and it wasn't *courting*, I can tell thou that. I sent him packing wi' a flea in his ear. I'll not rue t'day he was taken."

"I see," said Holmes. "Perhaps, though, since Mr Gramascene's fiancée is now in town, this information might be best kept between ourselves for the present."

Ben scowled even more fiercely than before. "Wasn't me come in here raking it up, was it?"

"No indeed. You may rely upon our discretion. If I might ask, though, Mr Scorpe, would it be possible for us to speak to Effie on this matter also?"

"She's not home, and I'll liever see thou in Hell," Scorpe promised us grimly. "Now, get out on my inn, t'both on you."

We left, with some regret on my part. It was, as Holmes had observed, the only hostelry in town.

As we walked back along the high street towards the Mereside Hotel, I cast a look over my shoulder at the Serpent's

Arms. A face was watching us from an upper-storey window, but vanished from view at once, the moment it saw my glance. It seemed that Effie Scorpe was at home after all, but speaking to her against her father's opposition would be quite a task.

# CHAPTER TEN

In the morning, as Holmes had suggested, the two of us hitched a ride on a brewers' cart as it returned around the lake from a delivery at the Serpent's Arms, with the intent of visiting the Ravensfoot Palaeontological Museum. Constable Batterby had told me, after all, that I might go anywhere I pleased around the shores of Wermewater.

As ever, the shore near Wermeholt was damp and muggy, with a miasma of mist retreating into the mere as the morning wore on. However, as we rounded Wermewater to the west, following the path that I had taken on my first arrival in the town, the sun grew brighter and our surroundings more cheerful. The lake began to glitter prettily in the morning light, and the forested shores of Glissenholm began to look more scenic than sinister. Needless to say there was no sign of any creature disturbing the water. As we approached Ravensfoot, the shores around Wermeston Hall, also thickly wooded, came into view.

Holmes called to the driver to halt, and we dismounted, passing the fellow a tip to show our appreciation, although in truth it was the carthorse who had done the additional work. I wondered whether the driver knew more about the incident that had done for poor Dr Harpier, but when asked he told us that, while he recalled talk of the accident, he had been nowhere near Wermeholt at the time and was no wiser than we.

We walked the final half-mile into Ravensfoot, and entering the town, remote though it was, made me feel as if we were rejoining the civilised world. We took morning tea at a shop on the lakefront, looking across to Wermeholt, and I was struck again at the contrast between its picturesque appearance from such a distance, tucked cosily beneath the slopes of Netherfell, and the dank reality of the place in which I had spent the past days.

From our new vantage point, it was possible to see directly into the estate that was so feared by the townsfolk of Wermeholt, although Glissenholm stood in the way of any view of Wermeston Hall itself. On my previous visit to Ravensfoot I had had little reason to consider it of greater interest than any other part of the scenery, but now I gazed carefully, trying to map and memorise its terrain, as I might once have done on looking down from an Afghan mountain pass into the valley below. However, the ground between the wall where I had encountered Modon and its counterpart protecting the other side of the estate was thick with trees, obscuring all but the broadest contours of the landscape.

Though larger and more bustling than its neighbour, Ravensfoot was no cosmopolitan hub of activity, and the museum was a small one, tucked away on a back street, identified to potential visitors only by a brass plaque. We knocked, and after quite a lengthy wait were admitted by the elderly curator, who introduced himself as Samuel Wexworth. "Heavens, I'm popular this morning," he said gaily as he let us into a narrow hallway where the shells and bones of extinct creatures were mounted. "Sometimes whole weeks go by without anybody disturbing my old bones."

I wondered whether he meant his own or those in his care, but then I realised that this must be an habitual joke with him.

As we made our way, Holmes and I had to duck down to pass beneath the vast head of some primordial elk, with outlandishly enormous antlers, but Wexworth was a small man, bent with age, and the beast presented him with no such impediment.

We entered a larger room, where the wall-mounted specimens were fewer and the space given over primarily to glass cases. Some items in the collection were striking indeed, including the skeletal foot of some vast lizard that, when alive, must have stood higher than the building. My attention was captured by the intact skeleton of a snake, still embedded in the rock where it had been found. It looked to me exactly as I would, from my position of almost complete ignorance, expect a modern snake's bones to look, but the plaque told me that it was an extinct species of python.

"*Discovered in Java by Marcus, Lord Wermeston,*" I read, "*and donated to the museum in 1852.* Was Marcus Lady Ophelia's father?" I asked.

Mr Wexworth nodded. "Oh, yes. That particular holding was a bequest to my predecessor, since his lordship died well before my time. He was well-travelled, as I understand, and a highly respected zoologist. Palaeontology was not his primary interest, but from what I gather he was very proud of this specimen. He was most keen that it should be displayed locally."

I remembered Sir Howard Woodwose telling Summerlee and myself that Lady Ophelia had travelled widely with her father before his death. "Was he in the East Indies often?" I asked.

"Their fauna were his particular interest," Wexworth said. "As I understand it, he was exploring the Malay Archipelago when he died. Lady Ophelia was with him, as she often was, and she returned his body to England for burial."

"On Glissenholm, I presume?" Holmes asked. Wexworth looked blank.

"We understand the Wermeston family burial ground is there," I explained.

"Oh. Well then, I suppose so," he agreed, but it was apparent that he knew less of the matter than we.

Holmes asked, "Is it possible that your python does not represent the whole of Lord Wermeston's fossil collection? Might further specimens be held at Wermeston Hall?"

"I wouldn't know. Lady Ophelia is a very private individual." Mr Wexworth nevertheless looked eager. "If you find out that there are such items, however, do please put in a word for our museum. As I have said, my predecessor had friendly connections with her father. We are always on the lookout for new holdings, and it would be terrible to think that something of genuine scientific importance might be lost through ignorance on the part of Lady Ophelia's executors. Although God willing she'll be with us for some time yet, of course," he added as a rather perfunctory afterthought. The curator's mind was obviously full of the fossil treasures that might lie hidden in Lady Ophelia's hermitage.

Recollecting himself, he asked us, "Were there any holdings that you were particularly hoping to see?"

Holmes replied that we had a special interest in teeth and jawbones.

"I see, I see. Well, we have some rather fine examples in that line." He led us over to a bank of wooden drawers, one of which he slid out to display a set of sharp stone objects under a sheet of glass. "These are petrified sharks' teeth, from various species both extinct and still surviving. They're actually among the most common fossils – sharks have existed for aeons, you see, in forms very like their present ones. Since they regularly shed their teeth, the ocean floor must be positively littered with them."

We peered at the teeth. Though I should certainly not have liked to be menaced by a jaw full of them, each one individually would do a person considerably less damage than a penknife.

"Surely it's not a shark," I murmured under my breath. Holmes shook his head impatiently, and I had to agree. While I was hardly an expert on the creatures, as far as I knew they were ocean-going predators. A saltwater fish would hardly be at home in Lake Wermewater.

"Have you any intact jawbones, Mr Wexworth?" Holmes asked.

"Other than my own, you mean?" Wexworth replied jocularly. "Not from a shark, alas. They are much rarer than the discarded teeth."

"From any prehistoric predator, then," Holmes suggested.

"Perhaps particularly an aquatic one?" I ventured.

Holmes shook his head again. "That is not germane to our present purposes," he pointed out, and I remembered that we were searching, not for the extinct kin of a living beast, but for an inanimate murder weapon.

Some rummaging on Wexworth's part produced the petrified jawbones of various long-departed creatures. Some were larger than others, but the largest of all, belonging according to the curator to a kind of toothed bird, was still too insubstantial to have caused the damage we had observed on Gramascene and the boat.

Without explaining our reasons, Holmes showed Wexworth a sketch he had made depicting the marks that had been left on the vessel, alongside a foot rule to supply the scale. The man frowned and shook his head.

"We have never held anything like that," he said. "If it is indeed a fossil, I might suggest an ichthyosaurus, or perhaps a mosasaur." The former, he explained, had been a fish-like lizard, the latter a kind of ocean-going crocodile, but both were presumed to have been wholly aquatic and subsisted on fish, making them poor candidates for our sheep-worrying Hagworm. "If you discover who owns it, please let me know and

I shall make them an offer."

"Could it be a plesiosaur?" I asked.

"A plesiosaur?" Wexworth's jovial face developed a frown, and then his manner changed. Coldly, he asked, "Do I gather from the tenor of your enquiries that you are with that charlatan Creavesey?"

Holmes surprised me with a laugh. "We are decidedly not of the professor's party," he reassured the curator, "though we are acquainted with his current, very eccentric project. I gather that you have had the pleasure also."

"He came to me a few weeks ago, gibbering of plesiosaurs," Wexworth acknowledged peevishly. "He told me, with great protestations of secrecy, that he intended to find the Wermewater Hagworm, if you please. An absurd and backward superstition, far less prevalent among the townsfolk here than their rustic counterparts across the mere, I am pleased to say. I am bound to add that it is not the sort of thing I should expect a man of science to treat with any seriousness. But from what I can gather, Professor Creavesey is not the man his colleagues believe him to be. He—" He bit his tongue very belatedly. "Oh, dear. Perhaps I have said enough."

"Then we shall not press you further, sir," said Holmes kindly. We left the elderly curator standing among his collection like one more fossil, a troubled look upon his face.

We luncheoned at an inn whose fare was considerably superior to that available at the Serpent's Arms, before walking back to Wermeholt. We retraced my steps around the lake, watching Ravensfoot recede into the distance behind us. As we rounded a spur of Ravensfell, a tall, stringy figure came into view ahead, taking the same route. I recognised Professor Summerlee's walk, and said as much to Holmes, but the man was too far away to hail. A minute or so later, he glanced back towards Ravensfoot and seemed to see us. Rather than pausing to allow us to catch up with him, he quickened his steps and hastened onwards.

"That is not very sociable of the professor," Holmes observed.

"He is not a very sociable man," I explained.

"Mr Wexworth implied that we were not the museum's first visitors of the morning," Holmes noted shrewdly. "I am not given to betting, Watson, as you know, but I would lay money that we were preceded there by Professor Summerlee."

The professor's haste began to look positively furtive as we followed him, although he must have been well aware that we had seen him already. I wondered whether he felt as if we were pursuing him. Had he perhaps discovered something at the museum, some information or even material evidence that he was now concerned to keep concealed from us?

As we approached Wermeholt, however, the damp seemed to rise from the lake and chill my mood, and I lost interest in our ungainly precursor. Instead I kept a weather eye on Glissenholm, and once I saw stirrings among its trees that I thought there was not the wind to account for. The lake's surface remained untroubled, except by the passage of the occasional boat.

At length Professor Summerlee disappeared among the cluster of buildings that formed the margins of Wermeholt, and shortly afterwards we reached the same point, passing by Woodwose's cottage and shortly afterwards the churchyard. After we had called in at the post office to find out whether there was any response to Holmes's telegram to Dr Mossbaum (which there was not), my friend was all for pressing on and attempting once more to gain ingress to the Wermeston estate, there to speak, if we might, with Lady Ophelia herself. At my insistence, however, we first stopped off at the Mereside Hotel.

There we found Professor Summerlee awaiting us in the lounge, much as he had been on my original arrival in the town. "Dr Watson," he said, as calmly as before. "And Mr Holmes, unless I am sorely deceived. You must forgive my not awaiting you on the road. I did not care to have the conversation that I knew must ensue out in the open. Perhaps we might retire to the privacy of one of our rooms?"

Holmes was lodging at a nearby boarding-house, Mary Topkins having taken over her fiancé's former room at the Mereside, so I entertained both men in my own, rather cramped bedroom. Although Holmes seemed to accept Summerlee's explanation for his evasiveness at face value, I could not help reflecting that the professor had had the time since his return to the hotel to conceal any item that he might have borrowed from the museum – although, had he been carrying a jawbone of the size we had been considering, he could not easily have hidden it about his person during the walk.

"I am pleased to meet you, Mr Holmes," the professor said without preamble, once we were ensconced in my room. "I have mentioned to Dr Watson that I greatly enjoy his accounts of your exploits – not, to be sure, for their literary qualities," he added, with his usual punctilious adherence to fact and indifference to the sensitivities of others, "but for the insight they give into the workings of a deductive mind. I think that you and I are similar in some respects, in that we aspire to the qualities of objectivity and accuracy in our observations and reasoning. I do not claim to anything resembling your expertise in the criminological field, naturally, which is why I am glad that you have come here."

Holmes smiled lazily and began to fill his pipe. "From what Watson tells me, Professor, I believe you are correct. I know that your journey this morning was to the Ravensfoot Palaeontological Museum, and I can only suppose that you were undertaking some detective enterprise of your own, relating to the work of your colleague Professor Creavesey. May I enquire what it was?"

Summerlee nodded quickly, his goatee waggling. "You called at the museum yourself, I suppose. And not on the same mission as I, or you would now be telling me my business, not asking it. Surely you were not investigating Topkins' absurd theory that the legendary lake creature is some kind of living prehistoric relic?"

"Not exactly," said Holmes. "I am pursuing a line of inquiry. You said, though, that you were pleased that I was here, and alluded to my criminological expertise. Might I conjecture that these irregularities to which you allude may have a criminal element?"

Summerlee looked thoughtful. "At present I would say not, although I am willing to be proved wrong. I refer to the need for justice for the late Henry Gramascene. I would have expected that to be your first supposition, in fact, as it is a very obvious one. I have no objection to telling you more of my suspicions regarding Creavesey, Mr Holmes, but I would appreciate your not attempting to draw me out with subterfuge."

Watching these two remarkable intellects taking the measure of one another put me in mind of the conversations I had witnessed between Sherlock Holmes and his brother Mycroft, the one man whom he acknowledged as his superior in matters of reasoning. Summerlee was not, outside his own field at least, of Mycroft's stature, but he was just as willing to take Holmes to task for his lapses as was Sherlock's elder brother.

"Very well, Professor," Holmes said. "I promise to deal honestly with you. And as an earnest of my good faith, the errand on which Watson and I visited the museum was to enquire after the local availability of dinosaur jawbones."

"As a murder weapon, you mean?" Summerlee asked at once. "The thought had occurred to me, but I had dismissed the idea. Jawbones in such an intact condition are extremely rare. Anyone who was in a position to acquire one would understand as much, and would be reluctant to ill-treat it in that way, for reason of its monetary if not its scientific value."

"Still," said Holmes, who was not accustomed to such

cavalier dismissal, "if the reason were strong enough it might overcome such scruples."

"Possibly," agreed Summerlee, "but the fact remains that such a rarity would be very difficult to come by."

"Very well," said Holmes. I thought him a little disconcerted at the force of the professor's argument. "Then let us move on. What exactly is it that you suspect of Professor Creavesey?"

"I cannot be exact, for I do not know with any great accuracy," said Summerlee. "You must understand that his area of specialism is not mine, though we have overlapping interests, and in much of what I tell you I am trusting to the word of colleagues in his discipline.

"They inform me that Creavesey has been for most of his career a mediocre scientist, and that his publications have more than once included mistakes that others have been obliged to correct. I do not mean that he was exceptionally inept – there are dozens of such men at every faculty, proficient enough to gain tenure but indifferent to developing their talents once it is secure. There are far greater charlatans than he at work in the field of palaeontology," he added, with a frown that made me suspect that there must be some particularly challenging professor to whom he referred. "However, it seems that over the past few years his work has improved markedly, to the point where it has been generally excellent, and often quite inspired.

"All men gain experience and wisdom over the course of their careers, of course, but such a radical leap in ability is virtually unheard of. In person – as you can confirm, Watson – he does not give the impression of a man of genius, his foolish obsession with the Hagworm being a case in point.

"I am afraid that there is talk of plagiarism, disgraceful though that would be. Creavesey's colleagues fear that he may be taking the credit for the work of some exceptionally brilliant student. If this is the case, they naturally wish that the young man in question should be freed from such exploitation, and enabled to make his own contributions to the field. Some of my informants have noted that young Topkins, who is considered the most talented of Creavesey's current students, has yet to publish work of his own. It was partly to observe the relations between the two, on their behalf, that I agreed to join this absurd expedition."

"Good Heavens," I said.

"Indeed," agreed Holmes. "Why did you think that a visit to the palaeontological museum would help you in this inquiry, Professor?"

"I had heard that Mr Wexworth took a dim view of Creavesey's presence at Wermeholt, and I wondered whether he had some concrete reason for it. I thought that as an expert in Creavesey's own discipline he might know more to his discredit than the self-evident folly of his current venture."

"And does he?" I asked. "He seemed to hint to us that Creavesey was not reputable."

"I do not think so," Summerlee said. "He seems to have taken offence that the first visit to the museum by such a renowned figure in the field was motivated by so frivolous an enterprise. I tried to suggest to him that his first impressions might be ill-judged, but I fear I could do little to shift them."

"It is odd," I said, "but this is not the first hint of academic intrigue that we have heard in this out-of-the-way place. Do you remember Woodwose mentioning Dr Harpier, the historian who previously occupied his cottage? Mr Felspar told us that his papers went missing at the time of his death. I don't suppose there could be any connection?"

Summerlee shook his head. "What relevance would the research of an historian have to the work of a palaeontologist? The periods they deal with are radically different."

"His work would have to have taken a most singular turn," Holmes agreed. "It scarcely seems likely, Watson."

"Yet disciplines intersect," I pointed out stubbornly. "Woodwose told us about the legend of St Hilda and how it relates to fossil sea-creatures, and I suppose folklore and zoology might equally meet in the Hagworm. Could not Harpier's historical researches have turned up something in the local record that supports the dinosaur survival theory?"

"I should not suppose so for a moment," Summerlee replied severely. "No, I imagine we have heard all the historical evidence that exists, and more, from Woodwose."

"Well, I stand corrected," I said with all the grace I could muster, although I was not convinced that I did.

"Your investigation is an intriguing one, Professor," said Holmes, "and I should be glad, if you would like, to put you in touch with a certain literary scholar, with whom I have worked on detecting forged manuscripts through their stylistic features. He might be able to advise you on what to look for in the writing of a scholar who has started plagiarising another's work. For my own part, I confess that you are right to suggest the matter's interest lies mostly in its relation, if any, to Henry Gramascene's death."

"The question has occurred to me, of course," Summerlee acknowledged. "But as I have said, I am an ignoramus in the field of crime."

Holmes said, "If Creavesey were stealing Topkins' work, that might indeed have given Topkins a reason to kill him. Alternatively, if Creavesey were worried that the truth would come out, he might kill Topkins. But neither of those is what occurred. Both men are still alive, to the best of my knowledge, and from what you have told me, remain on friendly terms."

"I sincerely doubt that Gramascene was the student being plagiarised, if such a person exists," said Summerlee. "He was a personable young man, but academically unremarkable."

A little nervously given my previous dismissal, I suggested, "Might he have discovered this secret of Creavesey's, perhaps from Topkins? If he were blackmailing Creavesey, that might once again give the professor sufficient motive for murder."

"If that is the case," Holmes observed coolly, "then Topkins himself is in danger. After all, if Gramascene heard the secret from Topkins, then Creavesey would know that Topkins' discretion could not be trusted. But from everything I hear of the professor, he seems an unlikely murderer. He is not, I believe, a physically powerful man."

"Certainly not," I admitted, seeing his direction of thought at once. "And Gramascene was young, fit and strong." I could, perhaps, imagine an enraged Topkins setting about his friend with the jawbone of some animal, but the professor was even slighter and frailer than he. "If Creavesey killed him, he could hardly have acted alone."

"Well, I didn't help him," Summerlee snorted. "And I can't see any reason why Topkins would, if the motive was as you describe."

"Still, Wermeholt is not a prosperous town," admitted Holmes, "and its inhabitants do not seem especially well off. Perhaps a would-be murderer could hire disinterested local help."

"Or perhaps there was another motive," I speculated, struck suddenly by a new idea. "We've been supposing that Gramascene might have been killed in such a way as to give the appearance of a Hagworm attack. At present the manner of his death is the most convincing evidence we have for the Hagworm's existence. Is it conceivable that that is by intent? Could Creavesey, or Topkins, or both, have staged the death in order to vindicate their theories?"

"It would be a remarkable *folie à deux* if so," Holmes observed. "And it hardly explains why Creavesey's student and

Topkins' prospective brother-in-law was chosen as the victim rather than some boatman unknown to them."

"We know that Topkins and Gramascene quarrelled—" I began, but I was interrupted by a thunderous knocking on the door of the room. I had already heard raised voices downstairs, but had been too intent upon my theorising to pay close attention to what they were saying.

Much to my surprise, when I opened the door I saw Peston the verger, flushed and panting. "Dr Watson!" he exclaimed. "Mr Holmes! Young Batterby sent me to find you." He paused for a moment to catch his breath.

"What is it, man?" I asked, alarmed. "Has there been another attack?" Then, considering his obvious agitation, "Another death?"

"Aye, a death," Peston gasped. "But not in t'mere, not this time. It's t'vicar, Doctor! He's throwed hissel off on t'kirk tower!"

# CHAPTER ELEVEN

Though the cause of his death was certainly quite different, Gervaise Felspar's body lay disconcertingly close to where Henry Gramascene had perished, a few feet from the grave of the priest's eighteenth-century predecessor. I remembered my first fleeting impression that Gramascene, too, had fallen from the stony turret above.

Again Constable Batterby stood by the deceased, surrounded by a small group of townsfolk. The sense of familiarity I felt as I knelt down to inspect the body was quite eerie.

This time, though, I had Sherlock Holmes at my side. Summerlee had remained at the hotel, declaring that he would only clutter up the scene. "Stand back, all of you!" Holmes cried. "Allow the good doctor some space to work."

Reluctantly, the crowd shuffled backwards, and Holmes, his eyes as sharp as ever, pounced with a cry on something their receding feet revealed lying in the grass. "The key to the bell-tower, I declare!" he cried, brandishing an old iron key that did indeed look like the one that Felspar had used to let us into the vestry the previous day. Peston the verger, who had returned with us from the Mereside Hotel, breathlessly confirmed that it was.

"We've already tried to get up there," Batterby grudgingly admitted. "It's locked."

"Who found the body, pray?" Holmes asked as I turned my attention to Gervaise Felspar's ruined frame.

"Well, as thou says *found*, that was Archie Peston here," said Batterby. "But it was Ned's lad Luke saw him first, wasn't it, Luke?" He nodded towards the younger of the two boatmen who had gone out after Creavesey's party on the morning of Gramascene's death.

"We was out on t'mere," said Luke excitedly, "when I saw something in t'kirkyard, all black and hunched up, just where that Mr Gramophone was found."

"That's Gramascene, Luke," Batterby reminded him sternly.

"Well, we come in to see what's what," said Luke, "but by then Mr Peston was here. We heard him cry out as we was tying up at t'jetty."

"I assume there was no sign of life remaining?" Holmes asked.

"No," said Luke seriously. "Vicar was deid as a squashed snail."

A few minutes' inspection sufficed to convince me that the priest had, indeed, died by falling from the church tower above – and some hours previously at that, probably around midnight. Whether this abrupt descent had resulted from his jumping, being pushed or simply losing his footing was quite another matter. I did not need Holmes to tell me that the key could as easily have been dropped by a member of the crowd as by Felspar before or during his fall. Among those present I could once again see Ben Scorpe, Mrs Trice and Mrs Gough (unless it was Mrs Jenkins), as well as the Mereside Hotel's own Mr Dormer, who had followed us here after seeing Peston's excitement.

I had not known the priest well, but I knew that he had lived a dutiful life, and not, I thought, one that had been especially happy. I could not mourn him as his parishioners would (or should, for at this point they were mostly standing around and gawping just as they had at the death of Gramascene, a stranger to the town), but I could and did feel sorrow at his passing, regardless of how he might have met it.

"Take him to the town hall," I suggested to Batterby. "Let's leave poor Gramascene on his own at Thorpe's for now. Did he have any relatives?"

"Never heard on none," the constable said. "His housekeeper will ken, but. Nora Gough as is." His eyes searched the crowd for her, but it seemed that both the sisters had slipped away.

"Come, Watson." Holmes was standing at the vestry door, still clutching the key he had found, barely able to contain his impatience. "We must examine the tower."

Batterby detailed some men to make the arrangements for Felspar's body, and Peston agreed to stay below to see that the priest was treated with respect.

With the constable in tow, Holmes and I entered the vestry, where the wooden plaque that Felspar had shown us the previous day was leaning up against a wall. There was no sign of any struggle or other disturbance. The stout wooden door that gave access to the bell-tower was, as Batterby had averred, locked shut. Holmes opened it and then handed the key over to the policeman's safekeeping. He ensured that he entered the tower first, even so.

The ringing-chamber was much as we had left it, with the bell-rope hanging down amid the accumulated clutter. Holmes ascended the ladder and I followed, leaving Batterby to bring up the rear.

Above there was a tall and empty chamber, housing nothing but a further ladder, the dangling bell-rope and the webs of an inordinate number of spiders. A thick layer of dust covered the floor with its two holes – one square for the ladder, one round for the rope – and Holmes examined it carefully, especially the signs of passage between one ladder and the next.

Ascending the taller ladder to the belfry itself, he asked the constable, "How often would someone come up here, in the normal course of events?"

"Ask Peston, not I," Batterby replied. "Don't see why anyone'd need to, but. Naught up here but t'bell, and they rings her from down below."

"There was certainly someone on the turret the night before last," I reminded Holmes. "I saw a lantern."

At the top of the ladder was a hatch. Holmes threw it open and we all stepped up into the belfry. The chamber was cramped, as it was dominated by the large bell that hung here. We had to keep near the sides, which was unnerving as there were large arches in each wall, open to the air, to allow the sound of ringing to be heard across the town. A chill wind blew constantly through the chamber, occasionally rousing a low murmur from the suspended iron bulk. No dust had accumulated here, though the wooden floor smelled dank.

In the corner was yet another ladder, which, after a brief examination of the room, Holmes scaled. He unbolted the hatch that led to the summit of the tower, giving me a significant glance as he did so, and threw it open.

At once a snake fell out, squirming and hissing, onto the wooden floor beneath. Batterby and I recoiled, and I cried out in alarm. "Stay back," Holmes warned us calmly. "There are more."

"More?" I repeated in disbelief. The snake writhed, rising up to glare at the constable and myself. It was an ordinary adder, I saw, dun-coloured with a zigzag pattern of darker brown along its back. It posed no danger as far as our lives went, but it could still give us a nasty bite.

With more resourcefulness than I might have credited to him, Batterby quickly removed his headgear and produced his truncheon, with which he proceeded to knock the reptile's coils into it. He immediately pitched the helmet out of one of the cavernous windows, with a cry of, "Watch below!"

"I hope they heard you," I observed, disapprovingly. I should not have cared to have a hardened container full of enraged snake falling anywhere near me.

Descending the ladder, Holmes said, "The danger is less than my immediate assessment suggested. I count two live snakes remaining. The rest are dead, or merely sloughed skins. Someone has been collecting rather assiduously." He slammed the hatch shut.

"Even so," I said, "I'm not overly keen to be sharing a turret with two live adders."

"Evidently the Reverend Mr Felspar shared that sentiment," Holmes observed, with the macabre humour of which he was sometimes capable.

We found a light wooden chest and a detached railing down in the ringing-chamber, and carried them up the tower with us. With Batterby's help Holmes was able to confine the two surviving snakes in the box.

"I imagine this was the one that was used," he observed. "It matches the marks I observed in the dust on the first floor."

I stood with Holmes and the policeman on the turret, surrounded by the snakes' dead brethren and the coiled skins they had shed. There were half a dozen of the former and twice as many of the latter, scattered across the small floor area between the battlements. With the three live creatures to give the impression that all were just as active, it was little wonder that a man with Gervaise Felspar's morbid fears had been panicked into taking the only escape open to him.

"I suppose he must have been up here already," I said. "He must have left the key in the door. Someone followed him with a box of snakes, tipped them onto the floor and then retreated, bolting the hatch and locking the door behind them. Then they discarded the key in the churchyard. What an unspeakably cruel prank."

"A prank is one word for it, Watson," Holmes observed. "Others might call it premeditated murder. How well known was it that Felspar hated snakes?" he asked Batterby.

The policeman shrugged. "Wasn't any secret. Nora Gough talks, especially til her sister. And thou kens what a secret's worth til Martha Trice."

"Mrs Trice is Mrs Gough's sister?" I was distracted by this. "I thought that was Mrs Jenkins, Woodwose's housekeeper."

Batterby shrugged again. "Three sisters," he said simply. Now that it had been mentioned, I supposed I could see the women's resemblance to the postmistress, though far less striking than between the two housekeepers themselves.

The turret of the tower was even more beset by the wind than the belfry, but the vista surrounding us took in the town itself, clinging to the lower slopes of Netherfell as its summit glowered above us, and the expanse of Wermewater stretching across to Ravensfoot and Ravensfell beyond. More peaks were visible in the distance, rising above Ravensfell. Only a corner of the Wermeston estate could be seen, lush with greenery, but Glissenholm was clearly visible, a bright hummock of vegetation in the still waters of the mere.

"Even so," I mused, "someone must have known that he'd be up here. They'd need to know the layout of the bell-tower, which is normally kept locked, and well enough to climb it in the dark at that, since all this occurred at night. And they'd need to have some reason to be approaching the church in the dark with a large box, if anybody saw them."

"Indeed," said Holmes. "I think at this point that you might do worse than speak to Mr Peston, Batterby."

"Aye, maybe thou's right," the constable muttered, and

clambered reluctantly down the ladder. Peering down at the graveyard below I could see that Felspar's body had indeed been removed, but the verger's black robe was still among the locals gathered about the bloody patch where he had fallen. Another figure was striding towards the crowd, tweed-jacketed with flowing white hair, and I recognised it as Woodwose.

"Why would Peston want to kill the vicar, though?" I wondered. "For that matter, why would anybody? He was a perfectly harmless soul."

"That is certainly a question that will bear consideration," mused Holmes. "I must say, though, that the view from up here is a fine one."

"Yes," I said, "this would be an excellent site for Hagworm-watching. I wonder whether any of Creavesey's party thought of it?" I imagined Thomas Wermeston, the sixteenth-century vicar, standing here when he caught sight of the apparition that foretold his death.

We descended again to the ringing-chamber, and thence through the vestry to the churchyard. With the vicar's body now gone, the throng of townsfolk had largely dispersed, and only a few remained in the hope of further entertainment. Batterby and Peston were not among them, and the remaining onlookers confirmed excitedly that the constable had taken the verger away to his office at the town hall. The blue shape of the policeman's helmet lay between the graves a few yards away, and mindful of its possible occupant I gave it a wide berth.

Sir Howard Woodwose had arrived, as I thought, and greeted us with barely muted bonhomie.

"Mr Holmes," he declared, "your formidable reputation precedes you. I firmly believe that you are one of the great men of our times. I am truly honoured to make your acquaintance."

If he hoped for some reciprocal praise, he received none.

Instead, Holmes asked him quite abruptly, "How well did you know Mr Felspar, Sir Howard?"

"Oh, Felspar was an old friend," Woodwose said at once, "though we had grown somewhat apart. We were at theological college together, you know."

"He mentioned the fact," I said, recalling that Felspar's account of their acquaintance had been a great deal less fulsome.

"The poor fellow has no living relatives," Woodwose confided in his usual boom. "There is only his housekeeper, Mrs Gough, and a few old friends like myself from his university days. I suppose that it will fall to me to arrange the funeral," he added doubtfully.

I shuddered at the idea of Gervaise Felspar being laid to rest in the town whose obsessions had taken such a toll upon his mental health, and had in the end killed him. The image of the serpent was inescapable even in the tombstones of this place.

"Were you aware of his extreme terror of snakes?" Holmes asked. "*Phobia* is, I believe, the medical term."

"The poor man." Woodwose shook his head. "I don't recall the matter being mentioned during our college days. Our university towns are not renowned for their reptile populations, unless you count some of the dons," he joked. "It would have been difficult to miss since his arrival in Wermeholt, however, even if Mrs Gough had not confided in my own housekeeper. On the one occasion when he visited my home, I am afraid my collection of primitive art reduced the poor fellow to a jelly."

"I see," said Holmes. I supposed that there was little likelihood in Wermeholt that the news of how the vicar had been induced to meet his end would remain secret, but he went into no further detail at this point.

"I wonder how well he knew the vicar of St George's in Ravensfoot?" Woodwose added thoughtfully. "He will have to officiate at the funeral, I suppose. I think his name is the Reverend Reginald Vangard. I wonder whether he is free on Wednesday?"

"Wednesday?" I repeated. "Isn't that rather soon for the funeral?"

Woodwose gave me an affable frown. "Merely to meet and discuss matters. Though I should need him to come here to Wermewater; I am extraordinarily busy at present."

Holmes said, "Wednesday is the twenty-first, I believe, Midsummer's Day. Will he not have celebrations in Ravensfoot to detain him?"

"Oddly, no," boomed Woodwose. "Wermewater has no solstice ceremonies of any note; they are not common in these parts. Really, Mr Holmes, you may trust me of all people to think of such things." The knight wandered off, muttering to himself, and Holmes and I left for the town hall, to participate in the questioning of Peston the verger.

By the time we arrived, however, Constable Batterby had let him go. "Archie Peston didn't ken naught," he told us sourly. "He says he was in bed asleep when all this happened."

"But he is familiar with the bell-tower's interior, and with Mr Felspar's habits," Holmes pointed out, exasperated. "We should at least ask him who else might share that knowledge."

"T'tower's been there a long time," said Batterby stubbornly. "Longer than Archie Peston. Lots on men and women in town'll have been up there in their time, one reason or another. He says vicar often ganned up, too. Anyone wanting to follow him'd just have to wait."

"This killing was carefully planned," said Holmes. "Collecting those snakes and skins would have taken time and effort."

"Aye," Batterby agreed. "Plenty on time to watch t'tower and see when vicar'd likely gan up there. Archie Peston don't ken nothing special. Little enough that's secret in this town, wi't'likes on Nora Gough and Martha Trice about."

"And if it should transpire that we need to ask Mr Peston further questions?" Holmes asked acidly.

"I ken where he lives," Batterby replied imperturbably. "He can't leave town wi'out someone seeing him, whatever way he gans."

And with that we had, for the moment, to be content.

Seething, Holmes returned with me to the Mereside Hotel. It was now mid-afternoon, and I for one felt that we had quite enough to think about, considering our excursion to Ravensfoot, Summerlee's revelations about Topkins and the whole sequence of events surrounding Gervaise Felspar's demise. I little knew how eventful the remainder of the day was to prove.

As we entered the hotel, we were waylaid almost at once by James Topkins. "Mr Holmes," he said in a determined voice that quavered only a little, "I wish to speak to you."

"Good Heavens," said Holmes sardonically. "To paraphrase a man I met a few hours ago, I seem to be unwontedly popular today. It was only yesterday, Mr Topkins, that you were finding my presence ghoulish."

"I still consider that it is, to be honest," Topkins replied shortly. "But it's evident that you're not going to leave, and I have my sister's feelings to consider. May we speak in private?"

Not caring to have my room invaded again, I suggested that we adjourn to the garden, where Holmes and I sat on a bench and filled our pipes. Topkins refused, professing to smoke only after dinner, and pacing in annoyance while we lit them.

"Now, Mr Topkins," said Holmes, putting an end to the young man's impatience at last, "pray tell me what it is that you hoped to dissuade me from discovering, which you fear will distress your sister, but which you now intend to confide to Watson and myself on the condition that we keep it a secret?"

Topkins stared at him, but rallied. "You have made a study of human behaviour, Mr Holmes. As a student myself, I respect that."

Hoping to elicit a similar reaction, I said, "We know that you and Mr Gramascene argued. Outside the Serpent's Arms at two o'clock in the morning of… it must have been Friday," I concluded, a little lamely.

Topkins sighed, and threw himself down on a nearby bench. "It seems that everyone in Wermeholt knows *that*, thanks to that ghastly postmistress," he replied peevishly. Evidently others had not had the same trouble as I in drawing the information out of Mrs Trice. "Yes, it's partly that I need to speak to you about. I was extremely disappointed in Henry, and I told him so."

"Perhaps you had better begin at the beginning," Holmes suggested.

"I suppose so," said Topkins. "Well, I've known Henry Gramascene for three years now. We met in the first week after we went up, and he's become one of my closest friends. I introduced him to my sister during a weekend visit home, and one thing led to another. I'm not much interested in matrimony myself, preferring to focus my energies on my work, but I know I'm the odd man out there. I was delighted, and so were my parents. Henry himself was an orphan, but my parents aren't proud people. As a suitor they found him perfectly eligible. I thought that he and Mary were very happy, and I was pleased for them.

"I was perfectly content, in fact, that my best friend was soon to be my brother-in-law, until we arrived in Wermeholt a few weeks ago. I hadn't expected him to come, to be honest – as you'll have realised, research was never his passion, and fond though I was of him I had no particular need for him to keep me company. When I told him that Professor Creavesey and I intended to go hunting lake monsters, he found the whole idea highly amusing. But when he learned that we would be visiting the Lake District, and Wermewater specifically, he said that he had always wanted to visit this part of the country, and asked to tag along.

"Shortly after our arrival at the Mereside, I noticed something furtive about his manner. I wasn't Henry's keeper, of course, and it was no business of mine if he was making friends in the town. But... well, when a man of our class strikes up a friendship with a country barmaid, and then begins to sneak away at night without telling anybody where he's going, I don't need to tell you how it may look."

"So he *was* seeing Effie Scorpe." Though Ben Scorpe had hinted as much, I was nevertheless surprised. I could hardly claim to know her well, but I had not thought Effie the type of young woman to justify her father's suspicions of her.

"Is that her name? The girl from the Serpent's Arms?" Topkins asked, rather dismissively. "If so, then yes, I believe he was. Her father certainly suspected it – he threw Henry out of the pub a few weeks ago, on some pretext or other. I came to think that he was right, and when I confronted Henry he made no attempt to deny it."

"This was after you followed him that night?" Holmes asked.

Topkins nodded. "I hoped to catch him in the act. When I caught up with him, he was about to throw some pebbles at an upstairs window in the inn. The Serpent's Arms does not take guests, and he could hardly claim that he was trying to rouse the publican.

"I asked him what people would think, and he laughed and said that he paid little heed to what people thought, especially in such an out-of-the-way place as Wermeholt. Which was like him, but the liaison itself was not. He told me, if you please, that I would thank him for it once he married my sister! Naturally we quarrelled, Dr Watson. I could hardly have done otherwise."

"What happened then?" Holmes asked. "You will understand the importance of the question, I trust, given that as far as we know this was the last time Mr Gramascene was seen alive."

Topkins coloured. "Well, I could hardly fight him. You know how fit he was, and as you see I am no heavyweight. I told him that I would be writing to Mary on the matter, and left him to his own devices. He told me not to be a fool, and that we should talk in the morning. In the morning, of course, he was nowhere to be found. I was extremely angry with him, as I dare say you observed, Doctor."

"I see," said Holmes. "With Mr Gramascene dead, you naturally concluded that it would do Miss Topkins no good to learn of his extracurricular activities, and such knowledge could indeed cause her considerable additional distress."

"Such was my thinking," Topkins agreed stiffly.

"I gather from your account that this behaviour was quite unlike him? He had shown no previous signs of succumbing to the attractions of other women?"

"As far as I was aware, absolutely not," said Topkins. "If he had, I should have confronted him before now."

"Indeed," agreed Holmes. "Well, Mr Topkins, I thank you for drawing this to my attention. We must certainly speak to Miss Scorpe on the matter. She may be able to tell us what Mr Gramascene was doing on the mere in the early morning, if not what befell him there. But I should like to ask you about another matter, if I may."

"Blast your curiosity! Haven't I told you enough?" Topkins snapped.

"There is a chance that it may assist us in determining how Mr Gramascene died," said Holmes. "I assume that you still wish that, for your sister's sake if not his own."

Topkins looked defiant for a moment, and then deflated. "Oh, very well. To my mind it's perfectly clear that Henry was killed by a surviving specimen of plesiosaurus, but I'm aware that that's a hard claim to get others to accept. I must ask you, though, to do all that you can to keep this matter of him and this... Miss Scorpe... from reaching Mary's ears."

"All that I may, certainly," Holmes readily agreed. "Although if the matter should come to trial, that decision will be taken out of my hands."

Topkins reluctantly accepted this, and Holmes asked his question.

"The suggestion has reached me that Professor Creavesey's published work may not be altogether his own," he said. "Unlike yourself, I have not the knowledge to assess this, so I have only the testimony of others on the point. I wonder whether you have an opinion, or better still some understanding of the matter?"

I could see from Topkins' face that he did indeed know something. "Professor Creavesey is highly respected," he said, awkwardly. "You surely can't believe that he would steal someone else's work." He was a poor dissembler.

"I do not profess to believe anything, Mr Topkins," said Holmes. "I am merely asking you what you believe. I will observe, again, that it may help us to identify Mr Gramascene's attacker."

Topkins looked prepared to bluster further, but then he subsided. "Oh, very well," he said again. "Once more, though, I must ask you to be discreet with what I tell you. Careers may hang in the balance."

"I can but repeat my previous assurance," said Holmes. "Insofar as the matter is under my control, I shall endeavour to keep it quiet."

"Well, then," said Topkins, "between ourselves, I know that you are right. The majority of Creavesey's best work, and his most brilliant ideas, are not his own. He has a private collaborator, who benefits from his academic standing and respectability to publish work that might not otherwise see the light of day. It's a mutually beneficial arrangement, not an exploitative one."

"And would this collaborator," I asked, tiring of his coyness, "go by the name of James Topkins?"

"I think not, Watson," said Holmes. "Mr Topkins may not

possess Professor Creavesey's long standing in the palaeontological field, but there would surely be no impediment to his submitting his research under his own name if his work warrants it."

"You're quite right, of course," said Topkins, who had looked simply bewildered at my attempt to surprise the truth out of him. "I've been remiss not to publish before now, but I'm waiting until my thesis is complete. I can't stand the idea of letting it out in bits and pieces. In the meantime, a positive conclusion to our endeavours here would make my name very satisfactorily."

I said, "So what obstacle would there be to another doing the same? You can't expect us to believe that Gramascene was this hidden genius."

Holmes said, "Again, there would have been no reason for Mr Gramascene to refrain from publishing any research he might produce, were it of sufficient calibre. You're barking up the wrong tree, Watson."

Topkins nodded. "You're right, of course, Mr Holmes. The collaborator is someone who simply wouldn't be taken as seriously without this subterfuge. Someone who would be patted on the head, complimented and told in no uncertain terms not to interfere in the proper business of scholars."

I grasped his meaning now. "You mean a woman," I said. "Mrs Creavesey, I presume?"

Topkins nodded, at last. "The Creaveseys have been kind enough to take me into their confidence," he said. "They both consider me a friend, and I am glad to reciprocate the sentiment."

"Edith Creavesey," I said. "Well, that is a surprise. Although she is certainly an intelligent and well-informed young woman, I had assumed she had no ambitions beyond being the professor's helpmeet."

Topkins nodded. "She's that, of course. Her affection for Professor Creavesey isn't feigned. But she's considerably his intellectual superior, and he admits as much. She had little luck persuading journals to accept her work as a student, and now she is a wife it would be assumed that any success she enjoyed was down to nepotism. I believe that they intend the truth to be revealed when the professor retires, in the hope that the substantial body of work that he acknowledges as hers will win her the acclaim she deserves."

"It is perhaps not the most firmly founded of hopes, if I know academics," Holmes observed regretfully. "Tell me, what view does Mrs Creavesey take of the professor's researches into the Hagworm?"

Topkins coloured slightly. "She is supportive, of course. As I have said, she is devoted to the professor, and both of them are fond of Woodwose, who originated the whole enterprise. But I believe that she does not share their optimism, or mine, regarding its success."

"She disbelieves in the creature?"

"She… has reservations, certainly," Topkins admitted reluctantly. I recalled the conversation I had partly overheard between him and the lady in question in the hotel's sitting-room. That Mrs Creavesey had said *You will not help me to dissuade him, even now,* lent weight to Topkins' account. At the time I had, I admit, wondered whether it might be a liaison between the two of them that they feared "the professor" finding out, but in retrospect they must have been discussing Summerlee's suspicions, not Creavesey's.

"James!" a woman's voice came from the door of the hotel, and I turned, expecting to see Edith Creavesey herself. Instead it was Topkins' sister Mary. Though still in the throes of grief, she looked a little more composed than she had been when we had seen her visiting her fiancé's body.

"I'm coming, Mary. I've finished speaking to Mr Holmes and Dr Watson," Topkins said at once. To us he added, "I presume that is the case, gentlemen?"

Holmes inclined his head. "Of course. You have been very helpful, Mr Topkins. If I need to know more from you, I shall know where to find you. I wonder, though, whether I might be permitted to ask Miss Topkins just one question?"

Topkins looked doubtful and disapproving. "Mr Holmes, my sister is in no state—"

"Oh, James," Mary sighed, "you really don't need to be so protective of me. I'm bereaved, not breakable. I can't say I welcome your presence here, Mr Holmes," she admitted candidly, "but I am perfectly prepared to be civil. I understand that you are looking into the circumstances of Henry's death, and I believe that we would all benefit from knowing that truth. What was it that you wished to ask me?"

"Simply this," said Holmes. "What was Mr Gramascene's connection to Wermewater? Your brother tells us that he had little interest in this expedition until he learned its destination. Did he give you any indication of its significance for him?"

"Oh, that." Mary Topkins gave a sad smile. "That was rather a foolish fancy on his part, I'm afraid. You know that Henry was an orphan – he was brought up by his maternal grandmother, Mrs Spencer, who died some years ago. Apparently she told him that their family originated in these parts, and he hoped that he might find out more by coming here."

"How interesting," said Holmes. "Was this her own side of the family, or another?"

"Her own, I believe," said Mary. "I'm afraid Henry never told me her maiden name, but I am sure you could find it out. He said, though, that she told him of a family legend that her ancestors were descended from a gentry family who owned some of the land around Wermewater. There was some romantic story that they moved away in order to escape some kind of curse."

# CHAPTER TWELVE

"Could it be true?" I had asked Holmes once we were alone. "Could Henry Gramascene have been the rightful Lord Wermeston?"

"If he was a Wermeston at all, then his descent was through the female line," Holmes had cautioned me. "Any claim he might have had would not have superseded that of Lady Ophelia. She, though a woman, inherited by virtue of her male ancestors. But, if there is any truth in this family legend, then he might have stood to inherit the estate, if not the title, on her death. I shall telegraph Mrs Hudson and have her make enquiries at Somerset House."

I imagined that our landlady might have more pressing calls upon her time, even in our absence. But I knew also that she was devoted to her celebrated lodger, and would carry out this favour with only a token complaint. She was probably the most able of our regular associates to carry out such research in Holmes's absence: our friends at Scotland Yard would be too busy with their regular work, Langdale Pike too indolent, and Holmes's brother Mycroft too inflexible in his routine. Shinwell Johnson specialised in entirely different kinds of information, and this was not the sort of task at which the Irregulars excelled.

For a moment I regretted leaving London, where so many excellent friends were available to assist and advise us, for such a backwater as Wermeholt, where we were surrounded by strangers more familiar with the lie of the land than we, and had to rely upon the likes of Constable Batterby and Sir Howard Woodwose, neither of whom seemed unambiguously willing to help us. But then I remembered my relief when I had seen Holmes the previous day. In his presence I could hardly feel isolated.

We also had Professor Summerlee, of course, whom I trusted despite his disinterested manner. When we had approached him with the plan that Holmes and I had concocted, in pursuit of which I was now loitering, unobtrusively I hoped, behind the Serpent's Arms, he had been game enough. If all was proceeding according to plan, the two of them would even now be sauntering into the bar, in search of a companionable drink together.

As I stood at the inn's rear, listening to the murmured voices drifting through the open kitchen doorway from the bar, I wondered who, if Henry Gramascene was indeed the heir to the Wermeston family estate and fortune, might have benefited from killing him. Not Lady Ophelia, surely, unless her isolation had made her so insane she could not bear the thought of a successor. Even then, she would not have acted personally, more probably sending the insolent manservant Modon.

Most likely, however, it would be whoever stood to inherit under her will, gaining her holdings if she died without familial heirs. Woodwose had suggested that that person might again be Modon. I wondered whether his jest had been nearer to the truth than I had imagined; if it was perhaps, indeed, no joke but an informed guess.

Either of these motives would of course apply only to a killer aware of the victim's relationship with the Wermeston family. While that had not been common knowledge, it was possible that Gramascene might have approached Lady Ophelia with the news of their distant connection.

However, he had been killed in such a way as to suggest that he had succumbed to the vengeance of the Hagworm, the very curse his ancestors had sought to escape. That practically invited those familiar with the legend to make the same connection, which could then lead them to the murderer's motive. That was unwise, unless the killer was, indeed, a savage, unthinking beast.

By now I could hear voices raised from inside the inn: Holmes at his most sarcastic, interspersed with the dry indignation of Summerlee.

"You speak of the science of deduction, yet you, sir, are no scientist," the latter was forcefully insisting. "Your lines of reasoning are the purest guesswork, entirely lacking in rigour."

"And yet I am so often proven correct," Holmes replied, with silky menace in his voice. "What says it for the value of your scientific method if it has little more to offer than my sheer guesswork?"

"On the occasions when they are correct, your conclusions simply state the obvious," Summerlee scoffed. "You are a charlatan, sir, with no claim to intellectual integrity, and any scientist of worth would say the same."

"Perhaps it is fortunate, then, that there are none of them here," Holmes purred.

"You scoundrel!" cried Summerlee, evidently beginning to enjoy himself. "I shall see you ruined for this!"

Judging that by now the attention of every person in the pub, especially its suspicious proprietor, would be turned towards the altercation between its illustrious customers, I slipped through the door and into the kitchen. It was not yet supper time, and the room was empty apart from the grey dog, which looked up hopefully as I entered and wagged its tail with recognition. I had prepared myself with a visit to the butcher's shop owned by Constable Batterby's father, and I passed the creature a pork sausage. The hound gave a sly glance along the passage to the bar where its master waited on his customers, then started to wolf down this surreptitious treat.

Avoiding the passage, I hastened to the inner door that led to the inn's back stairs. I quickly ascended the wooden flight, having already decided which upstairs room must hold the window at which we had seen Effie Scorpe that Sunday afternoon. It had been agreed between the three of us that, since I had already spoken with the young woman and established some degree of rapport, I should be the one to make our overture to her, while Holmes and Summerlee created the distraction I could hear continuing downstairs.

Ignoring the row, I tapped gently on the door I knew must belong to the young woman. "Miss Scorpe?" I said. "Effie? It's Dr Watson."

"Dr Watson?" came the young woman's voice at once. "I hoped it was thou – you, I mean. I saw you and t'other gentlemen in t'street."

"I'm hoping to ask you a few questions, Effie, if I may," I said. "It's about Mr Gramascene's death – and Mr Felspar's too," I added, remembering her fondness for the priest.

"Aye, poor vicar," Effie said immediately. "Why'd he do it, sir? Why'd he do a thing like that?"

"I'm sorry to say he was driven to it," I told her. "My friends and I are trying to find out by whom. May I come in?" I asked. It was improper enough for me to be up here in the first place, I thought, but entering the young woman's bedroom might make a scandal rather less likely than more, by somewhat increasing the slim chance of my leaving without being seen.

"He's locked t'door," Effie replied from behind it. "My da. He won't have me seeing anyone. He found out about Mr Henry visiting me, you see, sir. That Martha Trice told him after t'poor gentleman turned up deid. He hasn't let me out since, though heavens ken it's hard work for one man running t'pub alone, even with Auntie coming in to cook. He won't have me talking to outsiders, though, sir. He'd be in a rage if he found you here."

"I hope that we may avoid that," I told her fervently. "So Mr Gramascene did call upon you the night before his death?"

"Aye, sir, he did," she said. "He was looking to find out all I could tell him about the holm."

"Glissenholm?" I asked.

"Aye. Very interested he was, but he didn't want to talk to me in t'bar, where all might hear. I told him to find me later and we'd talk."

"And what did you talk about?" I asked.

"I told him that's where Lady Ophelia's family's buried, out by t'Hagworm's Stone."

"The Hagworm's Stone?" I asked. This was the first time I had heard such a feature mentioned.

"Aye, sir. It's a very old stone out on Glissenholm," she said in a matter-of-fact tone. "Mr Henry was more interested in the graves, though."

"And that is why he was calling on you so late at night?" I dare say I sounded sceptical, but I had not gained the impression that Gramascene's interest in Effie had to do with matters of local topography. I remembered, though, that he had been the keenest of the party to land upon the island during their proposed circumnavigation, and that Mrs Creavesey had dissuaded him.

"Well, it wasn't what my da thinks, sir, that's a fact," she replied indignantly. Though I could not see her face, I found the assurance in her voice alone convincing. "I'd got talking to Mr Henry one day when he was in t'pub, and he told me he was wanting to find out more about our local doings. He said his uncle – no, it was his grand-uncle – had come here a while ago, and died here."

after what I told thou about manhandling thy customers."

"That blackguard there's been sniffing around my Effie," Scorpe declared, gesturing wildly at me, "just like that last one."

"Aye?" asked Batterby sceptically.

"Aye, and these others made a set-to in t'bar so as I'd miss him going up to see her. They's in it together," he spat.

Constable Batterby looked at me. "Is this true, Dr Watson?" he asked me gravely.

A little dizzy still, I gathered my thoughts. "It's true I wanted to speak to Miss Scorpe," I said, "though I certainly wasn't 'sniffing'. I was seeking information of importance to our investigation."

"That's *my* investigation," Batterby observed angrily. "And thou didn't tell me naught about this. Thou says he went upstairs wi'out thy kenning, Ben?" he asked. "That's trespass, Dr Watson, as thou well kens."

"Nonsense," I said. "I was a guest of Miss Scorpe. It's her residence as well."

"Maybe, but it's her da's property, and t'man's wi'in his rights to throw you out," said Batterby severely. I had no ready answer to the point.

"Constable, if I may—" began Holmes, ready to smooth the ruffled waters, but Batterby rounded angrily upon him.

"No, Mr Holmes, thou may not!" he declared. "Thou's caused nothing but trouble since thou come to this town – upsetting t'bereaved, picking fights, mithering on about all kinds on nonsense from t'past. Casting dirt at t'likes on Archie Peston and Sir Howard Woodwose."

Holmes frowned. "I do not accept—" he began.

"Well, that ends now!" Batterby insisted. "Them in Keswick can do as they likes, I'll not have thou coming in wi' thy London airs, upsetting good folk and interfering wi' my work. Thou'll keep clear on all this from now on, Mr Holmes, if thou kens what's good for thou, and thou must count thyself lucky I don't arrest thou for trespass and conspiracy. And don't thou smirk either, Ben Scorpe," he added, rather lamely, "I've got my eye on thou."

"I wonder whether he ever really did contact the police in Keswick?" I wondered aloud, as Constable Batterby beat a self-important, if somewhat speedy, retreat.

Doing our collective best to ignore the amused looks of the townsfolk who had, as usual, gathered to spectate, the three of us repaired to Holmes's lodgings, which were closer by than the Mereside. There I told the professor and Holmes everything I had learned from Effie, though that was little enough.

"There was nothing of a romantic nature between Effie and Gramascene," I informed them. "So she maintains, and I believe her. He thought she could tell him more about his family history – and that of Dr Harpier, who was his great-uncle, apparently. He thought he might be able to find answers at the burial plot on Glissenholm. Ben Scorpe, as we surmised, considers their association scandalous and has had Effie locked up since he learned of it."

"That is not a great deal to show for our trouble," observed Summerlee, his high spirits apparently subsiding by now.

"One point, at least, bears considerable interest," Holmes noted. "We knew from the letter found on Gramascene's body that he knew Dr Harpier, but we were not aware that the connection was a family one. It accounts for the former's sudden interest in Professor Creavesey's expedition when he learned that Wermeholt was to be its destination. If Harpier was indeed of the branch of the family that believed itself descended from the Wermestons, then it also explains why he chose to retire here and make his researches into local history."

Summerlee said, "It is a questionable circumstance that two members of the family have died separately under unusual circumstances in Wermeholt."

"Most questionable," Holmes agreed. "And whatever killed Gramascene, the horse that trampled Harpier was no Hagworm." We all kept silent for a moment, considering this.

Then I said, "If Gramascene was merely using Effie as a source of local information, then perhaps it also explains why he said that Topkins would thank him for seeing her once he married Mary Topkins. That sounded like impudence of the lowest sort, but perhaps Gramascene simply hoped to prove the family connection to the Wermestons. If he managed to establish himself as Lady Ophelia's heir, then his wife and her family would undoubtedly benefit."

"Indeed," Holmes agreed. "He does not appear to have disclosed such hopes to Miss Topkins, but perhaps he feared disappointing her if he were proven wrong."

"Is there any way we can rescue the poor girl?" I asked, meaning Effie rather than Mary Topkins. "It seems most unjust for her father to keep her imprisoned so, for no fault of her own. I know that this is the country, and they do things differently here, but can the law not be persuaded to intervene?"

"Since the law in these parts is personified by the agreeable Constable Batterby, there can be no immediate prospect of that," said Holmes. "I agree with you that something should be done, Watson, but the girl seems to be in no urgent danger. She did not sound distressed to you, nor mention being hurt?"

"Well, no," I acknowledged. "I had the impression that she was mostly resentful at being locked up, as anyone would be."

"And this Hagworm's Stone?" asked Holmes. "What exactly did she say in that connection?"

I cast my mind back. "Only that Gramascene thought it related somehow to his uncle's death, and that she agreed with him. She did not say how, nor anything about it except that it is on Glissenholm and is an old stone."

"Some peasant superstition, no doubt," Summerlee decided. "Perhaps this stone is cursed, like the Wermeston family."

"Could Gramascene have visited Glissenholm that night?" I asked. "He had already established that the rest of Creavesey's party would not countenance landing there."

"It sounds as likely as anything else at this stage," Holmes agreed. "Well, gentlemen, I suggest we clean ourselves up and prepare for supper."

"Indeed," said Summerlee, preparing to leave. "Woodwose is joining us again for dinner at the Mereside Hotel tonight, I believe. Will you be dining with us?"

"Thank you, Professor, but I believe not," said Holmes at once. "Watson – one word more, before you leave. When in London I was unable to locate my binder of the *Illustrated London News* for the years 1882 to '84. I suppose you have no idea where it might be?"

Summerlee snorted. "I'll see you later, Watson." Shaking his goatee impatiently at my friend's triviality, he stepped out into the summer evening.

After he left, Holmes said, "Apologies for getting rid of the professor, Watson. He seems a sound enough fellow, for all his oddity, but for what follows I need a man whom I can trust completely."

By now I was longing for supper and an early night, but tired though I was from our most eventful day, I felt a thrill of promise at Holmes's words. I might have climbed a tower, trekked halfway around a lake, endured a museum, avoided snakes, attended at a second bizarre murder, had an illicit rendezvous with a publican's daughter, fallen foul of the law and uncovered well-guarded secrets about the Harpier and Creavesey families, but it was clear that Holmes had more adventures in mind for me yet.

"Constable Batterby accused us, with a modicum of justice, of 'casting dirt' upon Mr Peston," said Holmes. "But we have said nothing to my knowledge against Sir Howard Woodwose. I wonder whether he was anticipating an aspersion that we have not yet made. Sir Howard's only connection with our inquiries as far as we know relates to his occupancy of Harpier's cottage, and this makes me curious what evidence might be hidden there. In particular, I wonder about the fate of Dr Harpier's missing papers."

After our long acquaintance, there were occasions when I could follow the train of Holmes's thought as easily as he mine. I said, "You believe that Woodwose may have them still?"

"There is a reasonable possibility of it," Holmes told me with a smile. "And since it seems that Constable Batterby has made up his mind that I am a villain, I have little to lose by burgling the cottage while he is at supper and finding out. Will you assist me, Watson?"

# CHAPTER THIRTEEN

Though large for Wermeholt, Woodwose's cottage had not the space for his housekeeper, Mrs Jenkins, to reside on the premises, and in such a small town little inconvenience was occasioned by her living a short walk away and attending him during the day. We waited until we were sure that she had finished her day's tasks and left for the night, before addressing ourselves to our nocturnal mission.

We ensured that the street was deserted, with little likelihood of observation from the immediate neighbours, before creeping into the back garden of the cottage and trying the rear door. That it was locked was somewhat unusual in this rural setting, but perhaps not enough so to be suspicious, given the value of Woodwose's eccentric collection of artefacts. Holmes's lockpicks made short work of it in any case, and we were soon inside. Holmes had borrowed a pair of dark lanterns from the hotel, and we unshuttered them once the door was firmly closed behind us, taking care to keep the beam clear of the windows.

The serpent idols and carvings cast weird and sinuous shadows across the walls and ceilings of Woodwose's study as we carefully perused its contents, taking what pains we could to leave all as we found it. Although, as Holmes said, our discovery here would only confirm Constable Batterby's suspicions, being arrested would constitute a significant impediment to the investigation, and my friend had decreed that we should try our utmost to leave no evidence that might betray our presence.

One of the first things Holmes did was to inspect the decanters on the sideboard, identifying their contents with a sniff. "Port, brandy, sherry, gin, whisky... no laudanum here. However, there is a circular stain that would suggest there is normally another vessel in this row. Perhaps Woodwose realised, after Mr Felspar's unfortunate experience, that it was inadvisable to keep it about the place."

He started to look through the papers on Woodwose's desk, while I inspected our unwitting host's compendious bookshelves, running my eyes along such titles as *Traditions and Customs of the Bedouin Peoples* and *Shamanism in the Americas*. There was no time to flip through every such volume, and little hope of leaving the bookshelves looking unmolested if I had, but I did find a cluster of notebooks of different sizes, filled with dense and obscure notes in a cramped hand. A swift comparison with some of the paperwork confirmed that the writing was Woodwose's own, however, and the material related to his obsession with reptilia in world mythology.

Holmes was now checking the desk drawers, some of which were also locked, for hidden compartments and the like, while I moved on to another bookshelf. This one dealt more eclectically with matters outside Woodwose's own field and included some volumes of reminiscences by Lady Ophelia's father, Marcus Wermeston, relating to his travels in the Far East.

To my surprise, it was followed by two books that listed Ophelia Wermeston as their author. One was titled *Habitats and*

*Behaviour of Tropical Snakes and Lizards*; the other, *A Reptilian Taxonomy of the Malay Archipelago*.

"I say, Holmes," I began to whisper, but he interrupted me at once, giving a cry and brandishing a sheet of paper.

"This was tucked into the back of an accounts ledger in a bottom drawer," he exclaimed.

"Is it Harpier's?" I asked, still clutching Lady Ophelia's books in my two hands.

"No," Holmes replied. "It is mine."

He showed me the paper. It was a telegram from Dr Mossbaum the herpetologist, in prompt answer to the one that Holmes had sent the previous day. He regretted that he was committed all week at a conference in London, but recommended that we seek the advice of a local expert, the renowned herpetologist Ophelia Wermeston, who as luck would have it resided on our very doorstep. "Mrs Trice's duty to her customers leaves something to be desired, it seems."

I showed him the books, and he chuckled. "Poor Watson. So seldom the first with the news. It seems that old money and an old name will make a scholar of a woman after all. It is unfortunate for Mrs Creavesey that she has neither."

"But if Lady Ophelia is a student of reptiles…" I said.

"Then we must certainly consult her, as Mossbaum suggests," Holmes agreed. "It is not so remarkable, perhaps, given her father's views on the place of women, and his own particular interests. But it would be surprising indeed if, given this expertise, she had no views on the nature of her family legend – or, once we inform her of it, on the manner of Henry Gramascene's death. Recluse or no, we must obtain an audience with her as a matter of urgency."

"But why would Mrs Trice withhold Mossbaum's advice from you?" I asked. "For that matter, why would she pass the telegram to Woodwose instead?"

"That is certainly a critical question," Holmes agreed, "but perhaps one for when we are more at leisure than we are at present. Ha, what is this?"

At the bottom of the same drawer where the ledger had been, beneath a folded scarf, he had found a small iron shape. "The key to a strongbox, or I am much mistaken," Holmes declared. We had seen no sign of such a box in the study, nor in our brief inspection of the other rooms of the house. "If he keeps the key here, the chances are that it is in this room; that is, if it is in this house at all. He might hold it somewhere else altogether."

We resumed our search in earnest, looking under furniture and behind the books on the shelves, inside the fireplace and in the sideboard where Woodwose kept his tumblers. There was no chance now that our interference would go unnoticed, but Woodwose might return at any time.

The ceiling was crossed with wooden beams, and I stood precariously upon a chair to feel along the tops of them in case there was a strongbox hidden there. The room was heavily shadowed, and the shapes of the snake idols seemed to jump and writhe whenever the light of the lanterns flickered.

Meanwhile, Holmes had lifted the leather wall-hanging that portrayed the fearsome Aztec deity Quetzalcoatl. "Aha!" he declared, almost causing me to lose my balance.

I climbed down from my perch and joined him as he reached into a hollow in the thick stone wall. He brought out a sturdy metal box, which he set upon the desk. The key fitted it perfectly, and within was a clothbound notebook, on whose inner page the name *Edmund Harpier* appeared, in the same ugly scrawl as that we had seen on the letter in Gramascene's pocket.

"Harpier's handwriting was awful, though," I recalled in dismay. "That will make things difficult."

"It looks as if Woodwose has done some of our work for us,"

Holmes observed, flicking through the book. Though undeniably messy, Harpier's notes were interspersed with further comments, in a different-coloured ink and in a much more legible hand that I now recognised as Woodwose's. I saw the occasional date and mention of a local place name, and some surnames that I also recognised.

Holmes closed it with a snap. "Even so, I fear we have not the leisure to decipher this here. We must take the book with us, and hope that Woodwose does not remark its absence until we have made sense of it."

We did as he advised, and shortly afterwards we crept away again, as unseen as we had arrived. "Whatever we have here," Holmes noted as we parted company, to return to our separate lodgings, "it must be of importance, to Woodwose at least. If Dr Harpier's notes were worth a bequest to his college, there must have been a good deal of material. Yet Woodwose has selected this notebook specifically to keep to hand, and has spent considerable time and effort in deciphering it. Whatever has befallen the rest of the Harpier papers, this is what Woodwose considered worth preserving. If anything holds the secret of what led to the deaths of Edmund Harpier, Henry Gramascene and Gervaise Felspar, it will be this book."

I returned at last, exhausted from the rigours of the day, to the Mereside Hotel and my welcoming bed, where, for the first time since my arrival in Wermeholt, I slept like the dead for many uninterrupted hours.

When I awoke, I saw Sherlock Holmes sitting in the chair next to my bed, the stolen notebook on his knee, jotting notes of his own in the smaller notebook that he always carried.

"Ah, Watson!" he cried, full of his usual early morning cheer. He wore the previous day's clothes, which were somewhat rumpled, but seemed in all other respects to be as fresh as new-cut grass. "I had not the heart to wake you, my dear fellow, though you have slept late indeed. Why, it is nearly eight o'clock! But we shall need all our resources for the day we have ahead."

"How did you…" I began to ask, but then I saw the open window. The night had been chilly, and I had made quite sure that I had closed it before sleeping. "Never mind."

"The contents of this book are quite sensational, Watson," he declared cheerfully, and with little consideration for my own morning-tide befuddlement. "Dr Harpier was an excellent investigator. Had he turned his attentions to the present rather than the past, he might have made an adequate detective, at least by the modest standards of Scotland Yard."

"I'm delighted to hear it," I replied rather tartly. "Perhaps we might discuss this over breakfast, Holmes?"

"I hardly think that would afford us the necessary privacy. I shall tell you what you need to know while you ablute," he replied, and to my annoyance proceeded to do so.

He said, "As we surmised, Gramascene's maternal grandmother, Mrs Spencer, was Edmund Harpier's sister. Their own maternal grandfather was one Roger Royston, whom Harpier identified with Roger Wermeston. The latter was the younger brother of George, Lord Wermeston, who inherited the title in 1787. George was Marcus Wermeston's grandfather, meaning that Henry Gramascene was, if Dr Harpier's identification is correct, Lady Ophelia's third cousin once removed.

"Roger Wermeston served the King's cause as a lieutenant during the American Revolutionary Wars, but his loyalties came into question after certain details of British troop deployments fell into Yankee hands, and he returned to England under a cloud. After that he fell out of the historical record, but it was around that time that Roger Royston first appeared. Dr Harpier believed that the younger Wermeston brother did not re-establish contact with his family at Wermewater, preferring to change his name and lose himself among the population of London. He was buried in the churchyard at St-Martin-in-the-Fields."

"And not," I realised, "on Glissenholm."

"Indeed," Holmes agreed. "If Gramascene had been able to establish that Roger Wermeston was not buried there with the others of the family, that would strengthen his claim, though not prove it. As far as Harpier could establish, he and his great-nephew were the last of Roger Royston's descendants. When Woodwose told you that Lady Ophelia was the last survivor of the Wermeston line, he knew that there was a chance he was wrong. The death of Henry Gramascene placed the fact beyond dispute."

Despite Holmes's promise, none of this material had proven sensational thus far. I said, "I'm ready for breakfast now, Holmes, and my comprehension would much benefit from some coffee, at least. Can the rest of this wait until then?"

Holmes joined me, concealing Harpier's notebook in his satchel. He jiggled with impatience while I ate, and took nothing himself but some tea with lemon. Summerlee was nowhere to be seen, but James and Mary Topkins were just finishing their meal as we arrived. Disconcertingly, given Holmes's revelations, they were discussing where Henry should be buried. Mary found it intolerable that her fiancé should be laid to rest in the very cemetery where he had so horribly died, and they were discussing whether he should be interred locally at St George's in Ravensfoot or transported back to London, with the expense that would entail.

After I had consumed a barely adequate quantity of coffee and kedgeree, my friend all but dragged me out of the door to the hotel's garden, where we could walk free of curious ears. My irritation quickly gave way to astonishment as he informed me of what else he had discovered.

"Do you remember," he asked me impatiently, "the plaque we saw in the church, giving the dates of each of its incumbent vicars as far back as 1320? Harpier compiled that list, as Felspar told us. It was that, I think, that first interested him in a peculiar anomaly of Wermeholt's history.

"Because of its recent defacement, we found the last digit of each date illegible on the plaque. In hindsight, I suspect that the vandalism was carried out with that specific end in mind. If it had been left intact, then it would have been perfectly clear that there had been a change of priest exactly every century, for some five hundred years. Thomas Wermeston, as we know, died in 1599, his death supposedly foretold by the Hagworm. He was succeeded by Stephen Enderby. According to Harpier, in 1699 a new priest, Andrew Thwaite, arrived in January and died as soon as June, leaving the benefice to Simon Homerton. In 1799 our friend Laertes Wilfredson was buried in the churchyard, to be succeeded by Arthur Thorne.

"It is not altogether clear at this remove that John Hoop, who was succeeded in 1499 by Hugo Beard, died rather than retiring or moving elsewhere, but Harpier could find no later record of him. Robert White's decease is dated as circa 1400, but in view of what came later I think we can be fairly confident that the year of his death was 1399."

I interrupted this breathless monologue to say, "I'm not convinced by this, Holmes. You only have a record of three deaths in those years – Wermeston, Wilfredson and..."

"Thwaite," said Holmes. "He was a young and hearty man, who died a mere five months after taking up the benefice."

"Even so," I said. "You can't be sure about the earlier ones. Three could be a coincidence, surely?"

"If they merely died during the final year of each century, Watson, then perhaps. Since all three died on the twenty-first of June, Midsummer's Day, coincidence begins to seem unlikely."

"Good Heavens," I said, taken aback. "Yes, that is remarkable.

I say, though," I added, remembering a rather tedious discussion at my club, "the years ending in ninety-nine aren't the last of the century. The century won't end until the end of next year, 1900. There was correspondence about it in *The Times*."

Holmes sighed. "Mathematically, that argument is unassailable. The human mind is not so rational, alas. Harpier alludes to the widespread fears in 999 AD that the year 1000 would bring the apocalypse, and the transition from ninety-nines to hundreds catches the popular imagination in ways that the addition of a further digit cannot. I think it is clear, in any case, that we are not considering a phenomenon grounded in rationality."

"So what did Harpier consider was happening?" I asked. "What could lead to such precisely timed deaths so far apart?"

"The late doctor's researches, which began as a mere side-line to his investigation of his family history, reached a quite sensational conclusion. I imagine that his premature demise was what prevented him from sharing it with the world.

"He believed that there has been in Wermeholt, since medieval times at the very least, a cult based upon worship of the Hagworm, and that it was in existence as recently as a century ago. It seems that every century, on Midsummer's Day of the year ending in ninety-nine, a Christian priest is sacrificed to the beast."

"Sacrificed?" I repeated, incredulous. "But that's fantastical, Holmes. A town quietly killing its priest every hundred years, then carrying on as if nothing had happened? How could such a thing come about, and how could it go unnoticed?"

"A hundred years is a long time, Watson. The manner of these priests' deaths is not recorded, but even if they were thought suspicious, who would think to look for precedents from a century before? Who but a historian like Harpier, and he inconveniently died before the truth could out. One sees why a folklore specialist of Sir Howard Woodwose's standing would be interested in such a discovery, though he must have had at least an inkling of it to have gone to the trouble of sequestering Harpier's papers.

"As for how it came about… as far as I can gather from Woodwose's annotations, the practice is not unprecedented. He considers that many ancient religions involved a tradition of human sacrifice of some priest or king, who was seen as embodying a god. The victim's death was thought to reinvigorate the land and ensure the fertility of the crops. Indeed, by ancient standards one sacrifice per hundred years would be exceptionally restrained. I assume that the idea is to reassert the Hagworm's worship for the coming century.

"Harpier believed that the priests were killed in ceremonies that took place at the Hagworm's Stone on Glissenholm, and though he had not seen the site in question he gathered from descriptions that it was of quite ancient ritual significance. This suggested to him that the cult, and perhaps the Hagworm legend itself, may have evolved from some earlier tradition."

I said, "But if the plaque in the church was defaced to conceal this pattern, that means the cult still exists!"

"Quite so. Presumably Gramascene, like Harpier, discovered the truth nevertheless, and had to be silenced."

"I suppose that's why he was making for the church," I mused. "He knew that Felspar was to be the cult's next victim, and therefore that he was one of the few people in Wermeholt whom he could trust."

Holmes nodded. "It seems probable. The ancient god-kings of whom I spoke would have known their fate in advance, of course, but that hardly seems likely in this instance. The people of Wermeholt have no control over the priest assigned to them by the church, and could have little hope of converting any man of God to a pagan faith that demanded his own death. That would seem especially true of Felspar, given his particular fear of reptiles."

I said, "When Felspar was delirious, he spoke of his parishioners as serpents, and said both Harpier and Woodwose knew about it. I think he must have suspected something, even if he didn't understand exactly what fate was in store for him. Perhaps Gramascene had already confided some of his suspicions."

"Perhaps, Watson. But there is one important consideration. The deaths of Harpier and Gramascene are certainly more explicable, though the manner of Gramascene's is still mysterious, and we have as yet no clue as to the culprits' identities. But Felspar's death was *not* a sacrifice to the Hagworm."

"Not a sacrifice? But you said—"

Holmes shook his head impatiently. "I said that the past sacrifices had taken place on Glissenholm, and on Midsummer's Day. Today is June the twentieth, Watson. Midsummer's Day is tomorrow, and Mr Felspar died yesterday, in the churchyard. Someone killed him prematurely, for whatever reason. We know that the cult demands a sacrifice, but it cannot be Gervaise Felspar. Another killing is surely planned, Watson, and somehow we must prevent it."

# CHAPTER FOURTEEN

It seemed that James and Mary Topkins had resolved, for the time being at least, to accompany Henry Gramascene's body to Thorpe and Son's main branch in Ravensfoot, and would be staying there until the matter of his final resting-place was settled. Meanwhile, Professor Creavesey had received a telegram from his college, and despite the imminent arrival of his new boat, had reluctantly agreed to halt his pursuit of the Hagworm in order to attend an emergency faculty meeting in Camford. He and Mrs Creavesey, too, would be leaving that morning for Ravensfoot station.

"I'm glad the professor will be spending a while away from Wermewater," Edith Creavesey confided to me. "I've been worried that he would insist on hunting this blessed creature to his last breath, like Captain Ahab." I could see, though, that the redoubtable professor had every intention of returning to pursue his obsession, and I imagined that Topkins too would be back before very long, to serve as his redoubtable Starbuck.

Summerlee thus found himself at a loose end for the moment, and spoke of taking a few days' walking tour, but Holmes prevailed upon him to stay.

"We are, it seems, to consult a renowned scientist," he explained. "We shall need all the academic credibility that we may muster. If you please, Professor, you must reconcile yourself to what will be a rather unconventional visit."

There was little enough reason to hope that a request to Lady Ophelia for an interview would be fruitful. It was sheer luck that had enabled me, during my previous attempt, to speak even to the uncooperative Modon. Aside from the workers actually living on the Wermeston Hall estate, the local people held the place in superstitious awe, and we would gain no help from them. The wooden gates on both approaches stood locked and barred against strangers, and opened only for those authorised by Lady Ophelia herself.

Holmes had learned that boats with supplies were often seen approaching the estate from the far side of the lake, but his discreet enquiries in Ravensfoot the previous morning had garnered little information about who sent them or what they carried there. He had considered, but dismissed, the idea of taking a vessel across disguised as a boatman, with Summerlee and myself hidden among the cargo. His actual plan was simple enough, yet as he had hinted, was more what one might expect from a military campaign or exploratory expedition than a polite visit to the local gentry.

First, the three of us would bundle up a spare set of clothes each, along with certain other essential equipment, in a backpack. Next, I would walk out to the estate and climb to my earlier vantage point, where I could see across the drystone wall into the woods beyond, and should throw the pack over and into the trees before returning. The three of us would then put on our bathing-suits and make a show of setting off for a swim from the jetty of the Mereside Hotel.

We would swim out some way into the mere and then turn eastwards, striking parallel to the path that led to the estate, until we came level with the limestone wall. Though it stretched out some distance into the lake, it should be no trouble to swim around it and then return to shore a little way beyond. Once we had reclaimed the backpack, we would dry and dress ourselves and make our way through the woods towards Wermeston Hall.

There we would attempt to find and speak with Lady Ophelia before we were ejected by her staff. Privately, I hoped that we might also get a better look at the inlet where I had seen that scaly shape rise ominously and sink beneath the waters.

As I have said, there was little enough of Wermeholt beyond the Mereside Hotel, but as I walked through such streets as there were, both on my way to the estate and on my return, I found the stares of the townsfolk more unnerving by far, given what I had learned. I saw neither Mrs Gough nor Mrs Jenkins, but more than once I caught a passer-by making that surreptitious hand gesture of a striking snake in response to my presence.

I had, I admit, a greater terror of sharing the lake with whatever creature I had seen, whether or not it had also been responsible for the attack on Henry Gramascene. I told myself that we would be safe as long as we kept to the relatively shallow waters by the mereside, but then I reflected that the sheep and dog that had been found savaged had never even entered the lake.

Still, by that token I supposed that I was no safer on the shore than in the water. Holmes was coolly undisturbed by the prospect of taking a dip with the Hagworm, and Summerlee's stringent scientific objectivity left no room for concerns about his personal safety, so I made up my mind to display equal courage.

Accordingly, we swam out into the unpleasantly brackish water, far enough that our change of direction would be unlikely to catch the attention of any casual observer, and then set our course east towards the Wermeston Hall estate.

Our preparations had taken up the morning and it was by now early afternoon, with the sun blazing down from above.

Holmes swam with smooth, even strokes like an otter, while Summerlee made apparently haphazard thrashing movements that nevertheless propelled him with speed and efficiency towards our goal. I, an adequate swimmer only, fell a little way behind as we approached, but the others waited for me in the shadow of the limestone wall, lying with only their faces protruding above the shallow water.

We swam out and around the end of the construction, giving it a wide berth in case its foundations included any surprises for would-be intruders, then turned back towards the shore. This side of the wall, the path continued along the waterline a little way before turning towards Wermeston Hall, and we were terribly exposed for the few moments it took to surface from the waters of the mere and run for the treeline. No cries arose, though, nor any sign that we had been observed.

The most difficult part of the operation arose from finding and locating the backpack, which despite my best efforts had snagged in the branches of a tree. It took some little effort, and Holmes's arboreal skills, to recover it. A short while later, however, we were dressed, and our wet bathing things had been stowed in the pack and concealed with leaves to reduce the danger of discovery.

The atmosphere on this side of the wall, and of the spur of fell that buttressed the estate, was different from that surrounding Wermeholt. Where the air of the town was clammy, and tended to be cool even in high summer, here it was both humid and hot. Summerlee murmured something I could not follow about the valley's geography creating its own miniature climate, and Holmes noted that the abundance of trees, compared with the largely bare land on the Wermeholt side, would have its own effect.

Wermeston Hall itself lay some way off to our right, nestled between the folds of Netherfell. We had been walking only a few minutes when we saw the first snake.

It was perhaps four feet long and splotched in yellow and black. It slithered across our path with startling speed as we walked. I cried out in surprise, and so did Summerlee. Holmes kept his silence, but he, too, looked distinctly taken aback.

"I believe that that was a juvenile anaconda," Summerlee murmured, wary of creating any more noise. "They can grow a great deal larger than that."

"An anaconda?" I repeated incredulously. "In northern England?"

Summerlee shrugged. "There is no obstacle to importing such a specimen. It would find the climate here rather chilly, I think, but not otherwise inhospitable. There are rodents and frogs aplenty for it to eat."

We had not gone twenty paces before I noticed a bright green lizard on a tree trunk, with strange splayed feet. It blinked indifferently at us, flicked its tongue, then scampered upwards with blinding speed.

"A gecko," Summerlee concluded. "Not a European species, I think. Not that there are any that are found naturally within the British Isles."

As we proceeded, our eyes began to recognise that there were reptiles all round us. Most were mottled or speckled in colours that blended in with the trees, and made them difficult to discern against the background. Others, like the gigantic tortoise that creaked into view as we approached the wooded waterline, were impossible to miss.

"Good God," I said, "It's one of those Pacific island ones, isn't it? The ones Darwin wrote about." It was at least six feet from head to tail, and four across the shell.

"A Galapagos tortoise, I believe, or a near relative," Summerlee agreed. "You must understand that reptile zoology is not my speciality."

"It is Lady Ophelia's, though," I said, redundantly by this point. "It looks as if her studies are more practical than we realised."

"What is the lifespan of a creature like this, Professor?" Holmes asked.

"Considerable," said Summerlee. "Even an ordinary tortoise can live as long as a human being, and it is thought that such as these may live much longer."

"Indeed," said Holmes. "Then perhaps some of these specimens were brought home by her father. Others, I suppose, she may have bred from those he collected, or imported herself. I admit that I find myself keen to visit that inlet that Watson observed from his wall."

We were not afforded the opportunity on that occasion, however. A minute or two later – during which time I narrowly avoided treading upon a concealed puff adder whose venom Summerlee assured us was more than capable of killing me – we heard a crack of a twig and a cry of "Stop there, all on ye!"

The unsociable Mr Modon had appeared among the trees, clutching a lethal-looking shotgun which he trained directly at me. All of us raised our hands with great alacrity.

"So thou's trespassing now?" Modon asked me contemptuously. "So are ye all. I wonder ye made it so far wi'out one on t'snakes getting ye." He put two fingers in his mouth and emitted a shrill whistle.

"Yes, we appear to have lost our way entirely," said Holmes. "I wonder whether you would be so kind as to show us the way to the Wermeholt gate, so that we can return to our hotel?"

"No fear on that," the man growled, as I am certain Holmes had intended. "I should shoot t'lot on ye right now."

"You have only two barrels, Mr Modon," Holmes observed smoothly. "The third of us could surely make an escape while you reloaded."

"Not for long thou couldn't," Modon snarled. "Her ladyship can decide what we'll do with ye."

Two groundskeepers arrived at that point, with shotguns of their own, and I for one perceived little to gain, and much to lose, by not complying.

With his fellows at our backs and our hands still prudently elevated, Modon led us out of the trees to the path that ran through the estate, and thence to Wermeston Hall itself.

The Hall was old, a Tudor construction that had replaced the medieval castle once occupied by Sir William de Wermeston and his foreign witch-bride. A later, more whimsical owner had harkened back to those times by adding some fanciful turrets and battlements. Since then, ivy had been allowed to creep across the building's frontage and one entire wing had fallen into ruin, though the main house looked sound enough still.

At the front door was a flight of stone steps guarded by pillars bearing carvings of the Hagworm, similar to those we had seen on the gateposts, but larger and more fearsome. As we ascended the lichenous stairs, a large lizard watched us from the balustrade, its grey skin and its utter immobility perfectly matching those of its stone brethren. The creature was at least two feet in length.

"An iguana," Summerlee muttered to me, though the information was of limited practical use.

The three men led us up the steps and into the house, which was even warmer than the forest outside. This was so unusual in an old stone building that I supposed her ladyship, or one of her ancestors, must have installed some kind of hypocaust. An acrid smell enveloped us from the vestibule, reminding me of the reptile house at London Zoo, and here, too, there were creatures aplenty: snakes coiled around the curtain-rails, geckos scuttling up the walls, an indoor fountain teeming with terrapins.

From Summerlee's murmured commentary I gathered that the beasts kept in the house, at least, were neither venomous nor otherwise hazardous to human life, though one huge snake, taking up a great deal of a moth-eaten ottoman, looked as if it could easily crush me to death. I remembered the menagerie once kept by the malignant Dr Grimesby Roylott of Stoke Moran, including such prize specimens as a baboon, a cheetah and the venomous snake that he used to kill his stepdaughter Julia. The late Dr Roylott would, I thought, have been most jealous if he had seen the collection Lady Ophelia had assembled here, though it was clear she had little interest in apes or big cats.

At the rear of the house was a conservatory that had been kept in excellent repair. The trees beyond it had been cleared so that it could enjoy direct sunlight, and it was still warmer than the rest of the house – so hot, indeed, as to be stifling. There were few plants, mostly sparsely leaved trees, and in place of flowerbeds, the floor had been artfully piled with rocks and sand. Snakes and lizards were in abundant supply, and a pool, evidently fed by a beck diverted from Netherfell since the water chattered and babbled, was occupied by three quite small alligators, each about the size of Ben Scorpe's dog.

The other occupant was Lady Ophelia Wermeston.

She was as old as we had been promised, her white hair hanging loose about her shoulders, but the woman standing before us was no frail invalid. She was the tallest person in the room, and quite unbowed by age. Her lined and weathered face had once been very beautiful. She wore a long gown of an old-fashioned cut, in a vivid green, and a large snake draped around her shoulders like a stole.

"Why, Modon," she said chidingly, in a voice that was as sweet as that of a young woman, "put away that gun. Is that any way to treat visitors?"

"Not visitors, your ladyship," Modon reported, his normal surliness given way to deference. "Trespassers." He put up his gun nevertheless.

"Strangers, perhaps," Lady Ophelia conceded. "That does not mean we cannot make them welcome." She placed an arm on a nearby branch, and the snake she wore began slowly to creep onto the tree.

"This one was asking for your ladyship last week," Modon said, pushing me roughly forward. "I sent him packing."

"I'm glad to meet you at last, Lady Ophelia," I told her, with the greatest charm I could muster. "My name is John Watson, and these are Mr Sherlock Holmes and Professor Summerlee." Out of the corner of my eye I saw one of the alligators yawning ostentatiously at me.

Her ladyship showed no sign of recognising any of our names. "I see few people nowadays," she told us contentedly. "Few mammals, indeed."

I was taken aback at being described in this way, but the others took it in their stride. "You certainly keep company with a remarkable variety of reptiles," Holmes observed.

"I find them preferable," she agreed. The snake had almost left her now, only a coil of its tail wrapped fondly around her wrist. "They are very calming. My father taught me to find them fascinating, but he did not love them as I do. He was interested in them, but not inspired."

"Inspired?" Holmes repeated. "That is an unusual word to use."

"But an apt one," Lady Ophelia assured him. "Human beings are terribly hot-blooded. They are ruled by their passions and their needs, always so pressing, so frantic, so focused on the present moment. Some snakes need eat only once or twice a year, did you know that? What thoughts can fill the mind of a creature so free of urgency? What contemplations must be theirs, do you suppose?"

"With a few exceptions, reptiles are unintelligent creatures," Summerlee declared, didactically and, I feared, unwisely. "They are certainly not capable of contemplation."

Lady Ophelia gave a silvery laugh. "Yet if they were, how could we tell? They cannot speak to us, nor we to them. Even if we could teach a snake to mimic English like a parrot or a jackdaw, what could it tell us, when our lives unfold at such different speeds? The ancestors of my specimens ruled this Earth, gentlemen, for many millions of years. They built no castles, no empires, no libraries. Whatever knowledge they had took no material form. Yet how can we believe that those long aeons were mindless ones?"

"Were the dinosaurs intelligent? It is an interesting question," Holmes observed warily, "though unresolvable, I fear, at this remove."

"And yet their children are all around us! All around *me*, at least." Lady Ophelia laughed again, the tinkling laugh of a younger woman. I reflected that she had grown old in isolation, far apart from any peers who might have shown her how it should be done. "Their secrets must be buried within the egg, hidden in the seed their descendants pass from one generation to the next. With a concerted breeding project, one might re-establish an earlier strain."

Again, Summerlee opened his mouth to scoff, but Holmes shifted on his feet, treading as if accidentally upon the professor's toes. He said, "Your work is fascinating to us, Lady Ophelia. It is why we came to see you today. Tell me, do you have a complete catalogue of your collection?"

She smiled, and I was surprised to see how good her teeth were for a woman of her age. "It is not a *collection*, Mr Holmes, it is a colony. A little world, a mass of creatures living their lives, killing and feeding and breeding. Of course I have no catalogue."

"But you must know what kinds of animal are represented," Holmes pressed her. "They could not be here without your express wish, after all. What is your largest species, for instance?"

Lady Ophelia blinked, and I realised with unease that I had not noticed her do so since we had entered the conservatory. "I believe that your interest is not exclusively scientific, sir."

"A man has died," said Holmes. "A student of palaeontology, who shared your interest in archaic animal forms. It seems that something attacked him." He took from his pocket the drawing of the toothmarks found in Gramascene's boat, which he had made sure was secreted with our other belongings in the backpack. "Something with teeth like this. Are those familiar, Lady Ophelia?"

Lady Ophelia took the drawing and examined it. "I cannot identify these," she said serenely. Her whole demeanour since our arrival had been so odd that I could not tell whether she was lying.

"Are you certain?" asked Holmes as she handed it back to him. "They are a little reminiscent of the weapons your alligator friends are sporting." The beasts in the pool had barely moved since we arrived, except the one that had yawned wide, displaying a small but fearsomely bladed jaw.

Her ladyship shrugged. "If you say so, Mr Holmes. You will grant that none of these creatures could kill a man without going to a great deal of trouble, though. I can assure you that they would not consider it worth the bother," she added with a smile.

"I did not suggest that the culprit was one of these fellows," said Holmes. "Well, if you are unable to help us from your own knowledge, I imagine that you must possess a good many books on relevant matters. Perhaps we might be permitted instead to seek the owner of these jaws in your library?"

"Good Heavens, Mr Holmes." Lady Ophelia smiled again, and this time there was a hint of steel amid the silver. "I have made you welcome, despite the unexpected manner in which you arrived in my grounds, but you must excuse me if I cannot allow you the run of my property. This house's library was my father's sanctum during his lifetime, and since his death it has become mine. Domestic tasks aside, nobody save myself has set foot in it for longer, I suspect, than you have been alive. You will grant a solitary old woman her private space, at least."

"Perhaps we might borrow some books without entering the room, madam?" Summerlee suggested practically, but a little shortly. "I am sure your servants would be more than capable of carrying them out to us."

She gave another gay laugh. "You are most insistent, for intruders in my house. Very well, Professor Summerlee. You may borrow any volume of mine that you care to mention, save for my father's private journals and my own. Will that satisfy you?"

"It will," said Summerlee. Reluctantly he added, "Thank you, my lady, that is most generous," as indeed it was. "For now I shall require whichever comprehensive volumes of reptile anatomy you own, together with anything that specifically addresses the question of dentition. Accounts of predation techniques and other relevant behaviours we may consider later."

Again came the smile. "Very well, Professor, I will see that you and your friends are so furnished. Modon, please show our visitors to the gentlemen's smoking-room. I shall send the books to them there."

She swept from the room, the train of her green dress slithering after her. Modon kept his gun shouldered, but still his hand was significantly held on the stock. "Ye'd best come wi' me, then," he told us all with a scowl.

He led us along a passageway and unlocked the smoking-room, thick with dust and smelling more of neglect than of tobacco. With no gentlemen in the house it cannot have been used for a long time, although it had at least been kept free of cobwebs – or perhaps, thanks to the lizard population, merely of their builders. The casement windows were large, giving good light, and there was a reading-desk beneath one of them, as well as musty armchairs by the fireplaces. Summerlee, Holmes and I sat and filled our pipes.

"We might be here for a while," Summerlee observed. "It may take some time to narrow down the species from those textbooks."

"Might we request some refreshment?" Holmes asked Modon. "A pot of tea would be most welcome."

Modon spent a moment digesting this request. Then he replied, in a considered tone, "I'll see ye all damned first," and left us, slamming the door.

We heard the key turn in the lock, and his footsteps receded along the passage as the three of us exchanged looks of exasperation and dismay.

# CHAPTER FIFTEEN

"Well," Holmes observed philosophically. "I suppose it could be worse. As far as I can see, none of Lady Ophelia's more venomous associates is in here with us."

"Perhaps Modon only hopes to keep us from wandering again," suggested Summerlee, though his voice held little optimism on the matter.

"Perhaps, Professor," said Holmes. "And perhaps he will return at any moment with a pot of tea and a sponge cake. Such should not be our prevailing assumption, however."

"But this is surely an admission of guilt on Lady Ophelia's part," I exclaimed. "She must have played a part in the deaths of Gramascene and Felspar, and fears that we will expose her." I thought for a moment. "Unless it was Modon's own work, I suppose, and he hopes to prevent his employer from finding out."

"I fear we cannot even conclude that," sighed Holmes. "We are, as Modon reminded us, trespassers on Lady Ophelia's property. Under the circumstances locking us up is neither a surprising nor, it must be admitted, even an unreasonable reaction. It may be that she is merely sending for Constable Batterby – from whom I suppose we may expect little sympathy."

"This is quite exasperating," declared Summerlee as Holmes crossed to the room's large window. "With those books we might have had a real chance of identifying the creature."

"There are other sources of academic literature," Holmes noted, then tutted at the window. "Nailed shut," he observed. Moving instead to the door, he pulled out his lockpicks, which he had prudently included among the items smuggled across in the backpack. He peered into the keyhole and sighed. "And here the key is in the lock still." His attempts to poke it free proving fruitless, he returned to the window and examined it more closely.

"The sound of breaking glass would draw unwelcome attention," he noted. "However, the frame is elderly and somewhat rotten. Pass me one of those fire-irons, Watson."

I did so, and he began experimentally to lever at the window's wooden surrounding.

Summerlee said, "Can we not simply wait for Modon to return and overpower him? We are three against one."

Holmes shook his head. "He will be prepared for such an encounter. He will bring his gun, and probably his friends. No, we must make all haste away from here, in whatever way we can." Though not given to such fancies, I experienced for a moment an absurd vision of our making our escape riding on the giant tortoise.

Working together, we managed with great care and a minimum of noise to lever out the looser of the two casements from its frame, resting it on the reading-desk before lowering it gently to the floor. As we did so, light from the newly created opening fell upon a small lizard that I had not previously noticed high on a wall. The creature launched itself directly at me on gauzy wings.

The surprise was more than I was prepared for, and I dropped my corner with a cry of alarm. The frame fell and several of its panes shattered. We heard the sound of footsteps approaching urgently along the corridor. The flying lizard (a common species in the East Indies, as Summerlee would later assure me) changed its direction abruptly in mid-air and alighted to scuttle under a skirting-board.

"Quickly, now!" cried Holmes, and first Summerlee then I hurriedly climbed onto the reading-desk, squeezed through the space left by the removed casement, and dropped down into the overgrown flowerbed outside. As Holmes followed, I heard the smoking-room door crash open and a man's voice yelling. Holmes kicked the desk over and dived out after us, and the three of us fled together into the wooded undergrowth.

Holmes directed us downhill through the trees towards the mere. Behind us we heard crashes and cries of pursuit, but no shots. The wood was too dense with trees to allow a clear aim, and even a shotgun would have discharged its pellets harmlessly into bark.

I was not as young as I had once been, but my association with Holmes had had the advantage of keeping me remarkably fleet on my feet, and of the three of us it was Summerlee, rangy though he was, who began to fall behind. I hung back to hurry the professor along as Holmes went haring ahead to scout our path.

Quick, scurrying lizards and their larger, slower brethren, shelled and unshelled, hastened as best they might out of our path. Snakes draped pendulously from the branches of trees, and I was constantly aware of the danger of treading on one whose fangs could inject me with agonising poison. But, with Modon and Lady Ophelia's other thuggish retainers on our tracks, I could hardly wait to scan each patch of ground before I placed my foot there.

After a confused interval spent running in Holmes's wake, urging the dogged professor along with me, I emerged with Summerlee abruptly from the treeline near the shore. Glissenholm stood before us in the mere, nearer than I had seen it before, with Ravensfell rising beyond. Between the trees behind us and those that thronged the island was a stretch of deep blue water that, in this part of the lake, looked rather Mediterranean than the slate-grey of the waters around Wermeholt.

I heard a halloo from Holmes, and a short distance to our left I saw a jetty. Two of the rowing-boats tied up there had been cut free and pushed out into the lake, while Holmes was aboard the third, propelling it as fast as he could towards us.

The professor and I stumbled out into the lake and clambered aboard as, behind us, the first groundskeeper burst from the trees. The three of us ducked as a shotgun rang out, and I heard the cluster of shots sing as it flew above us in the air.

Holmes was up again at once, striking out towards the island. Two further pairs of blades were stowed in the bow, and I lent my assistance as best I could, but the boat was built for a single rower. Seeing quickly that my interference hindered as much as it helped, I desisted.

Behind us on the shore, the belligerent groundskeeper was reloading his gun, but stopped when Modon stepped out of the forest, followed immediately by the third man, and remonstrated with him. At this distance I could not make out the exact words they exchanged, but Modon's were reinforced with a solid punch to the other man's stomach, at which he doubled up. No further shots were fired, but the third man began to wade out into the lake to retrieve one of the other boats.

Holmes was striking out energetically still in the direction of Glissenholm.

"Holmes, we should make for Wermeholt," I told him, pawing ineffectually at my soaking trousers. "Perhaps even for Ravensfoot. We will surely find more sympathetic authorities there."

"While we are here," my friend replied between strokes, "and in a boat, I should like to take a look at that island."

"A further trespass will make no difference at this stage," Summerlee supposed. Again I thought I detected a surprising glee on his part at our present peril, which nobody who had met him only in the lecture theatre or dissecting-room would have suspected.

Behind us, the groundskeepers had retrieved one of the errant boats, but were hampered in their plans for pursuit by the fact that its oars were aboard our own. Modon threw what I assumed must be a choice sequence of oaths at us, but they were mercifully indistinguishable.

As I looked around our craft for any other equipment that might prove useful, a new notion dawned on me. "I say. This boat is exactly the same as the one we found at the jetty by the church, when Henry Gramascene died."

"The fact had not escaped me," said Holmes tightly. Given his present labours I excused his shortness.

As we pulled further away from the shore, I realised that our stumbling dash through the forest had taken us some way along a spur of land that formed one arm of the inlet that I had seen the previous week, from my vantage of the drystone wall on Netherfell. The mouth of this channel was coming into view now, with the limestone wall and serpent-surmounted gate of the estate visible beyond.

From this approach, it was clear that the small cove had been closed off by a series of stakes, between which a large net had been slung, woven from sturdy rope. The place where I had seen the creature rise and fall within the waters had been within the area of water thus enclosed.

"I see no more boats," Summerlee observed, peering the other way along the shore to the further wall of the estate. "It hardly seems likely that Lady Ophelia and her staff would need more than we have seen. To pursue us they will need to fetch another from Wermeholt."

"They might more easily have spare oars," Holmes observed, curtly again.

"That is true. Oars would be more easily mislaid than boats. Are you quite well, Watson?" Summerlee asked in concern, for I had been staring into the inlet as we passed it.

Beneath its waters, great shadows swam, ancient and ominous.

"Do you see?" I asked the others urgently. "I wasn't mistaken. I did see some creature there."

And as we watched, a giant beast breached the water of the inlet, roused by our wake. It opened its vast jaws and snapped at the net, which nevertheless held. Annoyed, the animal withdrew, and retreated beneath the surface with a flick of its great saurian tail. Its scaled back, replete with knobs and spikes, sank out of view.

"Good Heavens," said Summerlee. "What a size. I have never seen one so large."

"Can they even grow so big?" I asked. "Those jaws…"

"I have read that the male Nile crocodile is the largest known," observed Summerlee. "That one must have been four yards long." It was clearly a crocodile that we had just seen. "I say," the professor added with cheerful malice. "How disappointed Creavesey will be by this."

"Indeed," Holmes agreed. "I think we have identified Henry Gramascene's killer, at least. The weapon, if not the murderer," he added thoughtfully.

By now we were approaching Glissenholm. The men were gone from the shore behind us, and there was no sign yet of any waterborne pursuit. Holmes rowed around the island until we found a mooring, a little out of view of Lady Ophelia's grounds, where we tied up and disembarked.

My clothes were still soaked, and I had had little time to recover my breath after our run. Holmes, though, had been exerting himself with far more vigour and seemed miraculously unfatigued. "Come, gentlemen," he insisted, as Summerlee and I clambered out of the boat. "We may not have much time here."

A narrow, overgrown way, little more than a rabbit-path, led off into the woods of the holm, which to my initial trepidatious glances appeared reassuringly free of the reptiles that infested Lady Ophelia's sanctuary. The isle was not large, and I guessed that we could have walked the entire perimeter within twenty minutes. Holmes, however, was intent on following the path as it wound up the gentle slope. It would lead us, if all that we had been told was true, to the Wermeston family cemetery and the Hagworm's Stone.

Despite the lack of snakes underfoot, I found the island's atmosphere oppressive. Wherever we walked the woods seemed almost silent apart from our clumsy human tread, and yet whenever we paused, strange rustlings could be heard in the distance. The air had a rank smell not unlike that of Wermeston Hall itself. I had the sense of watching eyes. Although the trees were honest British oak and ash, I felt as if I were, like Lady Ophelia's father, an explorer in some exotic land with its own strange and hostile fauna.

As I contemplated this sensation, there was a crashing noise and a shaggy beast with horns and yellow eyes burst from the undergrowth directly in front of me. I fear that I yelled once again in terror, much to the mirth of Holmes and Summerlee, who were further from the creature and recognised it in the instant of its emergence as a perfectly ordinary black nanny-goat.

"Lady Ophelia's groundskeepers must graze them here," Summerlee said, as the animal bounded away from us among the trunks. "A way to keep the undergrowth under control, perhaps."

"At least that explains the movement I saw from the shore," I smiled, amused at my own embarrassment. "I was convinced it was the Hagworm, at large among the trees."

However, all our good humour evaporated a minute later, when we came upon a grisly assemblage of remains.

"My God," I exclaimed involuntarily. "What could possibly have produced that?"

When I was a boy, the gamekeeper on a schoolfriend's estate had shown a gang of us his collection of bird pellets – the dried balls of fur and bones that a bird of prey such as an owl will cough up, once it has digested all the nutritious parts of whatever mouse or other rodent it has swallowed whole. It was clear enough that this was the same type of object, but I fervently hoped that I would never meet the owl capable of regurgitating it. It was a greyish ovoid, lumpy and very irregular, and more than a foot long. From the pair of horns embedded in its hairy surface, it appeared to have once been another goat.

"A gastric pellet," Summerlee noted, with cool interest. "Many predators generate them, including certain reptiles. This one is dry and smells musty; it cannot, I think, be of very recent production. I cannot say that I have ever seen one of such dimensions before."

"Another crocodile?" I suggested, grasping at the hope of a mundane explanation.

"A crocodile might perhaps regurgitate a pellet of a similar size," the professor replied neutrally, "but they are not typically woodland animals. Where they can, they will take their prey beneath the water to consume."

"What creature did this, then?" I asked, rather wildly, but neither of my companions had an answer for me.

Considerably sobered in our outlook, we proceeded on our way. The path spiralled around the island until it reached its woody summit. Here was a grassy depression, partly clear of trees, and dotted with cairns. These piles of small stones stood at about the height of the white billy-goat that was grazing between them, and were the only monuments I could see that might mark the resting-places of Lady Ophelia's ancestors. None bore a marker, and many of the oldest stood tumbled and overgrown, so that they could hardly be distinguished from the ground around them. If Henry Gramascene had hoped to find a record of his ancestors here, he would have been disappointed.

In the centre of them all stood the Hagworm's Stone.

It was notably antique, its surface cracked and worn with age, yet kept free of lichen and other forest growths. It was, incongruously, made of marble, flecked in pink and black, and of a design I thought faintly familiar from visits to the British Museum. Its shape was that of a solid block like an overturned wardrobe, with carvings all across its front and sides.

Summerlee whistled. "I am most certainly no archaeologist," he told us, "but that is surely very ancient. To my eye it looks Roman."

Holmes said, "I believe I have seen this fellow before." He indicated the serpent that coiled in bas-relief across the stonework. "And not on Lady Ophelia's gateposts, either. Though I had little leisure to examine it, Sir Howard Woodwose had its relative in his study."

"By Jove!" I said, then winced at my thoughtless invocation of a classical divinity. I knelt to examine the carvings more closely. They showed a snake-like beast, not unlike the conventional Hagworm, but without the Hagworm's legs, and with a canine-looking face surrounded by a mane. Though rendered by a different artist, it was obviously the same being as depicted in the serpent statuette that Woodwose kept on his desk.

"You're right, Holmes," I said. "And you, Summerlee, I think. This is an altar to the Roman god Glycon."

It turned out that Summerlee had paid little attention to the folklorist's rather tiresome lecture that evening at his cottage, and so I told them what little I recalled of the deity. "His cult had thousands of followers, including the Emperor Marcus Aurelius, and… I think Woodwose said something about a glove puppet? I suppose the priests used it to imitate the god. Rather absurd, really."

As carved upon that altar, however, Glycon did not look absurd. His beady eyes were malevolent in his inhuman face, and his stone coils looked ready to lash out at any moment, thrashing us senseless. The long-dead sculptor had done quite as good a job as the equally devout successor who had carved the rendering of St Michael and the Devil in Wermeholt church.

"Well," I said, "I suppose this explains why the Reverend Thomas Wermeston wasn't buried in the family plot."

"I believe it may explain more still," said Summerlee slowly. "We must presume that some Romano-British clan settled here, and built a shrine to the god they followed. Perfectly ordinary behaviour on their part, no doubt, but somehow the local population kept their peculiar religion alive for centuries. It must have changed, as traditions do, and become the cult of the Hagworm, with all its associated legends."

"A speculative theory, but one that would account for a great deal," Holmes agreed.

"Woodwose must know of this already," I pointed out. "It is far too great a coincidence otherwise. I hadn't even heard of Glycon until last week."

"Quite," Holmes agreed gravely. "It seems that he is more familiar with this cult than we guessed. Hullo, what's this?"

"And to think he was deploring missionaries bringing foreign religions to Britain," I mused, but Holmes had bounded off to the other side of the altar. I followed him to find a large square of tarpaulin pegged to the earth, its area a little bigger than our sitting-room in Baker Street. The ground had apparently been cleared of trees and flattened for the purpose.

"Whatever is it for?" asked Summerlee, joining us.

"Concealment, surely," said Holmes. "Perhaps there is a Roman mosaic, too." He knelt to prise out one of the pegs. Immediately, a furious hissing noise emerged from underneath the tarpaulin, and we all three froze.

"A pit," I gasped. "There's something down there." The hissing continued, accompanied by a slithered whipping sound, as of a snake or lizard's tail.

"That is certainly no crocodile," observed the professor thoughtfully. Some metal poles and coils of rope had been stacked up nearby, and a ladder leaned against a nearby tree. I realised that it must be used for descending into the pit, though why one would wish to do such a thing I was too appalled to think.

"These pegs have been very thoroughly hammered in," said Holmes, unperturbed, still straining to free a corner. "Would you gentlemen give me a hand?"

But even with the three of us pulling, the peg would not give way. Eventually Holmes found a stout branch from which he cut a staff, and using that as a lever we were able to prise away a corner of tarpaulin. The pegs were spaced every two feet, and the fabric overlapped the edge of the pit, so we had only a narrow aperture through which to peer beneath us.

The light that reached us through the trees penetrated but a small way into the dark space, and afforded us little more than a confused glimpse of shadows, into which a mass of scales and teeth and bloody drool suddenly darted, hissing frantically. The reek of rotting meat assailed us, and we recoiled as one. I struggled not to void my stomach.

"We have not the leisure to investigate further," said Holmes, coolly replacing the flap. His face was, I thought, uncharacteristically pale. "Mr Modon and his comrades will be on our tails by now. We should make for land and gather our wits."

Neither Summerlee nor I wished to take issue with this, and at a pace that was barely more dignified than a run we made for the jetty and the safety of our boat.

# CHAPTER SIXTEEN

"Whatever was that creature?" I asked, after the professor and I had regained our breath. My mind was busily dredging up memories of dinosaurs at the Crystal Palace and the dragons of my boyhood storybooks, and combining them with the heraldic beasts on the gates to the Wermeston estate to create new horrors of its own.

"It was no Roman god," said Holmes, "of that, at least, I am certain." My friend, though grim-faced, seemed wholly untired as he worked the oars. His stamina was always remarkable, though as his physician I knew that he would pay for it later.

Summerlee seemed just as shaken. "The Wermestons have amassed a huge number of reptile specimens from across the world. Lady Ophelia spoke of… dinosaurs. Is it conceivable that Creavesey and Topkins are not altogether mistaken, and that somewhere, in some distant corner of our globe, those primordial fauna somehow survive?" He pressed gingerly at his ankle, and winced.

"If anywhere, why not here?" I asked. "The Hagworm cult has lasted for thousands of years. Might Glycon's worship have survived here because there was a real lake monster for his followers to transfer their devotion to? Perhaps that was the reason they came here in the first place."

"Gentlemen," said Summerlee, massaging his lower leg still, "I fear that I... oh, dear." His gaze had strayed to the shore of Wermeholt, whither Holmes had pointed our rowing-boat.

I followed Summerlee's eye to the town jetty, where a large party had assembled and was grimly watching the progress of our vessel. Meanwhile, two of Wermeholt's own boats had set out to intercept us. I recognised one of them as that belonging to the fishermen Ned and Luke.

"Are they all part of the cult?" I marvelled. "Was poor Mr Felspar's entire congregation one of pagans?"

"The ties of loyalty in such a town are always strong," Holmes observed. He had stopped rowing and turned to observe the scene, although our boat continued to drift in the direction of Wermeholt. "It need not take membership of a secret religion to unite a close-knit populace against outsiders."

"Can we still make for Ravensfoot?" Summerlee asked. "Have we time?"

Holmes glanced from the approaching boats to the far shore of the lake, making the calculation. "They would reach us before we were halfway. Even if we could somehow signal our distress to those in Ravensfoot, they would assume their neighbours were our rescuers, not our captors. We might make for the Wermeston estate's grounds instead, but I should prefer to place my fate in Constable Batterby's hands than those of Mr Modon. And I assume that none of us wishes to return to Glissenholm without a stout party of armed men."

"Certainly not," I shuddered.

"Then I fear our way lies with the good people of Wermeholt." Holmes smiled gravely. "You have faced Afghan tribesmen, Watson. I am sure that they will not be quite as fearsome."

Soon enough Ned and Luke drew alongside us, along with the other boat bearing their townsfolk, and between them they escorted us silently back to the town jetty.

The crowd awaiting us there held many familiar faces. I saw Ben Scorpe the publican and Mr Batterby the butcher, and Mr Dormer, our host at the Mereside Hotel, looking no more friendly or hospitable than his compatriots. In pride of place at the waterfront stood Martha Trice and her sisters, the housekeepers Mrs Gough and Mrs Jenkins, like the three fates of legend, their faces identically disapproving. At the sight of us, many of the crowd quite openly made the striking-snake gesture with their fingers.

At the mooring where Ned the boatman encouraged us to tie up stood Constable Batterby, nervously fingering his truncheon, and Sir Howard Woodwose, his eyes blazing with fury as he brandished the clothbound notebook that Holmes had removed from his strongbox, and which we had hidden before we left in Holmes's satchel at the very bottom of my hotel wardrobe.

"Mr Holmes," the knight began coldly before we had even disembarked, "from you I should expect such behaviour as this. It is of a piece with your ill manners, your conceit and your high-handed disregard for the feelings of the Topkins family. But in you, Dr Watson, I am disappointed. I welcomed you into my house as a guest, and you repay my hospitality with burglary!"

There was some gasping and tutting among the crowd, with Mrs Trice making a particular show of her moral outrage. I felt a twinge of guilt, but no more. Woodwose was correct to say that I had transgressed the rules of polite behaviour as well as the law of the land, but what we had discovered in the process amply justified our offence.

Summerlee, it seemed, had hurt his ankle during our rapid retreat from Glissenholm, and I helped him out of the boat. Coolly as ever, despite his exertions and the discomfort we were all feeling from our sodden clothing, Sherlock Holmes replied, "May I ask how you obtained that item, Sir Howard?"

"That's no concern on thou's," Constable Batterby interjected at once. "T'man's entitled to recover his property."

"Ah, but is it rightfully his property?" Holmes asked. "If intruding on someone else's premises may be justified on the grounds of recovering stolen goods, then it seems to me that Sir Howard and I are on equal ground. One cannot rob a man of that which does not belong to him."

Stubbornly, Batterby insisted, "Thou had no business breaking into Sir Howard's cottage while he was out at supper and taking things. That's burglary, Mr Holmes, no two ways about it. When we told Mr Dormer on it, he kindly allowed us to look at Dr Watson's room."

"Well, it seems that you have made up your mind, Constable," said Holmes, "though I would hope that the traditional process involving a judge and jury might follow in due course. I must point out, however, that Professor Summerlee was one of those dining with Sir Howard at supper last night, and must be considered altogether blameless in the affair. Sir Howard will agree with me, I am sure."

This was true only insofar as "the affair" referred to the burglary at Woodwose's cottage and not the trespass upon the Wermeston estate. However, Sir Howard nodded soberly, and the constable accepted it willingly enough. "Fair's fair then, Professor, thou can go," he said. "No leaving town, mind, we'll still need to talk to thou."

Summerlee looked indignant, and quite prepared to stay with us and insist on being arrested also, but Holmes said, "I suggest you return to the hotel, Professor. We may require your freedom as our advocate."

The professor reluctantly acceded, and hobbled off in the direction of the Mereside, leaving us with the constable, Woodwose and the crowd of locals.

"As there is no police station in town, I assume you have no cells," Holmes observed. "Are we to be locked in your office, Constable, or shall you finally be calling on the services of your constabulary colleagues beyond the confines of Wermeholt? I assume that your superiors in Keswick have not, after all, been notified of what has been occurring here."

"Old widow Arnott's cottage has stood empty since she died," Batterby replied shortly. "It'll serve t'night."

And so we were marched by the constable, with the townsfolk watching us silently, along the waterfront of Wermeholt and beyond the church to a small and very rustic cottage of slate and turf, whose interior we found made few concessions to comfort.

"T'next door cottage is mine," Batterby told us as he locked us inside. "I'll be watching, don't doubt it."

In the single room of the late widow's dwelling, which served as everything from kitchen to bedroom, Holmes found a straight-backed wooden chair and settled into it. "My arms are habituated to many kinds of exercise," he told me, stretching them with a grimace, "but I am not a regular oarsman. Perhaps I should partake more often of the sport."

"We really should have made for Ravensfoot," I observed ruefully. "Returning to Wermeholt seems to have been rather a cardinal error."

"Tomorrow is Midsummer's Day," he pointed out. "If the sacrifice is to take place, that is when it will occur. Even in Ravensfoot, it would take some time to persuade the authorities of our concerns, and longer to summon the assistance to intervene. At least this way we shall be on the spot when it happens."

"On the spot, but locked in a hovel," I said. Outside, the sun had long since vanished behind the slopes of Netherfell, and the slate walls, though sturdy enough to confine us, did little to protect us from the chill of the evening.

"It is uncommon enough that the door locks at all," Holmes observed. "The late Mrs Arnott can hardly have had many possessions worth stealing. And the lock is very recent, though not quite new enough to have been installed since our arrival here. Nevertheless, I think that somebody has been anticipating that its use as a prison might become a necessity."

"For poor Mr Felspar, I imagine," I sighed. "They couldn't have risked him leaving town before Midsummer."

"Poor Mr Felspar cannot be the intended victim now."

"Well, no." I shivered, which I sternly attributed to the coolness of our confinement. "I suppose it has to be a priest they feed to that thing on the island?"

Filling his pipe, Holmes said, "The centuries of precedent would suggest so. Though any religion may change its practices over time."

Again I said, "What *was* it we saw?" but Holmes did not reply, even to admonish me against the error of theorising from insufficient data.

At length I broke the silence. "Now I suppose I understand why Woodwose planned to ask the vicar of St George's to meet with him tomorrow here in Wermeholt. The poor man is their new sacrificial victim, I imagine."

Holmes said, "I am convinced that that is Woodwose's intention. I am not certain that the Hagworm's worshippers are altogether united, however."

I said, "Is *everybody* in Wermeholt part of this cult?"

"Batterby I am not certain of," said Holmes. "He does not strike me as a religious man, of any stripe. He might be simply in Woodwose's employ. We can be reasonably sure he is not in Lady Ophelia's, or he would have been as keen to imprison Summerlee as the two of us. But I am afraid that from what we have seen, we must assume the possible complicity of anyone from the town.

With the Creaveseys and Topkins out of the picture for now, the only person we can trust here is Summerlee."

"The only man, perhaps," I said, thinking of Effie Scorpe. However, as she too was still imprisoned as far as I knew, the point was somewhat moot.

We sat and smoked for a while, as the sky outside darkened and the cottage cooled further. The windows were tiny, too small for a grown man to pass through even were the glass removed, and though the hearth was broad enough, a cursory inspection determined that it narrowed to a chimney no wider than my head. The door was solid wood, and did not look as if it would yield to anything short of a battering-ram. From Holmes's attitude of indolence, I presumed that he had already considered and dismissed all these potential avenues of escape.

The house grew colder still. After a while, I found some moth-eaten blankets in an old chest and draped myself in one of them. Holmes refused one, apparently as indifferent to the chill as to everything else.

"We must suppose," he said suddenly, a while later, "that Woodwose came to discover the cult through the work of Dr Harpier. He would have had no reason to keep his notebook otherwise, or to annotate it as he did. He may have suspected beforehand, though, that the legends of the Hagworm concealed a more important truth, and that perhaps is why he came to know Harpier. It hardly seems likely that he would have killed him simply to gain access to his notes – that, surely, was the cult's response to Harpier's intemperate enquiries after local religious practices – but he was interested enough to have his papers abstracted and concealed from his executors.

"Meanwhile, he arranged legitimately to purchase and move into Harpier's cottage, intending to continue the late historian's researches. The notebook, however, would have quickly led him to understand that there was a fully fledged snake-god cult alive and active in Wermeholt. He could only have escaped Harpier's fate by assuring those he spoke to of his absolute sympathy with their practices, and his own devotion to the object of their worship. Indeed, from what we have seen he would appear to have inveigled himself into whatever hierarchy the cult follows, and become a respected enough figure within it to take charge of finding a replacement for Gervaise Felspar.

"It would have been expected by all, of course, that Felspar should become this century's victim, sacrificed like his predecessors to the Hagworm on the century's last Midsummer's Day, but his premature death put paid to that idea. By arranging for the Reverend Mr Vangard to visit tomorrow, Woodwose hopes to supply a replacement. This much is elementary, given what we have discovered, but it fails to address a most intriguing question."

"You mean, who killed Felspar, and why?" I surmised.

"Indeed. As we have established, his death on the nineteenth of June was of no use as a Midsummer sacrifice. On the other hand, anyone driven by mere malice against the vicar could simply have waited until the twenty-first to watch him die."

"Unless he had an enemy who was not part of the cult," I suggested. "They might not have known that he was due to be sacrificed."

"Perhaps, though it is difficult to imagine the man you have described as having mortal enemies. The only person who knew him before he arrived here was Woodwose, who we can be sure was aware of what was in store for him. In any case, for Felspar to fall victim to an unrelated murder, a mere two days before he was due to die in a conspiracy of many centuries' standing, would be a perfectly baffling coincidence. It is surely more likely that someone knew that Felspar was the appointed sacrifice, and intended to make him unavailable for the cult's purposes."

"I suppose so," I said. "They certainly weren't trying to save him."

"Indeed not. We must conclude, therefore, that somebody considered him inadequate as a victim. Perhaps they thought he was insufficiently pious, or found evidence that he was impure in some other way. Was he perhaps a widower, for instance? We know little of the other victims, so we can only guess what qualities they might have had in common beyond their holy orders, but when the tradition began, priests would have been presumed to be celibate.

"In itself, though, that would hardly be sufficient reason to hound him to death. Nor was there any need to silence him. Felspar had ample opportunity to confide his suspicions to you, and he was clearly too scared to do so. The only other purpose his death serves is to lure Mr Vangard here, and there would surely be ways to do so that would excite less suspicion.

"No. As I have said, we must posit a religious schism within the Church of the Hagworm itself, between those who supported sacrificing Mr Felspar to their deity, and those who felt that an alternative victim was necessary. His murderer knew full well that Felspar was to be the victim, and believed that that would be wrong – though not, as you say, from any concern for his wellbeing. Rather, one faction of cultists wished to place him beyond the reach of the other faction."

"It hardly seems credible," I said, "for a Church of England vicar in the year 1899 to fall victim to a holy war between rival worshippers of a Roman god."

"We have seen stranger things in our time, Watson," Holmes reminded me. "Who can forget the spontaneous combustions in the Canterbury morgue, or the grisly mystery of Barnaby Scruton, the piecemeal man? Or, for that matter, the case of—"

He was interrupted by a knock at the door – a rapid muffled

rapping, as of someone urgently, but surreptitiously, trying to attract our attention.

"We cannot admit you, I fear," Holmes called out idly. "The door is locked, and we have somehow misplaced the key. Most negligent, to be sure."

"Dr Watson! Mr Holmes!" came a voice, again urgent yet painfully hushed, and to my astonishment I recognised it as that of Ben Scorpe.

Holmes knew it too. We crossed together to the door, where we might speak more quietly. "Mr Scorpe," my friend drawled. "What an unexpected pleasure. How may we help you on this auspicious evening?"

"Don't antagonise him, Holmes," I hissed. "He may be able to let us out." Though his expression was invisible to us, I guessed from Scorpe's manner of approach that he was not here to gloat at our predicament.

"It's Effie, Dr Watson," Scorpe replied with concern, apparently considering me the more sympathetic member of our partnership.

"Effie?" I repeated in alarm. "Is she all right? Does she need a doctor?"

"She's well enough," the unseen publican replied, "for now. She's still at t'Arms. But Wermeholt's no place for her. She don't belong here, Doctor."

Based on what I had seen of the good-hearted Effie, and what I now knew of the poisonous environment in which she had grown up, I could not disagree with him. Nevertheless, given his past treatment of his daughter, his profession of regard for her welfare smacked of effrontery.

"Is that why you have her locked up?" I asked him angrily. "To protect her from Wermeholt?"

"Aye," he replied, either failing to detect my irony or caring nothing for it. "She's not safe here. She's too friendly wi' outsiders, like that Gramascene and thou."

"It sounds as if you fear her indiscretion," Holmes interjected, "and the response it might provoke from your fellow townsfolk."

"Put it how thou likes," growled Scorpe. "Wermeholt and Effie doesn't go together. Effie needs out, Doctor, and thou can help."

"What sort of help?" I asked, though the request was bizarre enough under the circumstances.

"Take her back til London wi' thou," he insisted. "Find her a position. She's a hard worker and she learns fast. Thou'll ken families need a maid or such."

"I'd like to help," I told him through the door. "But there isn't a lot that I can do locked up in here, Ben."

"Thou'll get out," Scorpe said. "Just promise me, Dr Watson, that thou'll help Effie, whatever happens. Aught as happens in Wermeholt ain't her fault."

Holmes said, "Before Dr Watson makes any promises, Mr Scorpe, an earnest of your own good intentions would be in order." Scorpe did not reply, but Holmes continued, in as conciliatory a tone as he could muster. "We are not, as you are well aware, occupying this cottage of our own free will. Constable Batterby holds the key, although I doubt that he is keeping it on his person. If you would be so kind as to locate it in his cottage and release us, then we will be most grateful, and delighted to discuss ways in which we might repay your kindness."

There was a long silence, and I wondered whether Scorpe had left us. Eventually, he replied, "I daren't."

"Oh, really, Mr Scorpe, a big fellow like you?" Holmes smiled. "I am sure that if it came to it you could cheerfully overpower a beanpole like Batterby."

"Horace Batterby's not what bothers me," muttered Scorpe. "Hagworm's neck's long, and her jaws are wide."

"Are you saying that the cult has a powerful influence?"

Holmes speculated. "Well, Mr Scorpe, if you cooperate with us then perhaps we can find a new situation for you also. There is always a demand for good barmen in London, and I doubt that the Hagworm has any great influence there."

"Thou doesn't see," said Scorpe. "I daren't," he said again. A moment later he hissed, "Someone coming," and we heard his feet rapidly receding.

Holmes and I exchanged a glance, and a shrug. "I had hoped that we might find an ally in Mr Scorpe," my friend said.

"Nothing ventured, nothing gained," I said encouragingly. I wondered, though, why Scorpe had been so keen for me to promise that I would help Effie, *whatever happened*. What was he expecting that I was not?

We heard men's voices from outside, too low to hear, and then Constable Batterby's voice at the door. "What was Ben Scorpe saying til you?" he asked.

"Oh, nothing of any great import," Holmes replied airily. "He came by to gloat at our predicament, as any conscientious citizen of Wermeholt might."

Batterby grunted sceptically. He repeated, "I'll be watching you," and his tread receded into the night.

It was some time before I slept, and I am not certain that Holmes slept at all. At his insistence, I took the widow's hard wooden bed while he sat upright in her equally hard chair. When I finally slumbered, I faced unspeakable dreams of archaic creatures rising from their graves beneath the earth and overwhelming London, crushing bridges and levelling houses in their wake.

Near dawn there came another rap at the door, this time less diffident and more excited. "Holmes! Watson!" called Summerlee's voice. Though prudently hushed, it sounded almost gleeful. "I have been attacked!"

"Are you all right, Professor?" I asked sleepily, then stared in astonishment as Holmes, who seemed not the least bit tired, retrieved his lockpicks from his shoe and set to unlocking the door.

"Fit as a fiddle," called Summerlee, oblivious. "Oh, good morning," he added, as the door swung open a moment later. "I suppose I should not have assumed that a locked door would detain you long, Holmes." He hobbled inside, incongruously carrying a wicker laundry-basket, the twin of one that I remembered from my room at the Mereside Hotel.

"You had your lockpicks on you all the time!" I pointed out accusingly to Holmes, who frowned.

"But of course," he said. "Did you not see them yesterday, at the Hall?"

"But we could have escaped hours ago!" I insisted.

"As I have said, this is a sensible place to be for the moment. And we would not have had that interesting conversation with Mr Scorpe." Turning to Summerlee he asked, "Who has attacked you, Professor?" Despite his alarming words, Summerlee looked no worse for wear than he had the previous day, and indeed seemed thrilled by this latest turn of our adventure.

"This unfortunate fellow," said the professor cheerily, and tipped the wicker basket upside down, producing a crackle as of crumpled paper.

Holmes and I leapt back, and I cried out in alarm, as a snake fell at our feet, banded in cream and brown. A moment's inspection showed that the creature was beaten bloody, though, and quite dead.

The professor continued, "It is a rattlesnake of some sort. I do not recognise the exact species." I now saw the segmented bulge at the creature's tail that had created the rattling noise. "I quite laid into him with a poker, I am afraid. A pity; he was a beautiful specimen."

"Professor," Holmes asked patiently, "how did you come to encounter this snake?"

"I awoke a few hours ago to find it in my room," replied Summerlee blithely. "Fortunately I have visited Mexico, and am familiar with the creatures. The sound they make is unmistakeable."

"But how did it get in?" I wondered.

"Oh, through the window, I imagine. I sleep with it open, and there is a trellis outside that any snake could easily climb, or for that matter any person with a snake in a box. It was perhaps foolish of my would-be assassin not to select a more stealthy species, but this one is venomous enough to meet the need, had I allowed it to strike. I am lucky enough to be a light sleeper."

We contemplated the deceased animal for a few minutes, while clammy mist from the lake mingled with the stale air of the cottage. Then Holmes said, "One point intrigues me. We assume that the reason Mr Gramascene, at least, was killed was to silence one who had learned more than an outsider should have of the workings of the Hagworm cult. Dr Harpier's death ten years ago seems to have served a similar end, and I would venture that this was also the intention behind this attempt on the professor's life.

"Meanwhile, Watson, you and I have learned as much as any of the gentlemen in question, and we have spent the night locked in a cottage whose chimney positively invites the posting of venomous snakes. Yet during that time no attempt has been made upon our persons. Does that not strike you as odd?"

"I don't know what to make of any of it," I said frankly.

"Well, never mind for now," said Holmes. "As I have said, the sacrifice is to be made today. We are at hand, and we are, for the present, free. I suggest that we seize the moment and make our way to Glissenholm, before the town at large is awake, and there see what we may do to protect the life of the Reverend Mr Vangard of St George's, Ravensfoot."

Summerlee and I assented, and the three of us stepped out into the pre-dawn light of Wermeholt on Midsummer's Day.

# CHAPTER SEVENTEEN

We crept through the silent streets, avoiding the early morning stirrings around the bakery and especially the post office, and down to the waterfront. By mutual agreement, we made not for the town's main jetty, where we might be seen even at this hour, but for the mooring behind the Mereside Hotel, where we were likely to find the hotel's own boat unattended.

It was, but another was not. A little way out from the shore, a battered rowing-vessel bobbed in the stagnant waters. In its bottom lay a broad, tall, well-dressed body, unmistakeably that of Sir Howard Woodwose. There could be little doubt that he was dead.

"Was this the crocodile again?" I wondered, gazing horrified across the few yards of water that separated the boat from the jetty. From what I could see, the learned knight was in worse shape than Henry Gramascene had been, with his legs horribly mangled and his right arm bitten clean off at the elbow.

"More likely than not," Holmes agreed decisively. "This changes matters."

"How so?" said Summerlee.

"It seems that Woodwose's opponents within the cult have eliminated him," said Holmes, who had given Summerlee a précis of his more recent conclusions during our progress. "That may prove an error on their part. At least some of their co-religionists must support his cause, as, to the best of my estimation, does Constable Batterby. If we inform the constable of our discovery, we may find him more sympathetic to our own intentions."

"Or he may immediately imprison all three of us, on suspicion of murder this time," Summerlee pointed out sharply.

I said, "If we're seen fleeing the scene of this crime, he would be duty bound to do so, and it would hardly help our case when we come to make it to those outside Wermeholt. Whatever his shortcomings, Batterby is the legal authority here. We are obliged to report this to him."

Summerlee reluctantly acceded, and not without misgivings the three of us returned through the murky dawn to the policeman's cottage, which as he had told us stood next to the widow Arnott's. The slumber from which we roused him appeared to have been just as uneasy as my own.

His eyes widened with incredulity and rage when he saw Holmes and myself at large, but that expression changed at once when Holmes reported what we had seen.

"Sir Howard's deid?" he repeated incredulously when we told him our news. "Is thou telling me t'Hagworm got him?"

"That I can hardly confirm," said Holmes, "but he has most certainly expired, and not peacefully. If you would care to accompany us, we can show you."

By the time we returned to the hotel's jetty, other early risers had seen the body, and a small straggle of townsfolk stood nearby, looking hushed and cowed. With the help of some of these, we dragged the boat up the shore and lifted out Woodwose's remains.

It seemed that the knight's death had resulted from his very considerable loss of blood, which now liberally stained the craft's flat wooden bottom, rather than from a single trauma. A solitary oar lay beside him in the vessel.

"Was it his own boat?" was the first thing Holmes asked, and Batterby nodded mutely. Like Gramascene's, it was scraped and bloodstained at the stern.

"He has been dead for some hours," I noted after a swift examination. "Since midnight, I should say. Does anyone know where he might have been going on the lake at that time?"

Batterby and the other townsfolk exchanged wary glances. "Not many places he could go on Wermewater," one old man reluctantly volunteered in the end. I recognised him from one of my visits to the Serpent's Arms. "There's Ravensfoot, or t'Hall, or Glissenholm. There's nowhere else."

"There are large stretches of unoccupied shore between Wermeholt and Ravensfoot, and between Ravensfoot and the Wermeston estate," Holmes observed absently. "If Woodwose had made an assignation to meet somebody, it could have been at any identifiable point on the lake's circumference. Or, as you say, on Glissenholm." I shuddered at the idea of visiting that place at night.

"Doesn't matter where he was going, anyhow," muttered Battersby. "Hagworm'd get him anywhere."

The locals shuddered, almost as one, and I heard a lone voice mutter, as Ben Scorpe had, "Hagworm's neck's long, and her jaws are wide." The others made the now-familiar finger gesture to ward off the creature's wrath.

Quietly, Holmes said, "But why would the Hagworm choose to attack Sir Howard, Constable? Was he not its loyal follower?"

Another man, not one whom I recognised, said sharply, "Who told thou that?" before the old fellow from the pub elbowed him in the ribs. More furtive glances were exchanged. At least one woman left in a hurry, very likely to tell everyone she knew what was happening.

Very hesitantly, Batterby said, "Sir Howard was an outsider, see. He had his own ideas. There's some round here didn't like his coming in and telling them they'd got things wrong all these years."

"I imagined as much," said Holmes. "And you think the Hagworm concurred? Well, well."

Leaving Batterby to deal with the accusing looks of the locals, he knelt and spent some time examining the stains on the transom of the boat, and the cleat above it, where a single loop of frayed cable was tied.

"Watson," he said at last, "in your first observation of Henry Gramascene's boat, did you see a line tied like this? There was no such when I examined it."

"Why yes, there was," I recalled, surprised. "It had been cleanly severed. I didn't notice that it had been removed since. I assumed it had been used for tying up the boat."

"If it was like this, it hardly seems robust enough," Holmes replied. "I should not call it rope – it is little more than string. Besides, conventionally boats are tied up at the sides, where there are, as you will see, stronger cleats for the purpose." He was quite right, I realised. Seeing a cable tied to a boat, I had simply assumed that it was used to secure it at a mooring, and had not examined that assumption further. As ever, I had seen but had not observed.

"What do you think it was used for, then?" I asked, baffled.

"Never mind that for now. Who would have had access to the craft between its discovery and when I inspected it, Constable?" Holmes asked sharply.

Batterby stammered. "All kinds on folk," he said. "Them as was watching us at t'kirkyard. Them as carried t'boat there. Others as had business in t'town hall. Could have been anyone."

"An argument for the secure storage of criminal evidence, if ever I heard one," said Holmes bitterly. "It is as we suspected, Watson. This is the work of the Nile crocodile. My opportunity to examine its dentition yesterday was momentary, but sufficient for me to note the chief variations in size and shape. The breadth of the jaws, also, is just as we observed."

"Hagworm's jaws are wide," said Batterby at once.

"And her neck long? So I am led to believe," said Holmes. "Nevertheless, this damage, to the boat and to Woodwose, was inflicted by a mundane animal, albeit not one native to these inland shores. It seems that Lady Ophelia's pet has been given a little exercise."

"It is kept behind a giant net," I reminded him.

"Then presumably the net can be lifted or otherwise withdrawn."

"So this was just an animal attack?" Batterby asked, baffled. "Thou makes it sound like someone murdered him."

"The two are not invariably contradictory. I confess that the removal of this telling evidence," Holmes said, once again indicating the cable, "obscured to me the exact method used. I would suggest that a large joint of lamb or beef, lashed to this cleat and trailing blood in the water, would have been quite sufficient to attract the attention of our Nilotic friend, and equally to satisfy his appetite after the altercation that would inevitably ensue."

"But surely the crocodile would just eat the meat?" I objected. "Why should it attack the boat's occupant, with easier food to hand?"

"I assume that both Gramascene and Woodwose were unaware that their craft had been thus baited," said Holmes. "When they observed a gigantic beast bearing down upon them, its mouth open ready to bite, what should they be expected to do? Evidently both attempted to defend themselves, and were roundly savaged for their pains. After seeing off the challenge, however, the crocodile would as you say select the easier pickings, and return to its lair."

"A murderer couldn't be sure of how the animal would behave," I insisted.

"Not altogether, no. But that would be the favoured outcome, and the likeliest. The victim's death would serve a dual purpose, his elimination confirming the Hagworm as a real and threatening presence. Of course, the crocodile might instead decide to take the human prey, and that would most satisfactorily achieve the former end, though leaving the latter more a matter of inference."

"Or the victim might be lucky enough to survive," I objected.

"Possibly, but if so he could be expected to confirm the stories of a monster in the lake, at least. It would take a remarkably clear head to distinguish a crocodile from a Hagworm in the dark and the heat of the moment. And doubtless there would be ways to ensure that he succumbed to his wounds later."

"Is thou telling me t'Hagworm's just a crocodile?" repeated Batterby in disbelief. The townsfolk had dispersed by now, muttering darkly about the turn of Holmes's deductions, and the constable, too, looked terribly uncomfortable with the tenor of his argument.

"I am telling you, at least, that these deaths are not the doing of any supernatural monster," Holmes replied smoothly. "This tableau has been constructed for the benefit of credulous observers, who I fear are in plentiful supply in this town. Evidently, somebody who felt the concerns you mentioned about Sir Howard Woodwose's influence among the worshippers of the Hagworm, dispatched him in a manner that would demonstrate the god's displeasure."

"Aye?" Batterby seemed dubious still. "Aye, I suppose it could be so. But what about Mr Gramascene?"

"Before we come to that," said Holmes, "Professor Summerlee has something to show you."

We tramped back to the widow's cottage and Summerlee produced the body of his unexpected nocturnal visitor, at which Constable Batterby stared with great concern.

He said, "Where did it come from, but? Adders is easy to come by, but there's no rattlesnakes in England."

"Nor are Nile crocodiles among our native fauna," Holmes noted. "I presume that, like your fellow townsfolk, you have never visited the grounds of Wermeston Hall, Constable? I assure you, the absence of rattlesnakes would be an unthinkable oversight on Lady Ophelia's part. Her menagerie of reptiles is quite comprehensive."

"Aye, then," Batterby muttered. "Rattlesnakes and crocodiles. I's seeing some sense in this now, Mr Holmes, and I don't like it."

"No more do I, Constable," Holmes assured him. "I think, though, that under the circumstances it is your duty to apprise us of everything you know about the local worship of the Hagworm."

"Aye." The constable's tone was sobered and subdued. "I think I've let this go far enough."

At Batterby's invitation, Holmes, Summerlee and I adjourned next door to his own cottage, similarly poky but with more modern fittings, and kept by him with bachelor neatness. We older men sat and puffed at our respective pipes while the policeman, nervously smoking a cigarette, gave us what amounted to his life story.

"As you'll have guessed," the constable began, "I was born in Wermeholt. Most families round here's had Wermeholt folk as their foregangers for generations. There's some gans til Ravensfoot, or further, and a few Ravensfoot folk moves here, but precious few. Most on t'families living here has been Wermeholt folk since t'days on old Lord William de Wermeston hissel. And all on us kens about t'Hagworm.

"I kens how other folk grows up in England, and how they believes in God and Jesus and all, because that's what t'kirk teaches them. And I kens that folk abroad grows up to be Muslims or Hindus or what-has-thou because of what they's taught. Most folk doesn't think so mickle, I reckon, but just believes t'things they're told by t'folk they trust.

"Folk here is just t'same, only what we're taught to follow is t'Hagworm.

"Vicar tells us all about his God, see, but that's a god for outsiders. Maybe he's real, maybe he's not, but he's not t'god for us in Wermeholt. Your God's up in t'sky or somewhere, and no one ever sees him, but ours is under t'water, right there in t'mere, and folk sees and hears her all t'time, outsiders sometimes too. Our god's real, is what my da says, but who'd ken aught about that other one?

"Stories say t'Hagworm's old Lord William's bride, and maybe that's true, but t'Hagworm's Stone is older than Lord William, and t'Hagworm's been here for ever, t'true ruler of Wermewater. Maybe that lady as made hersel a worm in olden times slithered off to become its bride, and our Hagworm now's their great-great-grandchild. Who kens? She's real, that's t'thing, and she's our god. Them who tells us otherwise... well, most on t'time we listens and nods along, and maybe some on us even says our prayers each night like good Christian folk, but Saturday nights in summertime we rows out til Glissenholm to give t'Hagworm her dues too. And when t'time's at hand we all kens who our true god is."

Holmes, who had nodded sharply when Batterby made his comments about the unthinking habits of believers, was showing signs of impatience with this religious talk. Summerlee, whose primary interest was in the structure of organisms rather than their behaviour, seemed still less enthralled. Even so, we all understood what it must cost the constable to unburden himself thus, and we continued to listen with respect.

"All that's what my da told me, and what I grew up believing," the young man continued. "And I kenned stories, too, of how every hundred years a Christian priest goes til t'Hagworm to show that this is t'Hagworm's place, not Jesus's, and however big your Christendom gets, our Wermeholt ain't part on it. And I believed it, too, but I never kenned it would happen in my lifetime. That wasn't part on what my da told me, at least.

"And then I joined t'police, and over angry my da was. And I thought then I'd put it all behind me. I'm no Christian, I'll admit, that's still not for me, but I thought as I could put t'Hagworm out on my life. Coming back to live here, but... T'Hagworm's all around in Wermeholt, in names and pictures and folk's hearts, and in t'Wermeston family arms and all. I kenned most folk in town followed t'Hagworm, and some incomers too, like Sir Howard Woodwose."

He paused to light a third or fourth cigarette, and then continued.

"It was young Effie Scorpe come til me and told me they was going to give Mr Felspar til Hagworm on Midsummer's Day. I told her not to be such a fool, but she said her da kenned all about it, and my da too, and others – Martha Trice and Nora Gough and Edna Jenkins, t'Modon sisters as was, and Ned Henson and his son Luke, and all on them – and Sir Howard t'leader on them all, she said."

"Wait a moment," I said. "You referred to the *Modon* sisters. Mrs Trice and those two housekeepers – is their brother Modon, Lady Ophelia's manservant?"

"Aye," Batterby confirmed. "All three was born on t'estate, and moved til t'town to marry. Now they're all widows, though that's not so unusual. Saul Gough was took by t'scarlet fever, and Ezekiel Trice by t'flu, and Stan Jenkins fell down a scree herding his sheep one winter and wasn't found for three weeks.

"Any road, young Effie was so sure on hersel that I talked til my da, and he took me to see Sir Howard, who explained it all til me. 'The Hagworm requires propitiation,' is what he said." The constable's imitation of Woodwose's booming voice was rather good. "'She must take a Christian priest to assert her dominance over Wermewater for the century to come, as she has each century since classical times.' He said a lot of other things too, about how once our Hagworm was worshipped across t'Roman Empire, but now it's just us here in Wermeholt keeping t'old ways alive. And... well, he sounded so wise, like he really kenned what he was saying was true. And I believed him.

"Poor Effie – I let her down, and no mistake. Effie always liked Mr Felspar, but then she likes anyone who can tell her about life outside Wermeholt.

"I talked til some on t'older folk, whose own granddas and grandmas would've remembered last time a priest was given til t'Hagworm, and told them on it when they was small. They told me how that goes.

"T'folk all gather at t'corpse-gate jetty at t'kirk, and they brings t'vicar out and binds him, and they all rows out til Glissenholm, where t'Hagworm's Stone is. And there they kills him by beating and strangling and drowning, as they calls it t'threefold death, and then they leaves his body for t'Hagworm to take, and then they all rows home. And always he's gone by morning.

"That's what I thought'd happen this time, but then I started hearing how Sir Howard was changing things. I never went til them Saturday nights out on Glissenholm, even after our talk, because it still didn't feel right to me, but others did, and they talked about how it made them unhappy.

"Thou sees... t'Hagworm's real, aye, folk sees her all t'time, but she ain't a tame beast, and she never used to come when thou called. Sir Howard said as t'Hagworm had a true form, but she also had different shapes she took – like that snake wi' hair on t'Hagworm's Stone, and that snake wi' legs on t'gates at

Wermeston Hall, and others too. And since Sir Howard's been in charge of Saturday nights… them forms started being seen. Serpents. Things wi' legs and wings. They came when he called them, and folk worshipped them like they was t'Hagworm hersel.

"Now I guess, from what thou's told me, that all them forms on t'Hagworm was just snakes and lizards and t'like, that Sir Howard took from Lady Ophelia's collection out at t'Hall. But folk believed.

"Some saw how Sir Howard had changed things and didn't like it at all, said that wasn't how things was meant to be. But Sir Howard said these was signs and wonders for a new age, and t'twentieth century would be t'time on t'Hagworm, and on Midsummer's Day we'd all see t'Hagworm in her true form. From how he made it sound… well, it'd be big, that's for sure. Big and horrible. Perhaps it'd be that crocodile thou spoke of, though folk round here ain't so daft they wouldn't ken a crocodile if they saw one.

"Still but, Sir Howard said as she's come, t'true Hagworm, and that folk would see her eat up t'vicar this time, no drowning or beating or strangling for him, and they'd believe. And many folk was sure that what he said was true. I didn't believe at first, but then your Mr Gramascene turned up deid, savaged by some beast, and then… then I believed in t'Hagworm again. And I feared she'd ken me for an unbeliever, and she'd come for me. And so, when I should have called t'county police in Keswick and asked them to send help, I'm sorry to say I didn't do aught on t'kind. They still doesn't ken aught on this, though I'll have to tell them now.

"And then Mr Felspar died. Sir Howard was spitting fierce about it, but he said we'd just get Mr Vangard over from Ravensfoot and all'd go as planned. But others said as someone else had plans on their own.

"And that's all I ken, gents, I'll swear it. I've not killed anyone, but I stopped Mr Gramascene's death from being investigated all right, and I was planning to turn a blind eye when Mr Vangard went. I'll answer for that all right. I thought Mr Gramascene was killed by t'Hagworm, just as I said, and when word came this morning about Sir Howard I thought t'same. Now thou's told me about t'crocodile, Mr Holmes, I don't ken what I think any more. But I don't ken any more than thou about who killed Mr Felspar, I swear it."

The three of us paused to digest this remarkable testimony. Constable Batterby was a callow, rather graceless young man, and he had shown himself a weak one. But even so, it must have taken remarkable courage to confide in us, three strangers to the community where he had spent his life, knowing that in doing so he was betraying his friends and relatives for the sake of his police calling. The moral fibre he had shown was all the more remarkable since he had confessed to being no Christian.

Holmes had been jotting something down on a piece of paper, which he now folded carefully. He said, "Constable Batterby, did you remove the rope from the cleat on Mr Gramascene's boat?"

"Not I," said Batterby at once. "I didn't even notice it was gone. I'd no idea what it meant till thou told us all just now."

"And why," my friend continued, "did you let Mr Peston go following Mr Felspar's death?"

Batterby hung his head. "I thought he kenned naught, like I said. He told me he'd been keeping t'vicar safe for Midsummer, at Sir Howard's orders. He thought he'd be safe, up in t'tower."

"And is that what you think now?"

Batterby shook his head. "I don't ken what I think, Mr Holmes," he said again.

Holmes nodded. "That is always an excellent starting position. We appreciate your confidence, Constable, though I fear that you may expect to face consequences for your complicity in this conspiracy."

Batterby nodded miserably. "Reckon thou's right."

I said, "Batterby... did you gain any sense from Sir Howard of what this 'true form' of the Hagworm's might be?" I saw Summerlee shudder as, like me, he remembered the unseen creature that we had glimpsed upon Glissenholm.

The constable shrugged. "A big snake, maybe? Doesn't they have some in t'tropics as are yards long, and can crush a man in their coils?"

Holmes said, "That is speculation. Woodwose himself gave you no particulars?"

"Nay. Just that it'd be a form fit for t'god."

I thought again of the thing – no snake, surely, and no crocodile either – that had assaulted our senses from its pit on the island the previous day. If it was supernatural, it was not Glycon, the Roman glove puppet, but something more like the dragon that St Michael fought in effigy in the church vestibule.

And that, of course, was no God, but Satan.

If anything, the idea of a predatory dinosaur somehow surviving to the present day was a more comforting one. However fearsome that might be, it would at least be nothing more than a mere animal.

# CHAPTER EIGHTEEN

"It is clear enough," said Holmes, "that all these killings are the work of the Hagworm cult. However, there are internal politics at work that make the assignation of responsibility the more interesting.

"Dr Harpier's death preceded the recent schism, of course, since it happened before Woodwose's arrival. But we must assume it served the same end as Henry Gramascene's, that of preserving the secrets of Wermeholt from the outside world. Mr Felspar's death must have been arranged by the counter-Woodwose faction within the cult, since we know Woodwose favoured keeping him alive as a sacrifice. So, of course, must the slaying of Sir Howard himself. However, we cannot rule out that Woodwose was complicit in Gramascene's killing before the same method was turned against him. And then there is the attempt on Professor Summerlee's life, occurring on the same night Woodwose died.

"Now we turn to the animals involved – first a carthorse, then later an unseen crocodile, a native species of snake and finally a rattlesnake. The attempted murder of the professor is the first that has overtly involved an exotic reptile. This suggests—"

But at this point a riotous thudding came at the door, amid shouts of, "Come out on there, Horace Batterby!"

"I feared as much," said Holmes quickly. "Constable—"

Then the door was flung open, and in burst Ben Scorpe, with Ned and Luke, Peston the verger and a dozen other men from the town, who quickly filled the single room of the cottage. All four of us were seized at once, each by two men, with little opportunity to resist.

Ben Scorpe was not one of those holding us. Instead he marched up to Constable Batterby and glared into his eyes, all his diffidence of the previous night forgotten.

"Thou's a traitor, Horace Batterby," he spat. "Thou's a filthy traitor til thy folk and town."

He landed a punch in the policeman's stomach with the force of a charging bull, and Batterby doubled up, choking. His captors let him go, and he fell on the floor, whereupon Scorpe kicked him viciously in the stomach, back and head.

"Stop it!" I cried. "You're killing him!" I looked around desperately for Mr Batterby senior, hoping that he, at least, would object to this treatment of his son, but the butcher was nowhere to be seen.

"Ain't all t'killing as'll be done today," said Peston, darkly.

Eventually Scorpe finished his assault, and Batterby lay on the floor, bloodied and gasping but still, thankfully, alive.

"Allow me to examine him," I insisted. "For pity's sake, I am a doctor." Scorpe gave his head a dismissive shake, and my arms were held as firmly as ever.

"Then I shall," snapped Holmes, slipping somehow from his own handlers' grasp. He knelt at the side of the brutalised constable, but was able to do little more than loosen the man's clothing before he was pulled away.

The young boatman Luke made to hit Holmes in turn, but Scorpe growled, "Not him!" and Luke backed away at once.

Our hands were tied. Then, leaving the unconscious

policeman bleeding on the floor of his cottage, Holmes, Summerlee and I were dragged outside, not gently, and hustled back along the waterfront.

This time, our destination was the churchyard, and its corpse-gate jetty. Among the gravestones had assembled the largest crowd of townsfolk I had yet seen, a hundred or so faces new and familiar, from babes in arms to toothless elders, all staring at us in malevolent silence. Remembering Felspar's estimate of the parish population, I supposed that virtually everybody in the town must be present.

Certainly Batterby the butcher was there, a grim expression on his face as he saw us arrive without his son. At the forefront of the crowd were Mrs Trice and her sisters, who scowled and spat like tricoteuses at the guillotine, Mrs Trice's monosyllabic daughter standing mutely behind them. Mr Dormer the hotelier looked down as Summerlee and I approached, and failed to meet our gaze. The ironmonger was there with his assistant, and the town hall clerk, and the maids who had cleaned my room and served my breakfast. Other than the constable, of all the living townsfolk whom I might have recognised only Effie Scorpe was absent.

Beyond the lakeside gate a positive flotilla of vessels bobbed in the mere. It looked as if every craft that could be gathered here had been, whether from Wermeholt or the Wermeston estate. I even saw the scraped and bloodstained rowing-boat that had witnessed the death of Howard Woodwose, pressed back into service.

Around the mooring was assembled a small troupe of servants from the Hall, including Modon and the groundskeepers who had pursued us across the estate. In their midst, framed by the corpse-gate itself, stood Lady Ophelia Wermeston in another emerald-green gown, as unnaturally calm as ever.

"Doctor, Professor," said Lady Ophelia, her sweet voice mocking us. "My welcome. And to you especially, Mr Holmes."

There was, I noted, no sign of any priest. It seemed that the services of the Reverend Reginald Vangard had been dispensed with.

"Come with me now," said Lady Ophelia more loudly, ostensibly to the three of us, but for the benefit of all those assembled. "It is time to keep our appointment with the Hagworm."

Holmes, Summerlee and I were bundled into one of the larger sailing-boats with her ladyship, and with the disagreeable Modon and two groundskeepers to guard us. The boatman and his mate trimmed the sails and set the tiller, and we embarked at the head of the little fleet for Glissenholm. Behind us, sails flapped and oars plashed, as the population of Wermeholt and the Wermeston Hall estate followed in our wake.

Somewhere in the nearer boats a drummer and a piper began a rather sombre jig. I supposed that it would carry over the water to Ravensfoot, but to any observer there or on the fells above us, the expedition would appear a harmless town outing; perhaps indeed a Midsummer celebration sponsored by the lady of the manor, but one whose murderous purpose would be quite disguised by jollity.

Wermeholt began to recede, and the shore beyond it came into view, while in the distance across the mere the trees and banks of Glissenholm grew larger. I shuddered as I recalled our last visit to that ill-fated isle. Were we finally to be introduced to the slavering, hissing beast that we had glimpsed beneath its tarpaulin, in the pit that stood next to the Wermeston family's memorial cairns? I could only suppose that we were, in which case Summerlee with his twisted ankle would have even more cause to be fearful than Holmes or I.

Despite his assumed insouciance, Holmes had been, I thought, as unnerved by that monstrous apparition as I had – more so, perhaps, since he placed all his faith in a rational, explicable world, and it was all too easy to believe that the presence we had half seen was an irruption into that world of the unnatural and unknowable.

For the moment, though, having been captured by merely human villains wishing him ill, my friend was within his element. His demeanour as he sat on the planking of the boat, his hands tied behind him, showed not the slightest hint of discomposure.

"Tell me, Lady Ophelia," he asked her amicably, "was it before or after Watson arrived in Wermeholt that you realised that Mr Felspar would make an unworthy sacrificial victim?"

I disliked, to say the least, the implication of this remark, but from Lady Ophelia it elicited no more passionate response than her familiar satisfied smile. "It was not a decision, Mr Holmes, but an understanding," she replied. "And it was one that I had held for some time. My father and I alike inherited the family's affinity for reptiles, but in Papa it took the form of purely zoological fascination. Most people assume that mine is the familiar name they find in Shakespeare, and I allow them to believe so, even using it in my authorship. But Papa named me Ophidia, after the order of classification to which snakes and serpents belong.

"Though he was taught about the Hagworm at his nursemaid's knee, he had no interest in her or her ways. He abandoned our family traditions for the religion of science, and I, too, believed that our forefathers had no more to teach us. In that I was wrong, as was he. When he died I returned to Wermeston Hall and begged that same nursemaid to tell me everything she knew about our family's ancestral faith.

"She was the grandmother of Modon and his sisters, and her family serves me faithfully still," the noblewoman continued sweetly. It had not escaped my notice that the ominous trio of Mrs Trice, Mrs Gough and Mrs Jenkins were following in the vessel immediately behind our own. Mrs Trice had donned the same black as the eerily similar women to each side of her, and the three of them looked fitted to the role of nuns or priestesses of some diabolical religion. Following her ladyship's reference to Shakespeare, I could not but think of them as her personal Weird Sisters.

Lady Ophelia – or, as I supposed I must correctly call her, Lady Ophidia – continued.

"Papa considered that the revelations and discoveries of natural philosophy had rendered all gods obsolete, and he cared no more for the Hagworm than for any other. Like you, Mr Holmes, he trusted only in theorems and evidence, in what might be argued and proven. In that, I believe he lived – and died – before his time. The nineteenth century has been an era of transition, but the twentieth will belong to the men of reason. The creed of the world outside Wermewater, against which we shall guard the Hagworm's realm, will no longer be Christianity, but scientific rationalism."

Holmes inclined his head. "So I had surmised," he replied. "It seems your ladyship is quite the religious reformer."

"Any faith, however ancient, must evolve if it is to survive," her ladyship said. "Religions and organisms have that in common. The creatures in which I specialise may appear ancient to us, relics of some past age long gone, but they have persisted where their peers perished because they were able to adapt when their circumstances changed."

"And yet Woodwose disagreed with you about the manner of that evolution," Holmes suggested, guiding her gently back to the point. "He was perfectly content that a Christian priest should be given to the Hagworm on this occasion, as so often before."

Lady Ophidia smiled sadly. "Sir Howard had held a grudge against the church since his youth. He understood that the institution was becoming irrelevant, but he could not overcome his personal antipathy. He, too, refused to change, and so…" she sighed.

Holmes refrained from pointing out that it was not changing

circumstances that had killed Sir Howard Woodwose, but the very tangible crocodile sent after him upon Lady Ophidia's orders. Instead, he said, "But he made innovations nevertheless. He had read about the priests of Glycon deceiving the god's believers with glove puppets, and thought that he could go one better."

Lady Ophidia gave her silvery laugh. "The Hagworm is not Glycon, Mr Holmes, any more than she is the wife of my ancestor Lord William, become a wyrm through witchcraft. Sir Howard told me of his theory, and I respectfully disagreed with him. Oh, I understand that the designs upon the Hagworm's Stone depict the Roman deity, but the site was sacred long before his worshippers arrived here. They came to Wermewater seeking a god who had been known as long as men had lived on these shores – one whose form was like Glycon's, but who otherwise resembled him only superficially. They sought a serpent god, and lo, a serpent god they found. But the Hagworm is older than Glycon, older than the Roman Empire. Older by far."

"So what *is* the Hagworm?" I asked, intrigued to know what this woman believed herself to be worshipping.

"She is the spirit of the distant past," she said, with utter serenity. "The Goddess of Nature, not as Nature shows herself in our own era, but as she was incarnate in the Age of Reptiles. The Hagworm is the vital spirit of those ancient creatures' strength, their savagery and their majesty. She is all that survives of those magnificent beasts.

"Your friends, Professor Summerlee, foolishly believe that they are seeking a surviving dinosaur. Far from it. The Hagworm is the God of Dinosaurs."

There was a lengthy pause, during which we digested this information, and re-evaluated our respective views of Lady Ophidia's mental state. Behind us in the other boats, the pipe and drum continued unabated in their monotonous dirge.

"Be that as it may," Holmes said at length, "Woodwose borrowed reptiles from your menagerie and made them stand as proxies for the Hagworm. Quite apart from his cavalier approach to your property, such blasphemy must have infuriated you."

Her ladyship gave that tinkling laugh again. "Far from it, Mr Holmes. Again you approach the question as a rationalist, not a believer. A Christian knows full well that what he consumes in the communion service is just a sip of wine and a mouthful of bread, but he knows through faith that their use in the sacrament means they are also the blood and flesh of Jesus. For him, the context in which the lie is spoken turns it into the truth. So, too, with Sir Howard's use of my specimens as his Hagworm familiars.

"On my estate, among its brethren, a horned lizard may be merely an individual of the species *Phrynosoma asio*, but in a ceremony of true worship it would become, indeed, the vessel of the Hagworm herself. Male or female, adult or juvenile – such particularities would become irrelevant. It would be no longer itself, but the extrusion into the world of the god. It is the exact same principle whereby the priest, whatever his personal qualities, stands in for Christ during the communion – and, for that matter, when we sacrifice him to our own god. So Sir Howard believed, and I had no quarrel with him on that score."

"I see." Holmes was, I could tell, thoroughly annoyed by the irrationality of this, though in comparison with what Lady Ophidia had been telling us previously it seemed to me to verge on reasonableness. "And was your Nile crocodile the Hagworm's instrument when it killed Woodwose himself, or Henry Gramascene?"

"No, Mr Holmes." Lady Ophidia's lunatic serenity did not waver. "That arrangement was a purely pragmatic one. It was unsanctified by any sacramental context."

"That makes sense, of course," said Holmes ironically.

"I take it that the arrangements for Dr Harpier's death were equally secular? A carthorse would make an unlikely vessel for a dinosaur deity."

Lady Ophidia sighed. "Dr Harpier was on the verge of submitting his findings to a journal. Dear Martha had already arranged twice for his submission to be lost in the post, so he intended to deliver it in person. Modon was obliging enough to ensure that the horse slipped his traces as the doctor was passing by, and that the manuscript was not found on his body.

"No, I had no thought at that time of using my animals to encourage awe among the Hagworm's children. I have always kept my menagerie secret from all but my intimates, to avoid sensation-seekers. The local people's dislike of the Hall grounds has assisted with that, of course, and with that, too, my friends in the town have helped. No, the inspiration to use my specimens in such a way was Sir Howard's alone."

"And so you made use of that insight when it came to Henry Gramascene's death," Holmes observed. "Thanks to your crocodile, his demise could serve a threefold purpose, if not a sacramental one. It silenced another who, like his great-uncle, had learned more about your quaint local customs than you could tolerate. It served as an example of the Hagworm's holy wrath. And, with Watson on the scene to witness it, it could be used to lure a victim into your clutches who fitted your own specifications more closely than poor Mr Felspar.

"It must have seemed most fortuitous when Gramascene was seen wandering the Hall grounds that night. He had been told that the answers to the questions he was asking lay on Glissenholm, but had been warned that merely rowing there from Wermeholt would draw attention, and all kinds of awkward questions. He must have scaled your wall, intending, I assume, to purloin a boat from the grounds and approach the island from there, giving the impression to any observer that he was one of your own groundskeepers.

"Whatever then transpired – whether your men caught Gramascene and allowed him to escape by boat, or whether they merely allowed him to carry out his original plan – you had them prepare the craft he used by attaching to it the crocodile bait. After he left, the crocodile was released; at your order, certainly, but I presume not by your hand. Your work again, Modon, I suppose?" he asked sharply. The manservant gave him a thunderous scowl, but said nothing.

"Modon is blameless," Lady Ophidia insisted at once. "He is my loyal right hand. In all instances, he was merely acting on my instructions."

"I dare say," said Holmes, "but I do not think that is how the law would apportion the responsibility. Nevertheless, in comparison with this elaborate plan, which you returned to in Woodwose's case, the attempt on Professor Summerlee's life was almost rudimentary. My apologies, Summerlee," he added, with a good-humoured nod at the professor.

"Not in the least," Summerlee agreed. "I myself was insulted by its simplicity."

"By then, of course, you knew that the three of us had seen the fauna on the estate, and there was no further value in secrecy. Exactly which of your confederates in Wermeholt introduced the snake to the professor's bedroom is rather a moot point at this stage," Holmes noted drily, gesturing at the modest armada behind us, uniting as it did the entire town in the conspiracy. "Since Mr Dormer was on the spot, though, and knows the hotel better than anyone, he would have been the obvious choice.

"The most intriguing death, however, is that of Mr Felspar. The manner of his killing, though fiendish enough, is not in doubt. He had a dislike of boats, so the crocodile would not have availed in his case. His fear of snakes, however, meant that it was possible to use a harmless native species to persecute him to suicide, rather than revealing the presence of exotic specimens in Wermewater.

"Mr Felspar had, I imagine, been ascending the tower frequently, to observe the trips his parishioners were taking to Glissenholm. We know that Saturday nights had seen the regular ceremonies at which Woodwose and his Hagworm familiars presided, and I dare say that with Midsummer approaching there were rehearsals and other preparations which entailed nocturnal visits. With information from the reliable Mrs Gough it would be easy enough to know when to find him there.

"Again, it little matters who introduced the snakes and locked him up there with them, though again the man with the greatest knowledge of the building, in this case Peston, would seem the most likely. Whoever it was, they acted upon your orders and directly against the wishes of Woodwose.

"I had imagined that your intention was simply to rule Felspar out as a sacrificial victim, but if all along you hoped to substitute a victim of your own, then that would be insufficient, and therefore unnecessary. Woodwose was more than capable of procuring a replacement priest, and so it was he whom you needed to remove to get your way in the matter. As we can see, in his absence these good people defer entirely to you.

"If Woodwose was always to die, then, why the need to do away with Mr Felspar? Were you after all concerned to secure his silence? I think not. He had learned the truth from Effie Scorpe, and had discussed it also with Henry Gramascene, but his questionable mental state would mean that, even if he had told others what he knew, he was unlikely to be believed.

"Effie must have believed that Felspar himself would be the Hagworm's sacrifice, and I suppose that she would have warned him to flee the town. He evidently refused this prudent course of action, presumably out of loyalty to his flock and calling. But if he realised that she was wrong, and that another was to die in his place, would he have stood by and let it happen? I think he would have done all in his power to prevent it, and you could not risk that."

"We feared that he would try to stop the ceremony," Lady Ophidia admitted. "For all his frailties, Mr Felspar was a sincere servant of his faith, and even a courageous one."

"Well, your respect for an opponent whom many would have underestimated does you some credit, at least," said Holmes. "So who was to be your sacrifice, before you developed the scheme to lure me to your domain?"

Again, Lady Ophidia gave bell-like sound to her amusement. "Your presence is most welcome, Mr Holmes, but it was hardly indispensable. Wermeholt was already playing host to men of science. It is true that you, with your deductions and your data and your compulsion to reduce reality to rigid rules, are a particularly egregious example of the type of man the outside world would have us admire, but either of Professors Summerlee or Creavesey would have made an adequate substitute for Mr Felspar."

"Thank you, I am sure," said Summerlee.

Lady Ophidia continued. "Since you unexpectedly survived the night, Professor, I have been torn, I admit, over whether to offer Mr Holmes to the Hagworm alone, or to make a triumvirate of sacrifices this time – a scientist, a doctor and a detective. It was our ancestors' practice to grant one victim a threefold death, but on this occasion we have the luxury of three ambassadors from the realm of the rational, all of them gifts for the Hagworm's appetite."

I shuddered once again. Holmes merely elevated his eyebrows. "Then I am not, after all, the perfect victim? I admit that my pride is wounded.

"One question, then, remains, and I confess that it is one whose answer continues to elude me. The promised 'true form' of the Hagworm, befitting a god, which Woodwose planned to show to these good people today… it is, of course, just another beast from your collection, the one that you have quartered on the island ahead of us, presumably to keep it from preying on its fellows at the estate."

We were approaching alarmingly close to Glissenholm now, and the gloom of the trees was beginning to loom above us. To distract myself from our impending fate, I wondered how so many visitors were expecting to alight there.

Holmes continued, "This creature has been loose on the island at times, since we saw the remains of one of its meals there, and Watson attests to a shaking in the trees that would certainly have been beyond the power of any goat, but it must also have been allowed visits to the shore. The grisly deaths of sheep and their unfortunate canine protector over the past year were, I suppose, experiments on your part, to determine its abilities and behaviour as a predator. How you were able to confine it in the excavation we saw I cannot say, but based on the equipment at the site it must have been quite a task. I would guess that you drugged its water supply, since you would not wish to feed it before today. You require your god to be hungry for the sacrifice."

Lady Ophidia's smile confirmed nothing, and Holmes reluctantly returned to his primary question. "Regardless," he said, "I must admit to a certain scientific curiosity as to the species that Sir Howard deemed sufficiently godlike to warrant such a role in this eccentric passion play." Only one who knew my friend as well as I would have detected the note of discomposure in his voice at the uncertainty he felt.

Lady Ophidia's smile widened, showing still more of her teeth. She said, "I told you that I had no quarrel with Sir Howard's sacramental use of my reptiles. The instrument he proposed for conducting this particular sacrifice was a departure from tradition, but it was a most apt one, and I was happy to assent to his suggestion. Like him, I believe religion must move with the times.

"I told you that I was once an unbeliever like my father, Mr Holmes, and I told you that it was his death that changed my mind. I did not tell you the manner of his death, nor what it was that killed him. Suffice it to say," she said, "that you and your friends will meet the Hagworm in her true form soon enough, and you shall see.

"And then perhaps, for the short time that remains to you, you will believe."

# CHAPTER NINETEEN

Our captors' boat tied up at the mooring that we had found during our own visit, out of view of Ravensfoot and Wermeholt alike, and we disembarked. The vessels that followed lashed themselves to ours, then to each other, forming a floating raft across which the townsfolk might step until they reached the shore. They did so reverently, led by the three Modon sisters, Martha, Nora and Edna, who had grown up on the estate in the cradle of the Hagworm's faith and seemed now to be its high priestesses, second only in their authority to Lady Ophidia. The men removed their hats, as if the holm itself were holy ground on which they were privileged to tread.

I saw little beyond the start of this process. We were marched away along the spiral pathway, the keening of the pipe and the pounding of the drum pursuing us up to the summit of the little island. With my hands tied, and those of our captors pushing at the small of my back, I stumbled frequently, but every time I was caught and hauled to my feet. They were even more solicitous of Holmes, and I remembered Scorpe's remonstration with Luke when the young boatman made to punch my friend. It seemed the Hagworm expected its sacrifice to reach it in an intact state.

At last we were dragged into the hollow of cairns where the Hagworm's Stone stood, with that dreadful pit, still covered by the tarpaulin, beyond. Holmes, Summerlee and I were tethered to trees like goats; not a happy comparison, given the remains that we had seen on our previous visit. The piper and the drummer joined us, and I saw that they wore footmen's livery, of the kind that had been in fashion perhaps half a century before.

"Welcome!" Lady Ophidia intoned, her voice joyful and solemn at once, and the musicians' funereal jig mercifully ceased. "Welcome to the grove of the Hagworm."

Her ladyship stood before us at the altar, while the townsfolk continued to bundle in behind us, dispersed among the cairns and occasional trees. There was no attempt at a ceremonial arrangement of bodies, no circle or pentagram and certainly none of the queues or processions one finds in church. As I had guessed, it took some time before the populace had all arrived to join us, and when they did the crowd they formed overspilled the hollow, filling the trees to some depth in most directions, though the area around that covered pit they kept meticulously clear.

Then, flanked by Martha Trice on her left, and Nora Gough and Edna Jenkins on her right, Lady Ophidia began her sinister ritual.

"Beneath the fell, around the holm, deep in the murk of the mere," she recited, and all those present chorused: "Dwells the Hagworm." Most voices were unsure of themselves, but a dozen or so were loud and confident, and the others followed their lead. Above them all the voices of Mrs Trice and her sisters rang out clearly.

"Among the fish, between the weeds, above the drowned and dead," the elderly priestess continued.

"Swims the Hagworm," the worshippers replied.

"Around the shore, between the rocks, across the fells and fields."

"Roams the Hagworm."

"The Hagworm's neck is long," Lady Ophidia declared.

"And her jaws wide," responded her congregation. On that point, at least, they seemed very firm.

At this stage, gambling upon our captors' preference for keeping us unharmed until the moment came, Holmes made his own contribution. "They are not, however, the jaws that killed Sir Howard Woodwose," he interjected, with all the force of his actor's training in his voice. "Nor, for that matter, Henry Gramascene. Those jaws—" However, this was as far as he was able to proceed before Modon roughly covered his mouth with a hand. Summerlee and I kept our silence.

More of the ceremony followed, with chants and prayers and responses just as in church, and psalms detailing the part played by the Hagworm in the creation of the local landscape and its people, its role in history and its implacable opposition to the Christian faith, in which I fancied I detected the late folklorist's hand embellishing the ancient words with some of his own opinions and prejudices. No explicit mention was made of Glycon; nor, though Lady Ophidia would have had ample time to edit Woodwose's bastardised liturgy further on the basis of her own preferences, of dinosaurs.

The townsfolk, the oldest of whom could not have been born when last this rite was performed in earnest, spoke the words with sufficient fear and reverence to gratify the leadership of any pagan cult, and we could see that there was little hope of any revolt on their part against the coming violence.

When recounting the Hagworm's deeds during the Middle Ages, the time of Lord William de Wermeston and his bride, Lady Ophidia spoke as if the Hagworm itself had become temporarily human, incarnating itself for the purpose of seducing her ancestor and binding itself for ever to the Wermeston family: "Her children in the mere share in our human heritage, just as those of us who live on these shores share in the heritage of the Hagworm," she averred. It seemed that Lady Ophidia's theology saw the woman's human form as the transformation, and her changing into a loathly worm as a reversion to its essence.

Such academic considerations might have occupied Woodwose had he been here, assuming that he had not written this part of the rite himself, but at the time my chief interest in them was their function in delaying what seemed my inevitable and painful demise, alongside my best friend and one of England's foremost anatomists. This near eventuality pressed ever closely upon my mind as Lady Ophidia recited the history of past sacrifices to her god, naming the vicars Robert White, John Hoop, Thomas Wermeston ("a betrayer of his family and faith"), Andrew Thwaite and Laertes Wilfredson. She also referred to "Priests of older ages, of Christ and other gods before him, their names now lost to us."

During the rites, Modon and his fellows from the Wermeston Hall estate had been labouring with crowbars to lever up the pegs that held the tarpaulin in place, to the sound of furious hissing from the pit. Now only the four that pinned it at the corners remained, with a man poised ready to loose them at each extremity.

Lady Ophidia was working now towards the culmination of the ceremony, explaining in more formal language what she had told Holmes in the boat of our function as representatives of the rational world that the Hagworm would ritually destroy.

"The Hagworm is our god and our protector," she asserted. "She circles the mere and its people in her coils, like a mother snake her eggs." I supposed that the herpetologist was allowing herself some poetic licence here. "The world beyond our fells may follow Jupiter or Woden, Christ or Darwin as it pleases, but here in the valley of Wermewater the Hagworm holds sway."

The creature in the pit was becoming agitated now, its hisses and thrashings accompanied by crashes that suggested it was throwing itself at the sides in an effort to climb free. I did not envy whoever had had the task of confining it in the first place, and wished I had thought to ask Mr Felspar whether there had been any unexpected funerals of servants from Wermeston Hall in recent weeks.

"What follows," said Lady Ophidia, lowering her voice, "is a sight that few are favoured to see. The Hagworm comes, in her true form, and only we may look upon her serpentine majesty and live. It is a privilege and a burden for us all."

I guessed, though, that the view into the pit itself, where the "true form" of the Hagworm waited, would not be visible to everyone present. I wondered whether this would mean the entire community were not technically direct witnesses to our murder. It would certainly have the effect of preserving the shape of the reptile deity from the eyes of any who might be sceptical of its divine reality.

The piper and the drummer struck up a new tune, more mournful still, with the cadence of a Gregorian chant, and I finally recognised the phantom music that had haunted my nights since my arrival in Wermeholt.

Modon and the other three men set to with their crowbars and withdrew the final pegs from the tarpaulin, to the sound of the subterranean monster's continuing rage.

"This creature's foremother killed my father," Lady Ophidia told us in a low whisper, her words not for the congregation now. "Papa had turned his back upon the Hagworm, had left her shores for some of the most distant lands the globe has to offer. Yet even there the god of reptiles found and punished him. She showed me the error of his ways and mine, and sent me back here into the Hagworm's bosom. I brought Papa's slayer with me, to live among the other specimens he had collected.

"I was certain that she would be the last of her line, but after she had been apart from her own kind for twelve years, she laid an egg that hatched into a male of the species. Parthenogenesis, in a terrestrial vertebrate! Professor Summerlee, at least, can appreciate how astonishing that is. Some reptiles are able to heal themselves, regrowing lost limbs, but this was a true miracle. A virgin birth, more provable and true than any the church teaches. Their descendant who lives today is once again alone, but perhaps she will repeat her ancestress's feat."

Summerlee indeed looked interested in this testimony, though like Holmes and myself his attention was preoccupied by the pit. Modon slashed at our wrists with a hunting-knife to sever the bonds holding us to the trees, though our hands remained tied. Then he and two other men led us roughly over to the pit, trailing our ropes behind us.

"But what species is it?" the professor asked, a little peevishly now. To die without knowing the identity of one's killer would, I suppose, be as frustrating for a scientist as for a detective, or for that matter a doctor.

"She is the Hagworm," Lady Ophidia insisted with lunatic conviction, as her servants gripped the corners of the tarpaulin and, grunting, heaved it away, rolling it roughly among the trees.

We looked upon the horror that Lady Ophidia Wermeston had reserved for us, and I yelled in terror and alarm. I am certain that Summerlee did so too, and it is only because of the racket we both made that I cannot say for sure whether Holmes did likewise.

The hole was deeper than I had realised, and the beast was huge, bigger than a bull, rearing up to hiss at us, its hind legs splayed and its tail whipping from side to side to create that horrible slithering thrashing sound. Its scaly skin folded about it like leather as it moved, and a trail of bloody slaver hung from its jaws. The stink of its breath passed over us in noxious waves.

As I beheld it, I understood perfectly Gervaise Felspar's terror of snakes. It was a predator, that much was unmistakeable, but its eyes betrayed no understanding of its prey. Lions or wolves will comprehend their quarry's terror, and will use that insight to predict its behaviour, and thus improve their hunt. This scaly visage showed nothing of such sympathy. The beast's eyes were as cold as its blood, indifferent to suffering or fear. They were no more hostile than they were friendly; they merely promised death. In that instance I believe I indeed saw the creature as its worshippers must have, a worthy object of veneration and terror.

Its neck was, as we had been promised, long. Its jaws were certainly wide.

"My God," I gasped. "It really is a dinosaur."

A great forked tongue flipped out of the beast's mouth as it tasted our scent upon the air, and its hissing became more frenzied than ever.

"Not an aquatic one, however," Summerlee noted, and I realised that what had held him silent was no such superstitious awe, but a fervent scientific curiosity that persisted even in the face of a death so painful as this monster promised. "One need but examine its feet to see that this is a terrestrial creature, as Lady Ophelia said."

"She is the Hagworm," Lady Ophidia repeated. "She is savage and relentless. If she has once bitten a goat or sheep, she will pursue it unto death, and with great speed. So I have learned."

"It is one of her ladyship's specimens, at any rate," Holmes observed aside to me. "In sacramental terms I dare say it may be the Hagworm, but scientifically it is a perfectly natural creature."

"Natural?" I repeated. "Look at it, Holmes! A beast like that should be dead and gone millions of years since!"

"*Should* avails us little here," Holmes sighed. "The fact is that this is the foe we face."

He said no more, because Modon gave him a violent shove between the shoulder blades, and he crashed down into the pit alongside the creature.

"The Hagworm lives!" Lady Ophidia cried ecstatically.

The three sisters surrounding her responded, "The Hagworm feeds!"

"Holmes!" I yelled in horror, but my friend had landed on his feet like a cat, and was already dancing away from the great beast as it turned to strike at him. Almost at once he shed the rope that had bound his arms, and gathered it up as well as the length that had tethered him to the tree. He twirled it round his arm almost insouciantly as he ducked and dodged.

There was nothing clumsy or lumbering about his bestial opponent, however, and Holmes was obliged to draw on all his acrobat's agility to evade its repeated lunges. Back and forth they darted, monster and man, Holmes somehow always just evading the snapping of the creature's bloody teeth. Their deadly dance took them towards the corner of the pit where Summerlee and I stood alongside Modon, who gazed down with rapturous malice as it did its terrible work. Across the pit, his sisters' expressions mirrored his own, and I shuddered to think that I had ever taken food or even tea from the housekeepers' hands.

I took advantage of their distraction, however, to begin rubbing my bound wrists feverishly against a sharp branch on a nearby tree.

Beneath us the dark drool hung from the monster's teeth like the beard of a Chinese dragon. I cried out as its great jaws struck again, and this time Holmes was not quite quick enough; the serrated teeth tore at his arm as he whipped it aside, drawing his blood. In ducking, though, my friend essayed a sudden roll beneath the belly of the monster. While its head was still seeking him where he had fallen, he clambered nimbly up onto its back and lashed out with his rope like a whip.

I thought he meant to lasso the creature's neck, to strangle it or somehow to control it, riding it like a Yankee cowherd on an errant steer, but his target had been Modon. The rope caught the manservant around the ankle and he fell, yelling in horror, into the pit directly before the predator. The monster struck again at Holmes, ignoring Modon, but the man continued to cry out in terror and alarm.

His sisters had begun shrieking too, all their eerie composure broken in their sudden alarm for their brother. "T'ladder!" Martha Trice cried. "Let him have t'ladder! Oh, quick, quick!"

The groundskeepers looked profoundly reluctant to take such a risk, and it was the three sisters themselves who rushed forward to the wooden ladder leaning against a nearby oak tree, laboriously lowering it for their brother to use. A moment later, Holmes had bounded up it and was out of the pit, shaking off the Modon sisters as they shrieked and clawed at him like harpies. Two of the groundskeepers were upon him immediately, and he knocked one aside before pitching the other down to join Modon below.

Holmes made a beeline for Summerlee, and I followed suit, pulling first one and then the other of my wrists free.

Modon emerged from the ground with great alacrity, shouting and swearing, and stumbled into the arms of his sisters. His unfortunate colleague followed, but just as he reached the top of the steps, he was shoved aside by the head of the terrible beast, as it breasted the rim of the pit.

I realised that the monster, too, now had a means of egress.

"The infernal thing can climb a ladder!" I gasped, as it rose. Between us we took the professor's tied arms in ours, and led him away in a shambling run for the woods. The screaming behind us redoubled in intensity, and there was the sound of frenzied crashing through the trees as the worshippers began to flee.

Then Lady Ophidia cried, "O Hagworm! My mistress and my god!"

Despite the urgency of our situation, we slowed and looked behind us. Modon was cowering behind the trio of widows, all his bravado forgotten, as their mistress faced her saurian deity. I realised that he was probably the youngest of the family, and imagined his older sisters instructing him in the Hagworm's ways, as their ancestors had taught the Wermeston family for generations. Amid my distraction, I wondered whether their ancient British forefathers had similarly educated the followers of Glycon, when they came here in search of their god. Did the relationship between the Wermestons and their retainers run back all the way to Roman Britain?

Here and now, though, a look of ecstasy infused Lady Ophidia's face as she raised her hands. "Take me!" she cried, clear and commanding. "Make me of one flesh with you, my lady! Unite our bloodlines once again, as you did in Lord William's time!"

"My word," declared Summerlee, as if at a new revelation, "the woman's utterly deranged." I had to bite back a hysterical laugh.

"Take me," cried Lady Ophidia again, but the Wermeston family's private god had no care for her now. It sniffed at her dismissively, its forked tongue flickering from side to side, and showed no particular appetite for her offer.

Then the beast's head whipped around, as if it had caught the scent it sought, and at the same time Summerlee said, "Holmes, you are bleeding."

The great reptile began to bear down through the trees and cairns in our direction, with terrific speed.

We fled. I cannot speak for Holmes or Summerlee, but I was seized by a thoughtless, overwhelming terror, the panic that I later learned is named for one of Glycon's fellows in the classical pantheon, goat-legged Pan. We ran, oblivious of the lashing of branches and the roots we stumbled over, unaware of the strain upon our legs as we hurtled downhill towards the island's shoreline.

A crashing and a splintering pursued us, accompanied by that ferocious hissing. As Lady Ophidia had promised, her specimen was shockingly fast and utterly relentless. Our only advantage was its bulk, which meant the woodland terrain impeded it more than it did us.

We charged downhill, crossing the path that we had ascended by. The stream of fleeing worshippers impeded us, keeping to the sanctioned route even in their flight. They shrieked and scattered as the great beast followed in our wake, and I saw one man trampled underneath its heavy tread. I thought it might have been the butcher, Batterby senior.

Precariously, we hurtled down the slope of the island towards its perimeter. "We must climb!" I managed to gasp at Holmes, as I narrowly avoided braining myself on a branch. "Shelter in a tree!" I doubted that Summerlee's ankle was up to the task, but Holmes and I might pull him up after us. It was, as far as I could see, our only hope.

"Scant refuge against a creature that is equal to a ladder, I fear," he replied, as short of breath as I.

"Then where are we going?" I expostulated. "They'll never let us onto the boats!"

"The island's other shore," Holmes panted, though I had seen no sign that he had taken any bearings during our frenzied flight from the clearing. "The Ravensfoot side."

"What then?" I asked. "We can't swim all the way." We crossed the lowest reach of the spiralling path, also populated by townsfolk in their flight for the boats. Their alarm at seeing the god they had been venerating was just as extreme, and I guessed that its demonic visage might drive more than one of them into the welcoming arms of St Michael's.

Then we were at the mere's shore. Leading the way, Holmes waded without pause out into the lake, and swam towards the rowing-boat that I now saw awaited us there. A sunlit peak lay ahead that first I took for Netherfell, but then I realised that it must, as Holmes had promised, be Ravensfell. Beneath it, gleaming in the summer sunshine, stood the town of Ravensfoot, its limewashed houses lining the waterfront beneath the tall spire of St George's Church, quite unlike the squat tower of St Michael's.

Without a moment's hesitation, Summerlee and I followed Holmes. I, for one, did not look back until we sat in the scraped, scarred rowing-boat next to the slight young figure of Effie Scorpe. Across from her sat Constable Horace Batterby, bruised and bloody, with his hands upon the oars and grim determination upon his face.

Once we were aboard I was able to do little more than sit panting on the planking, but Holmes, despite his injury, at once took charge of the rowing and began striking out for Ravensfoot, with his habitual swift, sharp motions of his arms.

Behind us, Glissenholm receded, and on its shore the giant reptile reared, hissing its frustration at being deprived of its prey... or so I supposed. A moment later, though, it slipped into the water and began swimming after us. I saw its neck and tail breaching the water in an elegant, sinuous curve.

"My God," I gasped, "what will it take to stop it?"

But it soon became clear that, as Summerlee had observed, the water was not the creature's native element. While it swam strongly, certainly more so than I could have in my current state, it could not keep pace with Holmes's rowing. It fell behind, and soon enough turned back. A minute later I saw it climb ashore once more and vanish into the treeline of Glissenholm, its whiplike tail flicking behind it.

I wondered whether it would take up Lady Ophidia's offer after all.

I became aware that Effie Scorpe was talking to me, quick and excited. "Mr Batterby did just as Mr Holmes told him, Dr Watson," she was saying. "Mr Holmes slipped a note in his pocket back in t'cottage, he says. It told him he'd to find me at t'Arms and let me out, then come after you all, in the boat Mr Gramascene was using when he died. It even said where we should wait for you. We had to drag t'boat down from t'town hall. We did just as Mr Holmes said, Mr Batterby and me."

"It was well done, Effie," I told her, with sincere gratitude. "I will repay the favour any way I can, believe me."

Behind us at the far edge of the holm, we could see some of the town's own boats emerging in a chaotic panic, and the shouts of those who had not yet left the shore came across the water to us. Nobody was of any mind to follow our vessel, or to do anything but save themselves, and perhaps their friends, from the rampaging beast. From this distance we could not make out individuals, but I could see nothing resembling the bright colour of Lady Ophidia's snake-green dress.

I sat back in the boat and listened to the firm, strong rhythm of Holmes's oar-strokes as we made for Ravensfoot, where the cult of the Hagworm held no sway, where a limewashed police station stood beside a telegraph office, and where all the other conveniences of the modern age awaited us.

# CHAPTER TWENTY

A few days later, Holmes and I stood on the railway platform in Ravensfoot, awaiting the service to Carlisle, whence we would take the sleeper train to Euston. After our perilous and exhausting adventures in Wermewater, I had little eagerness to continue my walking tour, and I had tacitly accepted Holmes's assumption that I would be returning with him to London. I would see in the month of July, and the year 1900 if I had any say in the matter, from the comfort of our rooms in Baker Street.

"I remember you telling me once," I reminded him, "that the vilest alleys in London do not present a more dreadful record of sin than the most beautiful countryside. After the past week, I believe you were right."

Holmes laughed shortly. "Oh, London's depravities are real enough, Watson, as are those of other cities. But I have never yet found a cult devoted to human sacrifice in Limehouse, Whitechapel or even Mayfair, and for that I am profoundly thankful."

While in Carlisle we intended to call on Constable Batterby, who was in the hospital there. Dr Kebbelwhite, the practitioner who had examined us all soon after our desperate arrival in Ravensfoot, had concurred with my assessment that the brave young man would make a full recovery. Professor Summerlee's twisted ankle was now mended, and the blood poisoning that I had feared from Holmes's bite had never materialised; apparently his attacker's teeth were less unhygienic than its rank smell had suggested. I had, to my own surprise, emerged from the whole affair with only a few scratches and bruises.

"The Church of the Hagworm shall not survive much longer, though, I am pleased to say," Holmes observed, continuing the conversation. "Its followers can no longer believe that their deity inures them against the outside world, and with this incident the outside world will be taking an unwonted interest in them."

Our terrifying escape from the monster of Glissenholm had been the climax of our adventure. The Ravensfoot police had proven surprisingly quick to believe the worst of their neighbours in Wermeholt, especially when the testimony of their brother officer was confirmed by the world's most renowned detective. They had telegraphed for help from their superiors, and on the morning of the twenty-second of June Holmes and I had accompanied the county police as they descended upon Wermeholt in great numbers, making a good many arrests. Ben Scorpe was in custody, as were Mr Dormer and Peston the verger. Since it had not been practical to arrest the entire population, the authorities had taken over the town hall as a kind of garrison, with plans to build a large and well-appointed police station at the earliest possible opportunity. Once again I was strangely reminded of the arrangements pertaining in Britain during the Roman Empire.

Holmes continued, "There can, I am pleased to say, be little hope that their beliefs will survive long into the twentieth century. Whatever scientist-priests may hold the cure of souls in Wermeholt in the year of 1999, they will be safe from the threat of sacrifice." The Reverend Vangard had assured me that morning that a new priest was being sought for St Michael's, one who had experience working as a missionary among heathen natives abroad.

"And whoever owns Wermeston Hall is hardly likely to demand it," I noted. Deserted by her followers, betrayed by her god, Lady Ophidia had finally retreated to the estate that was all she had known for so long, and had refused to open up the Hall's doors to the police. Her servants were hardly equipped to withstand a siege, however, and within a few hours they had surrendered on her behalf. Her ladyship was being held in the city gaol in Carlisle. One policeman had ended up in hospital with shotgun wounds, and several more with incidental snakebites.

Modon was not among those arrested at the Hall. He and his sisters had been among those left stranded on the island when the fleeing populace took away the boats. Since nobody in Wermeholt was at all inclined to return to the holm, they had had to wait for our arrival to be rescued, and were taken into the police's care in turn. By then, though, Martha Trice, Nora Gough and Edna Jenkins were all in mourning for their brother.

Modon had left his shotgun behind him in the pit, and had not dared to go back for it. During the melee there he, like Holmes, had been grazed almost in passing by the beast's teeth; and once deprived of its favoured prey, the monster had fixed his attentions on him instead, plucking him from Mrs Trice's arms and dragging him screaming into the forest. One of the police officers who had found the resulting gastric pellet had fainted, and the other was still being treated for shock.

The manservant, though, could hardly be considered a worthy sacrifice, and as Holmes said even the most fervent believer in the Hagworm could not credit that this latest iteration of their ritual had been successful.

"Watson!" A voice cried my name from the entrance to the station building, and Summerlee strode nimbly towards us.

He was accompanied by Professor and Mrs Creavesey, and by James Topkins.

"My sister sends her regards, but she is seeing to the funeral arrangements," Topkins explained, only a little stiffly. "The family have decided that Henry should be buried at St George's, and Mr Vangard is being most helpful."

It seemed the rest of the party intended to stay in Ravensfoot to see Gramascene buried. "After that, Mary will need me in London," Topkins added, "and my studies await."

"Shall you stay longer, Professor?" I asked Creavesey, but the old man shook his head sadly.

"I fear not, Doctor. It was foolish of me to embark on this expedition in the first place, and I should have called it off the moment we found Gramascene's body. He might not have been killed by the creature we were seeking, but for all I knew he had been – and yet I intended to press on regardless, endangering my other colleagues. The air of Wermeholt was rotting my brain, I fear. Returning to Camford lent me a perspective I could not have attained while there."

I already knew that the emergency college faculty meeting had not taken place, nor indeed had it ever been planned. The telegram had been supplied by Mrs Trice, using wording written by Sir Howard Woodwose, with the sole intention of removing the Creaveseys from Wermewater before the insanity of the Midsummer ceremony began.

"No," Creavesey sighed, "it is well past time that I retired. I have been a vain old man, pursuing my obsessions while taking credit for work that is not my own, and it is time the world was made aware of the fact. With any luck, the end of my career will help to launch another," he added, patting Edith's hand with a smile.

"I shall come back, though," Topkins said unexpectedly. "Even after all that's been discovered here, there's nothing that can truly explain the legend of the Hagworm. It wasn't any creature collected by Marcus Wermeston that those medieval monks saw, nor even Coleridge a hundred years ago."

Summerlee shook his head impatiently. "You are barking up a non-existent tree, Topkins. There are no plesiosaurs here. Even the beast on Glissenholm proved not, after all, to be a dinosaur."

Zookeepers had been brought in from London, Manchester and Bristol to take safe charge of all the specimens that Lady Ophidia had amassed at Wermeston Hall, and zoologists summoned from as far afield as Berlin and Stockholm, including our friend Dr Mossbaum. When I had collected my belongings from the Mereside Hotel, which a cousin of Mr Dormer's had taken over in his absence, I had heard a group of them excitedly discussing the exotic, and in some cases undocumented, species that had been brought to light.

These experts between them, working from the testimony of those of us who had seen it and their own observations, at a cautious distance, of the creature that inhabited Glissenholm, had deemed it to be no prehistoric monster, but a previously unknown species of giant monitor lizard. Unprecedentedly huge and predatory it might be, and its apparent capacity for producing young without a mate still puzzled everyone, but it was nevertheless a native of our own era. Examination of the records kept by Lady Ophidia confirmed that she had brought the original specimen home from the Dutch East Indies, specifically a small and obscure island known to the natives as Komodo, after it or one of its fellows had been responsible for the death of her father Marcus, Lord Wermeston, and for Ophidia's own perverse religious epiphany.

"It seems to be an example of island gigantism," Edith Creavesey observed now, "a paradoxical counterpart to the island dwarfism that I was remarking on before, Dr Watson, do you remember? Like the Galapagos tortoise you saw on the Wermeston estate. I have a theory that, while larger species when confined to islands will indeed grow smaller, those that are small to begin with may become larger. It will need to be confirmed by further observation, of course. Who knows," she smiled, "I may need to visit the East Indies myself."

"I should like to accompany you if so," said Summerlee, matter-of-factly and without a trace of gallantry. "This episode has reminded me of the value of such expeditions. There is much to be learned from them, even if our world is most unlikely to harbour surviving dinosaurs."

During this last exchange our train had arrived, and so we said our farewells and boarded our carriage. Soon we were pulling away and following the slopes of Ravensfell, bound for Carlisle.

I had already arranged that Effie Scorpe should follow us, once she had made arrangements for the running of the Serpent's Arms in her father's extended absence. Even as its landlady by default, she had no desire to remain in Wermeholt among the shamefaced townsfolk who had escaped arrest. I had promised to find her an opening in a household in London, though given the resourcefulness and courage that she had shown I hoped that it might be in a better position than maid. With training she might make an excellent secretary, or perhaps a nurse. I might even find her employment at my own surgery.

For the moment, Holmes and I had the carriage to ourselves. I stood to gaze out of the window, back towards Wermewater and the town and island that had so imperilled and terrorised us. The sun was glinting on the waters of the mere, and Glissenholm stood bright and verdant, its occupant left in peace to prey on nobody but the unfortunate goats. Behind it Wermeholt lay, dark and grim still, but with a chastened aspect. I knew that it would never again be the ill-omened place I had found it.

And, in the mere between them...

"Holmes, did you see that?" I gasped. "A head! Just like a snake's, rising up from the water!"

"The monitor?" he asked, languidly. "I would have thought it was still resting after its exertions."

"No, not the monitor," I insisted. "I'll never forget the sight of that thing swimming. And the crocodile's already been taken away to London Zoo. No, this had a humped back and a longer neck, rising up above the surface of the mere! It's gone now," I added, disappointed that my friend could not corroborate what I had witnessed.

He raised an eyebrow. "A floating log, perhaps? A boat? Or simply a trick of the light. You have had a trying week, Watson, to say the least. Doubtless you are a little overwrought. It would be best to leave such fancies behind, though, or at least to avoid Hyde Park until you are free of them. I shall not be responsible for the consequences if you start seeing sea-monsters in the Serpentine."

And so the train rounded Ravensfell, and I left the shores of Lake Wermewater at last behind me. For my part I have never returned.

# AUTHOR'S NOTE

The character of Professor Summerlee is borrowed from Sir Arthur Conan Doyle's *The Lost World*, which I've assumed occurs a decade or so after *The Monster of the Mere* is set. Personally, I prefer him to the more popular Professor Challenger. Challenger's arrogance and scorn for alternative views seem justified only because he is, by authorial decree, correct in his beliefs; Summerlee, on the other hand, adheres to the theories suggested by the available evidence, changing his mind when new evidence is presented to him. To my mind he's by far the better scientist.

Although the characters in the book refer to plesiosaurs as 'dinosaurs', this is a convenient shorthand. Watson, like many non-experts today, might consider them to fall within this category, but even in 1899 a palaeontologist would have distinguished between the land-based dinosaurs and their cousins, the marine reptiles. Meanwhile, the species found on Glissenholm became known to western science only in 1912, coincidentally the year of *The Lost World*'s publication – although it had, of course, been available to discover previously. Its remarkable ability, when kept alone in captivity, to produce male offspring through parthenogenesis was not documented until 2005.

The dialect spoken by the Wermewater characters is watered down for ease of reading, but draws on elements described in *Cumbrian Language in its Cultural Context* by Simon Roper. Needless to say, any errors are entirely Watson's.

Although most of Sir Howard Woodwose's lectures on the global mythology of serpents are substantially correct, the Hagworm legend is my invention, as are Lake Wermewater and its immediate surroundings. 'Hagworm' is in fact the Cumbrian word for a snake, usually an adder.

# ABOUT THE AUTHOR

PHILIP PURSER-HALLARD is the author of three previous Sherlock Holmes novels – *The Vanishing Man*, *The Spider's Web*, and *Masters of Lies* – and of a trilogy of urban fantasy thrillers beginning with *The Pendragon Protocol*. He also writes novellas and short stories, edits anthologies, and is an editor of and contributor to The Black Archive, a series of critical books about Doctor Who. He tweets @purserhallard.

# SHERLOCK HOLMES
## CRY OF THE INNOCENTS
*Cavan Scott*

It is 1891, and a catholic priest arrives at 221b Baker Street, only to utter the words "*il corpe*" before suddenly dropping dead.

Though the man's death is attributed to cholera, when news of another dead priest reaches Holmes, he becomes convinced that the men have been poisoned. He and Watson learn that the victims were on a mission from the Vatican to investigate a miracle; it is said that the body of eighteenth-century philanthropist and slave trader Edwyn Warwick has not decomposed. But should the Pope canonise a man who made his fortune through slavery? And when Warwick's body is stolen, it becomes clear that the priests' mission has attracted the attention of a deadly conspiracy...

### PRAISE FOR CAVAN SCOTT

"Many memorable moments... excellent." *Starburst*

"Utterly charming, comprehensively Sherlockian, and possessed of a wry narrator." *Criminal Element*

"Memorable and enjoyable... One of the best stories I've ever read." *Wondrous Reads*

## TITAN BOOKS.COM

# SHERLOCK HOLMES
## THE LEGACY OF DEEDS
*Nick Kyme*

It is 1894, and Sherlock Holmes is called to a Covent Garden art gallery where dozens of patrons lie dead before a painting of The Undying Man.

Holmes and Watson are soon on the trail of a mysterious figure in black, whose astounding speed and agility make capture impossible. The same suspect is then implicated in another murder, when the servant of a visiting Russian grand duke is found terribly mutilated in a notorious slum. But what links the two crimes, and do they have anything to do with the suicide of an unpopular schoolteacher at a remote boarding school? So begins a case that will reveal the dark shadows that past misdeeds can cast, and test the companions to their limits…

### PRAISE FOR NICK KYME

"A highly enjoyable book with plenty of action." *Fiftyshadesofgeek*

"An engaging and exciting story." *Talk Wargaming*

"An entertaining read." *SFF World*

# SHERLOCK HOLMES
## THE RED TOWER
*Mark A. Latham*

It is 1894, and after a macabre séance at a country estate, a young
woman has been found dead in a locked room.

When Dr Watson is invited to a weekend party where a séance
is planned, he is prepared to be sceptical. James Crain, heir to
the estate of Crain Manor, has fallen in with a mysterious group
of spiritualists and is determined to prove the existence of the
paranormal. Confronted with a suspicious medium and sightings
of the family ghost, Watson remains unconvinced – until James's
sister, Lady Esther, is found dead in a room locked from the inside.
Holmes is called to investigate the strange events at Crain Manor,
but finds that every guest harbours a secret. Holmes and Watson
must uncover the truth, and test the existence of the supernatural…

## PRAISE FOR MARK A. LATHAM

"Great fun… with a setting we love spending
time in." *Barnes & Noble*

"Lose yourself in nineteenth-century London
– you won't regret it." **George Mann**

"Victorian London comes alive in ways even Conan Doyle
could never imagine." **James Lovegrove**

# TITAN BOOKS.COM

# SHERLOCK HOLMES
## THE DEVIL'S DUST
*James Lovegrove*

It is 1884, and when a fellow landlady finds her lodger poisoned,
Mrs Hudson turns to Sherlock Holmes.

The police suspect the landlady of murder, but Mrs Hudson insists
that her friend is innocent. The companions discover that the lodger,
a civil servant recently returned from India, was living in almost
complete seclusion, and that his last act was to scrawl a mysterious
message on a scrap of paper. The riddles pile up as aged big game
hunter Allan Quatermain is spotted at the scene of the crime when
Holmes and Watson investigate. The famous man of mind and the
legendary man of action will make an unlikely team in a case of
corruption, revenge, and what can only be described as magic…

## PRAISE FOR JAMES LOVEGROVE

"Lovegrove tells a thrilling tale and vividly renders the
atmosphere of Victorian London." *Guardian*

"Another impressive read based on the
iconic detective." *Starburst*

"Delicious stuff, marrying the standard notions of
Holmesiana with the kind of imagination we can
expect from Lovegrove." *Crime Time*

**TITAN** BOOKS.COM

# SHERLOCK HOLMES
## THE VANISHING MAN
*Philip Purser-Hallard*

It is 1896, and Sherlock Holmes is investigating a self-proclaimed psychic who disappeared from a locked room, in front of several witnesses.

While attempting to prove the existence of telekinesis to a scientific society, an alleged psychic, Kellway, vanished before their eyes during the experiment. With a large reward at stake, Holmes is convinced Kellway is a charlatan – or he would be, if he had returned to claim his prize. As Holmes and Watson investigate, the case only grows stranger, and they must contend with an interfering "occult detective" and an increasingly deranged cult. But when one of the society members is found dead, events take a far more sinister turn…

## PRAISE FOR PHILIP PURSER-HALLARD

"A master craftsman. His stories are both cleverly constructed and wrought in the sharpest prose, and he's always a joy to read." **George Mann**

"A startlingly original premise with some bloody good storytelling. I'm in for the long run, and you should be too." **Simon Morden**

**TITAN** BOOKS.COM

# SHERLOCK HOLMES
## THE BACK TO FRONT MURDER
*Tim Major*

It is May 1898, Sherlock Holmes investigates a murder
stolen from a writer's research.

Abigail Moone presents an unusual problem at Baker Street. She is
a writer of mystery stories under a male pseudonym, and gets her
ideas following real people and imagining how she might kill them
and get away with it. It's made her very successful, until her latest
"victim" dies, apparently of the poison method she meticulously
planned in her notebook. Abigail insists she is not responsible, and
that someone is trying to frame her for his death. With the evidence
stacking up against her, she begs Holmes to prove her innocence…

## PRAISE FOR TIM MAJOR

"Tim Major is an exceptional writer." **Adam Roberts**

"The only novel I have read that made
my ears tingle." *The Times*

"Major has a special skill of weaving his
characters' inner turmoils into the perils
they face in the plot." *Morning Star*

**TITAN** BOOKS.COM

# SHERLOCK HOLMES
## THE MANIFESTATIONS OF
## SHERLOCK HOLMES

*James Lovegrove*

Maverick detective Sherlock Holmes and his faithful chronicler
Dr John Watson return in twelve thrilling short stories

The iconic duo find themselves swiftly drawn into a series of
puzzling and sinister events: an otherworldly stone whose touch
inflicts fatal bleeding; a hellish potion unlocks a person's devilish
psyche; Holmes's most hated rival detective tells his story; a
fiendishly clever, almost undetectable method of revenge; Watson
finally has his chance to shine; and many more – including a
brand-new Cthulhu Casebooks story.

## PRAISE FOR JAMES LOVEGROVE

"Pitch-perfect. Lovegrove tells a thrilling tale and vividly
renders the atmosphere of Victorian London." *Guardian*

"The reader [is] in no doubt that they are in the hands
of a confident and skilful craftsman." *Starburst*

"Lovegrove has become to the twenty-first century what
J.G. Ballard was to the twentieth." *The Bookseller*

## TITAN BOOKS.COM

# SHERLOCK HOLMES
## THE SPIDER'S WEB
*Philip Purser-Hallard*

It is 1897, and Sherlock Holmes is investigating a murder
that took place during a society ball.

Holmes and Watson rush to the scene, but are shocked by the flippant
attitude of the ball's host: the wealthy Ernest Moncrieff, a favourite
of high society who was found in a handbag as a baby. Suspicion
naturally falls upon the party guests, but the Moncrieff family and
their friends – including the indomitable Lady Bracknell – are more
concerned with the inconvenience of the investigation than the
fact that one of them may have committed murder. But behind the
superficial façade, Holmes and Watson uncover family secrets going
back decades, and a mysterious blackmailer pulling the strings…

## PRAISE FOR PHILIP PURSER-HALLARD

"This ranks among the top novel-length
Sherlock Holmes pastiches." *Publishers Weekly* (**starred review**)

"A very good locked-room puzzle." *Morning Star*

**TITAN** BOOKS.COM

# SHERLOCK HOLMES
## MASTERS OF LIES
*Philip Purser-Hallard*

It is 1898, and Sherlock Holmes is being drawn into a world of
conspiracy and subterfuge.

Holmes and Watson are called in to investigate the apparent suicide
of a senior civil servant, only to discover murder and a spiralling
conspiracy of deceit. What began as a favour to sure up national
security rapidly becomes something far more sinister: a conflict with
a murderous forgery ring, which may have ties to the very heart of
the British Establishment. As the truth becomes only more uncertain
and the web of blackmail, threats and violence draws around them,
Holmes and Watson are forced to consider who they can really trust…

### PRAISE FOR PHILIP PURSER-HALLARD

"Displays the author's remarkable facility at conjuring
the spirit of Conan Doyle's originals. Sherlockians
and Wildeans alike will embrace Purser-Hallard."
*Publishers Weekly* (starred review)

"The best kept secret in British genre writing."
*The British Fantasy Society*

## TITAN BOOKS.COM

For more fantastic fiction, author events,
exclusive excerpts, competitions, limited editions and more

VISIT OUR WEBSITE
**titanbooks.com**

LIKE US ON FACEBOOK
**facebook.com/titanbooks**

FOLLOW US ON TWITTER AND INSTAGRAM
**@TitanBooks**

EMAIL US
**readerfeedback@titanemail.com**